RECKLESS
Longing

Gina Robinson

Gina Robinson
SEATTLE, WASHINGTON

Book Layout ©2013 BookDesignTemplates.com

Reckless Longing/ Gina Robinson. — 1st ed.
ISBN 978-0615875248

For my college-age consultant
Thanks for all the help!

Also by
GINA ROBINSON
NEW ADULT ROMANCE
RECKLESS SECRETS
RECKLESS TOGETHER
RUSHED
THE AGENT EX SERIES
"Full of laughter, intrigue, and, of course, steamy
spies..." —*RT Book Reviews*

LICENSE TO LOVE
THE SPY WHO LEFT ME
DIAMONDS ARE TRULY FOREVER
LIVE AND LET LOVE
LOVE ANOTHER DAY

MORE ROMANTIC SUSPENSE
SPY CANDY
SPY GAMES

HISTORICAL ROMANCE
THE LAST HONEST SEAMSTRESS
THE UNION
THE ESCORT

WOMEN'S FICTION
PINK SLIPPER

CONTEMPORARY ROMANCE
ECHO BAY CHRISTMAS

CHAPTER ONE

Twilight was falling along with the outrageous hundred-degree heat of the late August day. The shadows were long and crisp and the summer colors vivid in a way that made life feel exceptionally real and every experience heightened.

It wasn't supposed to get this hot in Washington State. Just my luck the heat wave hit as I moved in. Maybe it was symbolic. Maybe it was a warning that I was stepping into a situation too hot to handle. I didn't care. I ignored that intuitive feeling that I was in over my head.

My dorm wasn't air-conditioned. I had put my sparse makeup on in front of a box fan blowing hot air at me. Now, even in the comparative cool outside, my crop top stuck to my body. I felt the neat lines of my eyeliner bleeding together and my meticulously applied concealer melting away from the red scar on my left cheek, leaving me exposed. I fought my habitual urge to touch the fresh scar, reminding myself I was trying to forget everything about it.

I approached the open mall in front of the student union building and the gyrating throng of people who would be my classmates, my fellow alums, my future network, with my roommate Bre. She was, by default of proximity and length of acquaintance, my new best friend on campus. By length of acquaintance, I meant two days. That tells you something about the newness and state of things. Two days was an eternity when everything, and everyone, was new.

The mall rocked with music, laughter, pickup lines, the smell of beer, and pulsing bodies. I paused on the outskirts of the crowd at the entrance to the mall, uncertain, for the millionth time, about the sanity of my plan. Yet determined to carry it out. No one had ever accused me of being cautious.

"Welcome to the Week of Welcome—WoW!" Bre took my arm. "Are you ready to meet a man?"

Men were the last and first things on my mind, but for Bre they were everything. She was like a wounded bird in her desperation to find a boyfriend. I felt both protective of her and totally annoyed. As emotionally banged and bruised as I was, I wasn't really in any shape to take care of her right now.

I'd transferred to this particular university precisely seeking a man. I knew he was here. Not because I was psychic, though I sometimes wished I were. Then I'd know where this was all headed and if I was doing more irreparable damage to myself than good. Were the risks calculated enough? Was the potential payoff worth it? Wreaking more havoc on my self-esteem and bruised psyche could very well crush what was left of me.

I knew he was here because I'd done my research. When I finally met him, and decided to reveal myself, I was going to turn his world upside down. But first, I had to determine if that was what I really wanted. And whether he deserved it, and a relationship with me, or not. I didn't need any more complications in my already complicated life. But I wanted to know. I *had* to know.

Bre was scanning the crowd, her eyes narrow and sharp with the look of a huntress. I wanted to tell her the expression on her face was enough to send any straight guy running. And maybe even some of the gay ones. But why ruin our friendship? I had to live with her, and in this early phase of our roommate-ness I didn't know how she'd take it.

The sense of competition hung heavy in the air. Poor Bre. She must be quaking with it. Everywhere I looked were girls who were skinnier, prettier, more confident than I was. Girls with flowing hair, perfect makeup, bandeaux tops over pert breasts, tight short shorts showing round butt cheeks with no cellulite. Abs firm and on display, sparkling with bellybutton piercings. Girls strutting their stuff. Girls who reminded me of my mother.

I suppressed a shudder. I was plain. By design. Because my mother was a ruthless competitor who never lost. And who never failed to compete with me, whether I participated or not.

I wasn't the daughter she wanted. I was the child who'd ruined her life. So I let her win, because it was easier and less painful and eased my guilt for being born. Life shouldn't be a competition. That didn't stop her. Nothing stopped her. Nothing quelled the deep unhappiness inside her. But this last time she'd crossed the line. I didn't think I could ever forgive her. And I wasn't in the mood to try.

Then there was the breakup with my boyfriend. I was still stinging and running from that. It was too fresh. The hurt colored my world darkly and made me cry at odd, inconvenient times. Like in front of my mother. I hated myself for that weakness.

I was, for lack of a better word, brokenhearted. And that wasn't likely to change any time soon. They say time heals all wounds. But they never say how *much* time. Lame, lame, lame. Lame antidote for pain. If you ask me.

Bre spotted her quarry in the crowd and bounced up on her toes, waving her arms over her head. "Dan! Jake! Over here." She grabbed my arm. "You're going to love Jake."

Which meant she thought Dan was the hotter guy and was keeping him for herself. Poor Jake was collateral baggage. The guy who came along as part of the package deal. Two friends for the price of one. I was supposed to take this extra piece of luggage off Bre's hands.

Bre had met Dan and Jake during her orientation week over the summer. She'd been texting Dan ever since, trying to heat something up between them. All the clues said she was failing. But at this stage of the game, a slight acquaintance was better than an abject stranger. Anything for some sense of belonging and community. Maybe Dan and Jake were hoping I'd be hot. Or that we'd introduce them to some of our hotter dorm-mates. Who knows what motivates guys?

Bre dragged me through the throngs toward two guys who were waving back at her. I sized them up, unenthusiastically. Since breaking up with Austin, no guy measured up. I thought my heart was dead. Part of me was, anyway. I'd lost that magical trill that makes life exciting and worth living. I was only at this Up All Night Week of Welcome event because Bre insisted. And I didn't want to start the year branded a lonely, loser hermit. But my heart wasn't in it. As soon as I'd stayed a respectable length of time, I was out of here.

"Dan!" Bre dropped my arm and threw herself into a hug with him. She reluctantly let him go and turned to his friend. "Jake." She air-hugged him.

I'd been right. Dan was hotter. Taller. Darker. Had a better smile. Jake was shorter. Stockier. Red-haired with freckles.

"Guys, this is Ellie." She gave me a shoulder-squeeze. "Ellie—Dan and Jake."

I nodded and forced a smile. Jake sized me up—ditch, friend, or date potential? The choices were written on his face. He was unsure.

The loud music made it hard to hear what anyone said. Bre was trying to say something to the two of them.

"Where should we start?" Bre yelled over the music. "Magic show? Dance?"

"Eat. Before they run out of free food." Dan pointed to a sandwich stand set up in the middle of the mall that ran from the library, past the student union building, SUB, to the street in front of the administration building.

And it was decided. Because Bre wasn't going to argue, not when she wanted to impress Dan. And the opinions of Jake and me didn't matter. Bre grabbed Dan's arm and let him muscle his way through the crowd. Jake shrugged at me. The two of us followed them, both of us with our hands in our pockets so there was no accidental touching. We joined the line and stared at each other and then looked away, gazing into the crowd, which I found infinitely more interesting.

The evening was going about as well as I expected. How likely is it in any given mating-game situation that the wingman will fall for the girl's moral support sidekick? In this case, given my mindset, the odds were exactly zero. With the pounding music, even trying to make idle conversation was pointless.

We got our subs and energy drinks and found an empty patch of lawn to sit on. Bre cooed to Dan. Jake and I were awkward and ate mostly in silence. My gaze landed on an Up All Night sign advertising the events of the evening.

Precision Piercing. Specials—Tonight only! Half off the usual price. Bellybutton, ears, cartilage, and noses only.

My heart pounded in my ears. I'd read enough. I knew what I wanted, what I had wanted for a couple of years now but was too rebellious to do—pierce my navel. To understand how not piercing my bellybutton is rebellious, you have to know my mom. It was what she wanted me to do, so it was exactly what I refused to do. But now I didn't care what she thought. I could pierce or not pierce at my pleasure. I was of age and didn't need her permission. She'd never know unless I wanted her to. And even then, she wouldn't be around to gloat and enjoy her triumph.

Anyway, that wasn't the way I saw it. Doing what I wanted without regard to her was my victory. I looked around at the party atmosphere that I should have been enjoying and found myself almost smiling.

Dan and Jake wolfed down their sandwiches and were ready to party. Bre wrapped the remains of hers, ready to toss it so she could get on with the evening. I'd barely touched mine, but that wasn't unusual. Since the breakup I'd lost my appetite for just about everything in life and ten pounds along with it. And I hadn't been overweight to begin with.

Dan offered Bre a hand up. "Dance or take in the magic show?"

"Dance!" Bre laughed and took his arm, smiling up at him coyly.

"Body piercing!" I said in unison with Bre as I stood and dusted the grass off my butt.

Three pairs of eyes turned on me. I kept smiling. "What? It'll be fun. It's not something you do every day. What better way to remember the start of our illustrious college careers here than with a new piercing?"

I spoke boldly for someone who only had her ears pierced.

Beside me, Jake shook his head. "Guys don't get pierced. Not at Up All Night." He spoke like an expert.

I ignored him and appealed to Bre. She shook her head. "The line will be too long by now. We'll miss everything else. You can get pierced any time. I'll go with you whenever you want."

"But not for half price," I said.

"Ellie, come on." Bre's eyes begged me to be reasonable.

I waved her off. "You guys go ahead. I'm off to get my bellybutton pierced. I'll text you when I'm done and catch up with you later. Have fun!"

Without waiting for an answer, I spun and ran off through the crowd toward the SUB, feeling free and exhilarated for the first time all summer.

My exhilaration lasted as I wound through the crowded first floor of the SUB, following the signs to Precision Piercing's station. Up the stairs to the second floor toward the ballroom, right until I saw the long line and my courage failed.

Jake had been an ass about things, but he was right about one thing—there were no guys in line for piercing. Bre was right, too. There was a good chance I was already too late. Any minute they'd be shutting off the line, saying they'd reached their maximum.

I stood there, not quite in line, staring and debating with myself. I'd just ditched my roommate and she was going to be pissed about it, especially if I came back without another hole in my body. On the other hand, I could claim I'd been turned away because the line was too long and she'd have gloating rights for the rest of the semester. Maybe even the rest of the time we knew each other. At homecoming twenty years from now, I still wouldn't hear the end of it.

"You'd better get in line before it's too late."

It took me a second to realize the sexy male voice was speaking to me. Startled, I looked around for the source. What was a guy doing here, anyway?

When I found it, my heart did an odd little flip. Sitting on a bench with an instant icepack pressed to his right eye was a guy that was too gorgeous to be benched. How could I have missed him? He had a wicked smile calculated to make girls melt, and his left eye danced with amusement as he watched me. He sat with his legs spread wide, just inviting a girl to stand between them and coo condolences on his injury. Touch his cheek. Offer him any comfort he wanted. He looked dangerous with one eye covered and the way a lock of dark hair fell against the icepack. Yet sympathetic at the same time, like you just wanted to take care of him.

Even though he was sitting, it was obvious he was tall and athletically built beneath the T-shirt and shorts he wore. "Well?"

I blinked. "I'm thinking."

"The window of opportunity is closing." He stood and walked over to stand next to me, so close I could smell the delicious scent of his cologne.

"Yes," I said. "I know."

He ignored any sarcasm that had slipped into my tone. "What do you want to have pierced?"

"My bellybutton." I just blurted it out, wondering why this complete stranger inspired my confidence. And why he cared.

He nodded. "Good choice. Bellybutton rings are hot. Every woman should have one."

"How do you know I don't have one already?"

His one-eyed gaze slid down my crop top to my abs in a way that sent tingles through me. He grinned and arched his left brow. "Kind of obvious. Even with only one good eye."

I looked down at my stomach, which clenched almost automatically, like it needed to be tight and firm for him. I spent half a second wishing I'd gone to the gym. Well, duh. He had me. I should have been embarrassed, but the easy way he said it was teasing and flirtatious. Like he knew the power he had over women, but wasn't flaunting it.

"Are you here alone? Where's your support person?"

I stared at him. "What?"

"Your best friend. The girl who's supposed to hold your hand so you don't chicken out." He pointed to the line.

I realized for the first time that he was right. All the girls were in pairs. Hope welled up in me. Maybe the line was only half as long as it looked.

I felt like a loser for being alone. I shrugged. "She ditched me. For a guy." Like that was so much better. None of these girls' best friends had bailed on them. "She promised to go with me another time. She thought we were too late and the line would be too long, anyway."

"It will be if you don't get in it."

I nodded again, not moving, mesmerized by him.

"Okay, you twisted my arm." He took me by the elbow and guided me into line. "I'll be your support person."

I looked down the length of the line, stunned and pleased. "Do you think you can handle estrogen central?"

He grinned, wincing in the process and pulling the icepack away from his eye. "I can handle anything."

Around me, girls were noticing him. Had been noticing him all along, probably. I wondered why he'd chosen me. Judging from their evil looks, they were wondering the same thing. Even with one bum, swollen black eye, he was the hottest guy I'd seen all night.

"I don't know," I said. "Can I trust you? You look dangerous with that black eye."

"That's part of my appeal."

"Modesty. I like that in a man."

He laughed.

"Seriously—how did you get it? It looks nasty." I paused and tried not to wince. "And painful."

"Do you think men who fight are sexy?" He switched the icepack to his left hand.

"No."

"Then I'll dispense with the lies and the really cool story I concocted to impress you. I had a run-in with a pool ball gone wild. Never play pool with Callahan when he's drunk. He's a wild man. And FYI, when someone yells 'duck!' in a poolroom, listen to them. They aren't kidding.

"If I hadn't had that third beer, my reflexes would have been quicker. As it is, I'm lucky I don't have a concussion, though the medic at the aid station said the jury's still out on that one. I'll know for sure within twenty-four hours."

"Why were you sitting up here? The poolroom's in the basement and the first-aid station is on the first floor."

"And filled to capacity with drunks and all their re-lated accidents. This was the only place I could find to sit."

"Makes sense. But where are all your friends?"

"They ditched me for a couple of hot sorority babes who came by." The way he said it made me laugh again.

"Nice."

"Yeah. Those chicks weren't into a guy with a black eye."

Their loss, I thought, half wondering if he was lying. Who could pass him up, black eye or not?

While we chatted, the line moved surprisingly quickly. We had started in the hall near the stairs. Now we were nearly at the door. Bre had been wrong about a lot of things, including there not being time.

"Well, support person, welcome aboard," I said. "I'm Ellie. You should know my name, just in case you have to comfort me. FYI, I prefer personalized comfort phrases like 'Hang in there, Ellie.' And 'You can do it, Ellie.'"

"Logan," he said. "In case you'd like to give me a personalized thank you, as in 'Thank you, Logan, for saving me from certain chickening out and regretting it my whole life.'"

"That's more like a speech. I hope I can remember it without writing it down."

He patted his pockets. "No paper on me. I'll refresh your memory when the time comes."

I couldn't believe I was smiling again.

We reached the door. A guy handed me a clipboard with a release form to fill out. It had a space for my address. I glanced over the shoulder of the girl in front of me. She hesitated at the address column, then wrote her school address in. I realized in an instant why—she didn't want her parents to be notified or find out.

"Don't know your school address?" Logan said beside me, seeming way too interested in where I lived.

I smiled and boldly filled in my home address. Let my mom find out. I wanted her to know and Logan to think I was mysterious. "I know it perfectly well."

"Whoa. Bold move." Logan had been peering over my shoulder. "The parents aren't going to go ape shit?"

"No," I said. "My mom's been wanting me to do this for a long time."

He looked like he didn't quite believe me. "Then why haven't you?"

"Because she wanted me to," I answered truthfully.

He grinned wider. "Rebellious. Excellent! A girl after my own heart."

I studied him. "Don't get along with your parents?"

"Mom's okay. Dad's a bit of a bastard."

"At least you have one," I said.

A girl approached and took my clipboard. She looked it over and directed me to a cashier. I pulled twenty-five dollars out of my pocket and handed it over. The girl at the register handed me a receipt and directed me to a line.

That was when it hit me that I was really doing this, thanks to Logan. That was also when I remembered my fear of needles and how petrified I was when I got my ears pierced. Of course, I'd been six. And I couldn't even see the piercing gun. But that quick zap of pain had been enough to give me nightmares for years.

In high school, I'd heard my girlfriends' stories about getting bellybutton rings, but I'd never paid real attention to the details. Because, like I said, I don't like needles or shots, or any of that stuff. Now I was confronted with the evidence.

We were in the ballroom. It was a big, open room with piercing stations set up throughout and lines before each. They pierced with precision, all right—assembly-line-like precision. As you stood in line waiting your turn, you could watch the current victim getting her piercing of choice.

I'd always thought I'd get to lie down on a table and look away while I tried not to think about that big-ass needle. Tried not to get even a glimpse of it. But that was not the case here. You had to stand and hold up your shirt while they worked. There wasn't a girl in line who didn't look scared. And the looks on the faces of the girls who were being worked on? Petrified.

Suddenly Bre's suggestion was looking a whole lot better and much saner. Screw the twenty-five dollars. I'd rather lose it than my lunch in front of Logan and everyone. I felt pale and cold.

Logan slid his warm arm around my shoulder. "Hey," he whispered in my ear. "They all look scared at first. Watch how thrilled they are when it's done."

"I hate needles." It was a bare whisper. As soon as I spoke I wished I could take it back. I sounded so pathetic.

"I'll be right here with you." He squeezed my shoulder. "Holding your hand."

Something about his voice was soothing and reassuring. He was so confident. And the thought of holding his hand...

That was dangerous territory. But at the same time, I didn't want to look like a coward in front of him. Or like he'd wasted his time trying to be nice to me. I wasn't going to make him a failure, too.

I nodded. "Hold on tightly. And don't let go."

"Never."

"Next!"

"You're up." Logan smiled at me, walking with me to the piercing station.

"What are we doing today?" the piercing guy asked as he read my paperwork.

"Bellybutton."

He nodded. "Good. Looks like you went for the jeweled stud."

I nodded.

"Stand right there." The piercing guy was friendly and reassuring in his own way. He grabbed a pen. "Pull up your shirt."

I looked at Logan. He nodded and smiled at me. I took a deep breath and pulled my crop top up a little higher, holding it just beneath my breasts.

The piercing guy stared at my abs, eyeing my stomach. "Hold still. I'm going to clean the area and mark where it should go. We don't want you crooked." When he was done, he reached for a pair of clamps that looked like a pair of scissors.

The sight of that clamp made me lightheaded, and I hadn't even seen the needle yet. I reached out my hand for Logan's.

He held his icepack in one hand against his side. But the hand he took mine in was warm and strong. His grip firm, but tender. "Just look at me. Eyes on mine." He was smiling and his gaze was mesmerizing, even one-eyed. The other eye looked awful—black and red and swollen shut.

He was so adorable and pathetic and brave. I bit my lip and stared into his deep brown good eye, thinking it was the most beautiful eye I'd ever seen, full of confidence and encouragement.

"There will be a pinch and then a quick stab of pain as I put the bar in," the piercing guy said. "Breathe in."

I took a deep breath and held Logan's gaze. I felt the pinch of the clamps. I gasped at the quick rush of pain that followed, trying not to imagine the needle going in.

"You're doing great." Logan squeezed my hand.

I forced a shaky smile and squeezed back, hanging on like my life depended on it.

"The bar's in," the piercing guy said. "I'll follow it with your ring. How are you doing?"

"Good." It came out a squeak.

Logan laughed. "She's doing awesome. Hang in there, El."

"Just keep looking at your boyfriend."

Boyfriend?

"Hang on to that one," the piercing guy said. "He's the first guy who's come in all night."

I opened my mouth to correct him.

Logan shook his head, silencing me. "She's damn lucky. But so am I. This shiner didn't turn her off."

"Okay. The ring's in. Now I just have to screw on the stud and you can look."

I felt a little tugging.

"All done."

I looked down and couldn't help smiling. "It's awesome." Spellbound by it, I let go of my crop top and made a move to touch it and make sure it was real.

"No! Don't touch it." The piercing guy shook his head.

I stopped mid-reach.

"You don't want to infect it." The piercing guy swabbed it again with cleaner.

I looked at Logan again.

"Gorgeous." His gaze was locked on mine, not my abs.

I went warm all over.

The piercing guy handed me a little bottle of cleaning solution and a page of instructions and I was done. And still clutching Logan's hand so hard it was turning white. Embarrassed, I tried to let go.

He shook his head and held on tightly. "Come on. There's a mirror over there. You'll want a look."

We walked to it hand in hand. In front of the mirror, I reluctantly let go of his hand and he let me. Framing my bellybutton on either side with my hands, like I was embracing a tenuous new life, I cautiously looked in the mirror. When I saw my reflection, I couldn't stop smiling.

"Thank you, Logan, for saving me from certain chickening out and regretting it my whole life." I turned to inspect my bellybutton jewel from another angle.

"Good memory," he said. "You *were* paying attention."

"And for letting me crush your fingers until they turned purple because I was so scared."

He smiled and flexed his fingers. "You're not as strong as you think. My hand's fine." He held his hand up and made a funny grabbing gesture. "See? It still works."

I laughed. "Seriously. I couldn't have done it without you."

He offered me his icepack.

I shook my head. "Thanks. But I don't need it. It doesn't hurt." I looked at him. His right eye was completely swollen shut. I took the icepack from him and gently applied it to his eye. I was so gentle that he only winced a little. "Your eye looks awful. Time for ice on." I smiled. "This will be an evening to remember."

He took the icepack from me and grabbed my hand. "Let's get out of here." He pulled me into the hall toward the stairs, past the dwindling line of girls waiting for their turns.

"Walker! Hey! Wait up."

It took me a second to realize someone was calling to Logan. He hesitated as a group of three boisterous guys approached us.

"Where have you been? Why didn't you text us back? We've been looking all *over* for you," the tallest of them said.

"Some thanks. We leave to get the invalid something to drink and you ditch us while we're gone," the blond one said. "This is getting warm." He shoved a can of energy drink at Logan.

Logan had to drop my hand to take it.

The three of them stared at me as I realized Logan had lied about being ditched by his friends. I couldn't decide if that was sweet or diabolical.

"What happened to your sorority babes?" I asked, ribbing Logan.

The guys looked puzzled. "What babes?"

I had Logan's number and he knew it.

"Guys, this is Ellie." Logan didn't seem embarrassed at all.

"Nice to meet all of you." My heart was pounding. I felt suddenly anxious. Things were moving too fast. Everything had been so perfect. At the same time, I didn't want it to end and I couldn't face the rest of the evening with his friends.

I went up on my toes and kissed Logan's cheek. "Thanks for everything, Logan Walker. Really. First week of college. I won't ever forget it." I gyrated my hips and flashed my new bellybutton stud.

While Logan was distracted, I waved to the guys and darted down the steps, melding into the crowd.

"Ellie!" Logan called after me. "Ellie! What's your last name?"

I didn't stop. I didn't answer him. It was better this way. *Really.*

CHAPTER TWO

My heart was still pounding when I reached my dorm room and shut myself in. It was stuffy and hot. The windows were already open and music from the mall boomed in, but the dorm itself was relatively quiet. Bre was still out. I texted her that I was tired and had gone back to our room. I turned on a fan and sat in the dark in front of it on my bed.

What had just happened out there? For the first time in nearly three months I felt something besides anger and hurt. I felt something almost magical and romantic for a guy with a black eye, and I was scared.

In some stupid, crazy way it was almost like I was being unfaithful to Austin. But wasn't he the one who had cheated in the most horrible way possible? Irrationally, it didn't matter. Feeling a spark with someone else felt like it invalidated what I'd felt for Austin, which had sure felt like true love.

I took a deep breath.

Logan Walker. I turned the name around in my head, viewing it from all angles.

In retrospect, his friends couldn't have shown up at a more opportune moment, and meeting Logan couldn't have happened at a worse one. It was better if I never saw him again. I remembered the first time I met Austin and how sweet he'd been, too. I didn't want this memory tainted by finding out just what kind of a jerk Logan Walker might really be. Besides, I was here for a reason and it didn't involve falling in love again.

I felt a stab of anxiety. My heart pounded out of control. No. I shouldn't worry about it. Logan didn't have my last name. He didn't know where I lived. He didn't have my number. And in a school of over twenty thousand students, what were the odds we'd randomly run into each other again?

A key rattled in the lock of our door. Our dorm was ancient and everything rattled, creaked, or wheezed. Bre stumbled in.

"You're home early," I said. "Get tired of Dan and Jake already?"

"Geez!" Bre flipped a light on and put a hand over her heart. "Are you trying to give me a heart attack? What are you doing sitting in the dark?"

"Recuperating." I lifted up my crop top and showed her my bellybutton."

"You got in?"

"Naturally."

She walked over and examined my stomach. "Nice."

I nodded.

"I should be furious at you for ditching me." She plopped on her bed, which was perpendicular with mine.

"Jake and I weren't hitting it off. It was better to set him free and do what I wanted to do." I paused. "What's your story?"

"The guys wanted to play pool. I watched for a while and then I bailed."

I grinned, thinking involuntarily of Logan. "Wise choice. Pool can be dangerous."

Bre looked at me like I was crazy. "What have you been smoking?"

"Nothing."

"What's this craziness about pool being dangerous as if it's an extreme sport, then? And why do you look like you're hiding something?"

"I'm not hiding anything but smugness," I said, trying to sound teasing. "I was right about the piercing." It was enough to throw her off the scent. I was intent on keeping Logan's memory to myself.

She shook her head like she was disgusted, then broke into a smile. "The boys want to meet up at the convocation tomorrow."

I was going to the convocation for one reason. And it had nothing to do with boys. Not that way.

Convocation is university-speak for a meeting. I quickly learned that people in academia like using big words for simple things. They love obfuscating the message. See? I know an SAT word or two, too. It was my theory that it made the people in charge feel just a little bit superior and brainier than everyone else. After all, while most of them had more degrees than the rank and file undergrad, there was no evidence they had higher IQs.

The Week of Welcome, WoW!, convocation was for incoming freshman and transfer students and parents if they wanted to attend. Mercifully, there were no parents in the group of us who tromped through the heat from our all-girl dorm to the performing arts center on the other end of campus. I'd had one year of college at a local school in Seattle, making me a transfer student. Because I'd gone to summer school and taken some college credits in high school, I had enough credits to make me a junior. Which allowed me to get my job with the university, the job that was a big part of the reason I was here.

My heart pounded as we entered the air-conditioned comfort of the performing arts building. Irrationally, I looked around for Logan, even knowing he was way too familiar with campus to be either a freshman or a transfer. And the odds he was helping out with this event were practically nil. Funny how I knew so much about him. And so little at the same time. As hard as I tried to tamp the feeling down, I wanted to see his smile and that twinkling good eye of his.

Bre was texting Dan the minute we entered the building. The stadium seated something like twelve thousand. Half of the people already there were waving and looking for someone who was just coming in. From a distance, many of the guys looked alike. I didn't give Bre great odds she'd find Dan. I would have lost that bet. Somehow she spotted him. The girl had eagle eyes when it came to guy she was interested in. It's a useful skill, I guess. Maybe I'd make her teach it to me. Or maybe I already had it. I just didn't want to admit it.

"Come on! There he is." Bre bounced on her toes as she waved to Dan.

I looked at Nicole and Taylor, my two other new best friends from the dorm, for confirmation we should play tagalong. The looks on their faces were clear— they weren't thrilled with the idea of sitting with Bre's prey and watching her circle for the kill. Or look like a fool trying. The guys around Dan, including the red-headed Jake, didn't look particularly promising to me. But then, no one looked promising after meeting Logan. Besides, I had that bruised heart. It took a mega-watt of shining personality and totally hot looks to jolt it into getting excited and actually feeling something.

"You don't need wingmen for this operation, sol-dier," Nicole said, taking my arm and pointing to a trio of open seats. "Go to it, girl." She gave Bre a little shove with her free hand.

Bre hesitated. "But—"

Nicole made a shooing motion.

"I can't go down there alone." Bre turned to me.

My defensive reflexes weren't what they used to be. She grabbed my arm before I could move out of the way. "I promised Jake you'd be there."

Her voice was plaintive and scared and I was the biggest sucker in the world. The three of us trooped

after her. Bre slid in next to Dan. I had to sit next to
Jake. Nicole and Taylor sat on the end.

"So we meet again," I said to Jake, using my friendly
tone.

He scowled back. "You ditched me for a bellybutton
ring." He sounded like a petulant man-child.

The bellybutton ring hurt when I sat. There was no
way I'd be doing crunches for a while, either. I was too
supremely aware of the bar through my navel. But it
had been totally worth it on so many levels. I had no
regrets. Not one. Not even when Jake gave me the cold
shoulder.

I shrugged off his pettiness and made a face at Nicole and Taylor, looking for sympathy for having to put
up with the jerk Jake. They rolled their eyes and smiled
back.

Nicole leaned into me and whispered. "We'll ditch
him on the way out. No way we're letting him ruin the
barbecue."

I sat through the university president's welcoming
speech with my mind wandering, my heart racing, and
my palms sweating. I'd only come to the convocation
because of the faint hope that he might be here and I'd
get a non-personal look at him from afar. The all-
campus barbecue afterward was my real objective.
More speeches by various university officials. Some
rah-rah pep talks. The band played. We sang the fight
song. Class was dismissed.

As we wound out of the performing arts stadium
toward the track and the barbecue, we were each handed a pin with the university logo and the current year,

our year of admission, on it. I pinned mine to my thin summer top so I wouldn't lose it. This year was going to be momentous for me one way or another and I wanted a souvenir.

"That was lame," Nicole said.

"And boring," Taylor added.

"And over," I said.

"But have you ever seen so many good-looking men?" Taylor said.

"You mean except for the ones we sat by?" Nicole shook her head. "Jake's a jerk. What did you do to him, Ellie?"

"Like he said, I ditched him to get pierced." I just hadn't expected Logan to prick my heart.

"And he's not the forgiving type, I take it." Nicole put her arm around my shoulder. "Good riddance." She gave me a squeeze. "But why do you get that goofy 'I'm in love' look when you mention your bellybutton ring?"

I was that obvious when I thought about Logan? I wasn't in love. But I was hanging on to that one perfect evening, the perfect memory that would never go bad. I had to work on my game face. I shrugged. "It's a long story. It has to do with my mom."

"Mama wouldn't let you get a piercing, huh?" She squeezed me again.

I didn't correct her.

"Sticking it to the authority figure! I love it. You and I are kindred spirits."

The smell of grilling burgers wafted toward us as we approached the track. The rest of the student body, those who hadn't gone to convocation, were already streaming in and milling around. Promise to feed a group of college kids and they will come.

Taylor looked around the crowd, staring at all the men who weren't freshman. The distinction was obvious: confidence, maturity, bulked-up bodies—hot, hot, hot! "Not a moment too soon. I'm starved." The way she said it, it was clear she was starved for more than burgers. "Let's get in line."

Grills and burger stations lined the perimeters of the track.

Nicole looked around. "There's a short one."

"It's as good as any," Nicole said. "The server looks cute."

And athletic. And built like a tight end. The football players were serving burgers while the profs grilled.

As we joined the line, I experienced another moment of panic. This was exactly the kind of place where Logan would be. Spotting, and avoiding, a guy with a black eye should be easy, right?

I wasn't hungry, but I got a cheeseburger anyway, topped with the university's famous gold cheddar cheese made by the food sciences department. And chips. And a cookie. I'd only come for the swag. And because *he*'d be here. And I didn't mean Logan.

"Did you see the guy who handed me my plate?" Taylor waved her hand, making a gesture that meant he was smoking. "I'm in love."

"Sucker. The university's evil plan worked. Now you'll have to buy an athletic pass so you can see him on the field," I said as we carried our plates to the center of the track just past the long-jump pit.

"Shut up!" Taylor said. "I bought my pass when I registered." She grinned. "Did you see the way he flirted with me?"

"It's his job to flirt," Nicole said.

"I thought his job is to play football and bring in money from the alums," Taylor said. "Flirting is a side benefit. Something he does for fun with gorgeous girls."

Nicole rolled her eyes. "Dream on."

We found a spot on the grass that was semi in the shade of the back of the football stadium that butted up against the track. We sat on the prickly grass and settled down to eat.

Besides being relatively cool, this was a strategic spot for me. The departments had set up booths to promote their programs and hand out swag at the end of the track in the shade of the stadium near us.

Being so near the booths distracted me. Ever since I'd found out the truth, I'd been searching for him on the sly behind my mother's back. It hadn't been easy. I was practically a pathological truth-teller by nature. I'd only learned to lie with relative ease with plenty of practice. And by watching Mom. She was the mistress of deceit. If she ever found out I knew and why I was here...

I suppressed a shudder along with the thought, not wanting to imagine how crazy she'd go. She'd ruin everything. Like she had with everything else in my life. This was my one good thing. Make that my one *potentially* good thing. My chance to see if I was genetically doomed to be a conniving bitch or if there was a chance, however slim, that I could be something more. Nurture or nature? Had I ever really been nurtured? I was banking on nature.

Rumor had it that the tech department handed out flash drives in the shape of the university mascot every year. As far as tchotchkes went, they were more popular than the purse-size plastic single bandage holders the College of Nursing handed out. Or even than the tiny foam footballs from the athletic department. Only the first few thousand students got them.

A long line was already forming in front of the tech booth. I wanted one. But more importantly, I wanted to see the director of university information services. He was said to personally man the booth, preferring it to barbecuing next to the provost. Observing him from a distance in his natural environment was the whole point of the exercise.

I wanted to see my father—the real him, untainted by the knowledge of me.

"Hey! Earth to Ellie." Nicole waved her hand in front of my face. "What are you staring at?"

I grabbed her hand and pulled it out of my way as she followed my line of sight. "They're supposed to hand out flash drives that are the hottest swag from the barbecue."

"Yeah?" It took Taylor a minute to spot the booth we were looking at. The banner with the picture of the flash drive gave it away. "I want one, too!"

He chose that moment to stroll down the path from the gym on the hill and into the booth. My breath caught. I'd studied his picture so often I knew it was him. I looked for any similarity, anything familiar about him. Something that linked us. I waited for my dad to look into the crowd and pick me out like this was a fairy tale. To be my white knight the way I'd dreamed he'd be when I was a little girl. Wondering at the same time if I was being fair. If I had met him on the street, totally unprepared and with no knowledge of him, would I instinctively know who he was?

As he stepped into the booth, he joked with some of the students who were already in line. He was tall with dark hair. Handsome, with deep-set eyes and square shoulders. Slim and nicely built beneath the university polo shirt he wore. He seemed at ease, looking happy as he tossed a few flying discs with the IT department logo into the crowd. He pulled a box of flash drives from beneath the counter and started handing them out, still joking and laughing with the students who were waiting for them. The line began to move.

I felt a total lack of air, as if all the oxygen had been sucked out of the atmosphere, leaving me to suffocate in my feelings.

He looked like his pictures, but better. Animated, his charm was evident and familiar in a way I hadn't anticipated. He reminded me of someone...

Then it hit me with the force of falling flat onto my face—he reminded me of Austin. I clenched my fist to keep from hitting something and swallowed hard to keep the bile from rising in my throat. I was trembling in the heat.

The curve of his smile. The crinkle of his eyes. The way he moved. Worse, he reminded me a little of Logan, too. I wondered then, for the zillionth time, if that was why I found Logan attractive. I was looking for another Austin. A better Austin. Or worse, a father figure.

"Who are you staring at? Where's the eye candy?" Nicole's gaze bounced back to the booth, scanning the line.

"No one." It took a supreme act of will to keep my nerves out of my voice.

"Liar! You're blushing." Taylor was looking now, too. "Hmmm, lots of prospects. But the hottest guy I see is the man manning the booth."

Nicole squinted. "*Nice*. But he must be thirty-five or thirty-six. A little old for you, Tay, isn't he?"

Thirty-six sounded about right. I was nineteen. He'd been seventeen when I was born.

"Thirty-six is a hot age," Taylor said, on the defensive. "All the sexy, older actors are in their mid-thirties. It's like the peak of attractiveness. They're real men."

They way they talked about him freaked me out.

Taylor looked at me. "You're staring at him. Why are *you* so interested in him? Don't tell me you're into daddy figures, too?"

"No. No way." I shook my head, icked out. "I'm curious, is all. He's my new boss. I recognize him from his picture on the university website." True. A good lie always begins with the truth. I learned that from my mother. She was the queen. "I'm curious to see how he is. Is he cool? Or uptight? No sense of humor?" Also true—I was dying of curiosity. "I'm trying to get the lay of the land before I show up for my first day so I'll know how to play things to impress the new boss."

"Good plan!" Taylor nodded her approval. "I can't believe you scored such a cushy job." She wrinkled her nose. "I have to work in the dining hall. Work study sucks."

Nicole laughed. She didn't have to work anywhere.

Nicole popped to a stand. "What are we waiting for? Let's get ourselves a free flash drive and meet your boss."

I shook my head. "No, thanks. Go on ahead. I'll wait here. I'd rather wait until Monday to meet him face to face. It would be awkward introducing myself in that crowd."

That was true, too. What a fantastic truth-teller I was.

But the better, deeper truth was that I didn't want to meet my father for this first time as one of a sea of faces that he handed a piece of swag to. I confess again to lying. I hadn't come to the barbecue for the swag, either. I'd come to see what I was dealing with and whether I could face him when the time came and not give myself away.

"Oh, look! There's Bre." Taylor pointed. "She and her friends are way up in line. Let's cut in with them."

"Get one for me, too."

CHAPTER THREE

Okay, I confess to Facebook stalking Logan. It was immature, maybe. In my defense, I waited nearly twenty-four hours until giving in to my morbid curiosity. Certain thoughts kept swirling in my mind, demanding an answer—was he really as hot as I remembered? What did he look like without that black eye? Was sympathy for him coloring my perception and memories of him? Deep down, women like me like a wounded hero. We have this nurturing nursing instinct that kicks in and suddenly we become Florence Nightingale. Helping the hurt is better than concentrating on our own problems.

And then there's being lonely and angry, which can impair your judgment as easily as being drunk, especially if someone white-knights you out of the blue the way Logan had. I'd been stone-cold sober when we met, but I didn't trust myself.

And finally, what if he really was a fighter? And his pool-ball story was pure crap?

I told myself none of this mattered. I didn't want to see him again, especially not after realizing that he looked a little too much like Austin and maybe I was transferring. Or trying to recapture something that should have died a long time ago. I was hanging on and mourning, going through the stages of dead relationship grief. This was probably just another stage, a dangerous stage. I had to keep my head and focus on my mission. I was here to meet my dad, not fall in love again. One major emotional upheaval was probably one more than I could handle right now. I needed two like I needed another lab class.

Despite all my terrific and logical arguments, I couldn't stop myself from playing FBI and looking Logan up on Facebook. He was easy enough to find. And drop-dead gorgeous when he had two good eyes. Buff, too, in his bro-tank.

So not good. I realized I was smiling as I stared at his picture. That wasn't good, either. I couldn't see his whole profile, not unless I friended him. I scanned his About section, hoping he'd listed his major or something. Nope.

Okay, this was maybe even more desperate, but I hopped over to the university missed connections Facebook page. To cheer me up. Or maybe depress myself with all those people who found other people hot and were looking to connect. Getting a mention was like a rite of status and passage and an ego booster. Maybe Logan Walker was looking for me, the girl who did a Cinderella on him. Wouldn't it be good to know if he was? And if he'd already forgotten me, I still had the memory of a perfect night.

There were tons of messages. Everyone was looking for someone they'd met at one of the WoW! functions.

Hey, beautiful girl in the red skirt who bumped into me at The Price is Right and spilled her pop on my sandals. I think you're hot. Bummed that I chickened out and didn't get your number. I'm the blond who won the football jersey. HMU...

I scanned down the list, smiling at the romantic sentiment of some, laughing at others, and getting more depressed, and, conversely, relieved at the same time. Then one message popped out.

Desperately seeking the gorgeous girl with the great sense of humor who got her bellybutton pierced at Up All Night. I'd like to hold your hand again. Hit me up. Seriously. Your moral support guy with the black eye.

There was no mistaking this message. This one was for me. *My* moral support guy.

I couldn't help it. I was smiling ear to ear, even as my pulse roared in them. "It's your black eye. It blurred your vision," I said aloud, as if he was in the room with me. "You couldn't see clearly. I think maybe you did get a concussion, because something messed with your mind." I paused. "I'm not gorgeous," I whispered just before I panicked and saw about thirty tags and over a hundred likes.

Shit.

I clicked on the message so I could see all the tags, worried that someone had tagged me and blown my cover.

Logan, buddy, this has to be you. You're the only guy I know who can get a black eye while playing pool. Babe, reveal yourself before my man goes crazy.

Message after message tagging Logan. No one knew who I was. I wasn't tagged once. I let out a happy sigh of relief. This was still my private thing. And—Logan's story about pool appeared to be true, or at least consistent. I took a screenshot of his message so I could look at it whenever I wanted.

I bounced back to his profile page. My fingers hovered over the Add Friend button like they had a mind of their own. Temptation is a bitch. I took a deep breath and reminded myself again what a bad idea it was to contact Logan. Not only did I not want to spoil that perfect memory, it wasn't fair to him.

Since I was on a Facebook binge, I flipped to Austin's page for comparison's sake. I'd unfriended him right after. We went from "in a relationship" to enemies in an instant. He'd updated his picture. My traitorous heart did a little flip when I saw it. He'd healed and looked good. Part of me was relieved.

I swallowed hard and studied his picture, trying futilely to convince myself he and Logan looked nothing alike. That I didn't have a type. That I wasn't looking for a guy like daddy. Until early this summer, well after I'd been dating Austin, I didn't even know what my dad looked like. And even if I did have a physical type, that didn't mean they had to act the same and all be lying scumbag cheaters.

The door to our dorm room shuddered open. Bre came in. I closed my browser.

"What are you up to?" Bre asked.

"Nothing. Just reading missed connections."

"Anything interesting?" She came over and plopped on her bed. "Were we mentioned?" She sounded too hopeful.

I shrugged and gave her a sympathetic look. "Why would you be mentioned? You made a connection."

"Some other guy could be lusting after my body." She grinned. "Why do you have that sappy look on your face?" She cocked a brow comically.

"I'm a sucker for a good romance. There's a lot of cute, romantic stuff on there. Missed connections galore. The course of true love never does run smooth." Yeah, I still remembered a bit of my Shakespeare. I snapped my laptop shut. "I'm starved. Let's get something to eat."

"Since when are you ever starved?"

Since now, when I was the teeniest bit irrationally happy that Logan was looking for me. It didn't mean anything. And I wasn't going to act on it. But I could hold onto that glimmer of happiness for a while. What was the harm in that?

On Sunday, we went to the rec center and spent as much of the day as we could in the pool. It was the only way to cool down. I wore my white bikini that showed off my new bellybutton ring. I wasn't exactly trolling, but I got a few looks. I kept a nervous eye out for Logan, wondering what he'd think of me in my bikini. He never showed. Maybe he was one of the lucky ones with an air-conditioned apartment.

Sunday night I cleaned my bellybutton super carefully. I wasn't supposed to have gone in chlorine, but the heat made me do it. Just before bed I checked missed connections again to see if there were any more tags and whether I'd been outed as Logan's mystery girl. A few more tags mentioning Logan. And this new message:

Hot guy with the black eye I saw at the creamery today with your three friends, how handsome are you in your normal state? I followed you back to campus, but not in a creepy stalker way. I was walking the same way at the same pace. I'm a blond Double Deltzee. I'd like to get to know you. Want to meet up?

I scowled. Delta Delta Zetas were sluts and the beauty queens of campus. They never wore their letters without wearing full makeup. Odds are this girl was truly gorgeous. And whether I wanted to admit it or not, I was jealous. Pea green, in fact, even though I had no right to be.

Monday morning I was up early. When I sat up in bed, my bellybutton ring ached, reminding me that pleasure doesn't come without pain. I winced and cursed Logan Walker for getting me into this bellybutton ring thing. Without his help, I could have backed out and been pain free. Then again, maybe I shouldn't have gone swimming in a chlorinated pool. I lifted up the tank top I slept in to check my piercing. My navel looked pink and healthy. I admired the ring—gorgeous! The jewel sparkled in the light streaming in past the edges of our blackout blinds and made me happy. As happy as I got, anyway.

Despite getting up early, I was still running late for my first day of class. My stomach was full of dueling butterflies, the vicious warrior kind that swooped and attacked each other. Today was not only the first day of class. It was the first day of my job and I was going to meet my biological father face to face.

I had no idea how I was going to react. Calmly, I hoped. I kept telling myself he was just a guy who had sex with my mother and never found out about the consequences. He didn't owe me anything. Maybe he owed my mom something, like back child support. But for all her evil ways, she'd never asked him for it. Of course, asking would have meant tracking him down and telling him about me. For some reason, Mom had never done it.

Even though I'd picked out my outfit the day before, now I had doubts. I changed and changed again in front of our rotating floor fan, tossing discarded clothes on my bed to blow in the breeze. The heat wave had only barely moderated into the nineties and the night had not cooled off like it should have. My room was heavy with the weight of the stuffy, warm air and nervous anticipation. When I opened my closet doors, I was hit by a blast of trapped heat. I could go to class in shorts and a tank top, but I couldn't go to work dressed like that. Not on my first day. Not to meet my father.

How should I dress to meet my father? For most people the clothing choice was simple—they meet them as babies in their birthday suit.

Then there was the sense of peer pressure. All the girls would be trying to look their best today. Without my mom around to compete with, I was not going to be outdone.

At last I changed back into my original choice—a cute summer skirt and lacy tank top. I applied my makeup in the heat, putting on more than I usually wore. Mom had taught me well how to apply makeup with the skill of an artist. I usually didn't bother with it on a daily basis. Especially not when she was around.

After I finished, I stared into the mirror at my reflection, looking for a resemblance to either of my parents. I didn't look like my mother. I had been all too aware of that my entire life. My first memory was almost literally hearing the words "It's a pity she didn't take after her mother. Melissa is such a beauty. She must look like *him*."

Him said with derision. Whoever him was. No one ever said. Sometimes I wondered if anyone besides Mom even knew.

My mother was a beauty, a siren, a sensual woman who turned men's heads, no doubt about it. Even now. Her hair was blond and sleek. Mine was naturally mousy brown with a hint of curl that gave me wings of bangs around my face. Growing them out didn't help, just made me look more like I was about to take flight. Her eyes were startling blue and wide. Mine were somewhere between light green and hazel, and slightly deep set. Her nose was petite and her cheekbones high. My cheekbones were muted versions of hers and my nose was wider. The only thing I'd really inherited from my mom was the general shape of her figure. And even still, I wasn't quite as buxom and she never failed to tell me that my waist wasn't as small as hers had been at my age. So, not quite the hourglass figure of hers.

I wasn't as good looking as Mom. In a crowd, you'd never pick me out as Melissa's daughter. This was the first time I could honestly say that was a blessing.

Mom had never told me why she and my biological father had broken up. Or even if they'd ever been a couple. She hadn't even told me who he was. But at least he wouldn't take one look at me and realize I was her clone. And maybe hate me on contact because of whatever had passed between them.

On the other hand, I didn't look like him, either. It wasn't like he was going to take one look at me and see his reflection, pull me into his arms, and say, "Hey, kid, welcome home." No, Jason Front wasn't going to recognize me as anything more than another kid working her way through college. And until I decided I wanted more, that was going to have to be fine with me.

Despite all my internet and social media snooping, there was so much I didn't know about my dad Jason Front. For being in IT, he was surprisingly private. His social media profiles were purely professional. Maybe since he worked for the university, that was the best way to protect himself from pranking. But it left me wondering things, like: Did he have other kids? Ones

that he knew about? Was he married? Divorced? Who
knew? The thought of finding out was both thrilling
and terrifying.

I might not be an only child after all. Maybe I have
half brothers and sisters. I wasn't sure how I felt about
that. It certainly would complicate any relationship I
might make with my newfound dad. It might even prevent me from revealing myself. I wasn't here to mess up
his life, just get to know him. I really didn't expect him
to be a real dad to me, even though I'd always longed
for one.

How *would* he react when and if he found out about
me? The thought made my stomach knot. Would he
accept me? Reject me? Deny being my father? Be over-
joyed?

What if he rejected me? Could I handle that? I
thought so. My mom was a complete wreck, a horrible
mother, and I somehow managed to live with that. But
I'd never know for sure unless I actually faced it. I
could freak and be crushed for all I really knew. I wondered—maybe holding the dream was better than facing reality. I was wary and cautious, extremely
cautious. I couldn't afford to make a mistake.

I had Chem 202 lecture at nine on Monday,
Wednesday, and Friday mornings. Chem lab on Tuesday afternoon. Chem 202 was one of those prereqs that
I needed for my minor in biology, needed before I could
take the more interesting upper-level classes of my
choosing. It was also the only sophomore-level class in
my schedule. There was one section of it, period. Why

else would I sign up for chemistry at that ungodly hour?

I rushed to the dining hall. It was hectic and packed. Everyone scrambling to grab a bite and running late. Taylor was working the coffee kiosk and playing barista. She already looked stressed and worn out. I got in the line behind everyone else who needed a morning jolt of caffeine to go from walking dead to semi-awake.

When my turn finally came, Taylor glanced at the clock overhead. "Aren't you supposed to be in class in five?"

"Yeah. Can you give me a rush order?"

"You'll have to take it black."

"Give me a shot of vanilla syrup and dollop of whip and I'm good to go."

She grabbed the whipped-cream canister, made a circle of cream around the coffee, putting extra whip on it, slapped on a lid, and handed it over.

"I owe you."

"Put a tip in the jar." She was already helping the next customer.

I raced to class, sipping coffee and moving as quickly as I could in flip-flop sandals. Chem 202 was, surprisingly enough, in the chem building in the big lecture hall. By the time I got there, the only empty seats were in the front. Breathing hard, I maneuvered my way toward the front and finally found an empty seat. "Is that seat saved?"

The skinny, nerdy guy in the seat next to me looked up at me. If he told me *It's saved for you, baby*, that would just make my day.

He shrugged. I slid in just as the prof, Dr. Rhonda Rogers, took the podium. She was mid-thirties, slender, well groomed. Not bad looking for a chem prof. And then she opened her mouth and revealed herself for the arrogant bitch she was.

"Most of you will *pass* this class. If you work hard. However, I give very few A's."

I frowned. This was going to be one of *those* classes. I was on academic scholarship and needed to keep my grades up to keep it. The last thing I needed was a jerk of a prof proving her superiority by wielding the grade card like a broadsword to create GPA carnage.

Then she launched into the lecture, flipping through PowerPoint slides solid with writing and data so fast there was no way to keep up with note taking. Despite getting an A in the chem class that was supposedly the prereq to this one, I didn't understand a word. Not many, anyway. The chemical symbols from the periodic table jumped out at me. Halfway through class, I was already on the university website, looking for an alternative class, and sending an email to my advisor. I wasn't alone. If the open browsers around me were any indication, getting out of this class was an urgently common theme.

There was nothing. It was either this, or another semester delay getting into the next class for my minor. I checked the prof's rating—1.2 out of ten over the past seven years she'd been teaching.

Get out fast! Run, don't walk! Drop this class before the first lecture ends. It only gets worse. Studied my ass off and barely got a C-.

And those were the uplifting and encouraging comments.

Dr. Rogers was some sort of research genius who brought in big grant money. So the university kept her. Fine by me, but why make her teach? Lock her in a lab somewhere and let her do her thing. Assign us an eager doctoral candidate who'd been a student recently enough to care about them. This was typical university-think—university first, students as second-class citizens as an afterthought. Funding and prestige were all. Come to our university. We have world-class professors. Never mind that they hate students and couldn't teach a kindergartener how to tie their shoe.

After an eternity of listening to gibberish, class finally ended. The skinny guy next to me turned to me. "We're trapped. There's no way out."

"You were checking, too?" I knew he had been, but I didn't want to look like an eavesdropper, or whatever you call it when you read over someone's shoulder. I'd seen his screen.

He nodded. "I knew it was futile. If there were any alternative, would any of us have signed up for chem at nine in the morning with the worst prof in the department?

"She's legendary for being a bitch. Word is she takes great delight in flunking students. It's not about teaching the material for her. It's about proving how much smarter she is than the rest of us mere mortals."

He shook his head. "But I had to convince, and kill, my optimistic self. I was hoping for a miracle, like so much demand that chem department had to open another section with a different prof." He grinned. "So much for youthful optimism. It met a quick death. We're stuck.

"Now it's time for battle strategy. We need a study group if we're going to defeat the bitch. An elite team of brainiacs. Either that, or a strategic team who can stage a takeover. Are you in?"

I was impressed with his grasp of the situation and attitude. And the foresight he'd had to check out the prof. I'd been too distracted to even think of it.

I liked the sound of a coup. I grabbed my backpack and made my way to the aisle. "Did you understand a word of what she said?"

He nodded. "About half."

Okay, he was the man for me. That was about half more than I did. "I'm in for the takeover. Not sure I'll be much help with the study group. You understood more than I did," I said as we climbed the stairs to get out of the auditorium.

"Can you bake?" he asked as we reached the top.

"That's a sexist question."

He shrugged. "I have a big appetite and I like warm cookies. I can do a lot of things, but I pretty much suck at baking. I blame my mom. She's a crappy cook. If you can bake, I'd be willing to take you on, even if you are a handicap."

"Who said I'd be a handicap? I'm pretty good at revolutions."

He smiled in a charming, endearing way. He had a sense of humor. I liked that in a man. Plus, I needed a smart, savvy ally.

"FYI, Dr. Rogers never hands back her tests, just posts grades. It's part of her diabolical plot to keep students in the dark and give them no opportunity or fighting chance at passing her tests. I, however, have been preparing for the inevitable. I have access to every test Dr. Rogers has given over the past five years." He paused for dramatic effect. "She likes to recycle questions."

"No!" I was pretty sure my eyes had gone wide. Now I was really impressed.

"I have my sources."

"In that case, I know how to slice cookies off a tube and bake them. And I have access to an oven."

He cocked a brow as we emerged in the hall outside the auditorium. "Cookies from a tube? That's supposed to impress me?"

"I can bake from scratch. I make a mean chocolate chip cookie. But it's not easy in the dorm. Have you ever tried to stock all the ingredients? I do, however, have a connection in the dining hall."

"Good enough. You're in." He extended his hand. "Dex."

"Ellie."

"I have a few other guys in mind for our group. They were sitting in the back."

Which I took to mean they weren't quite as nerdy as Dex.

"Military types or great brains?" I asked.

"Both."

"I guess I'll have to trust your judgment."

He whipped out his cell phone. "What's your number?"

I gave it to him and got his. This was either legit, or a really clever way of hitting on a girl. It didn't matter. Dex was cute in his own nerdy way and I kind of liked him. Best of all, he posed absolutely no danger to my heart. Chem was settled. Sort of.

I had another class, lunch, and a third class before work.

"I have to run," I said.

Dex nodded. "See you soon."

I nodded back. "Don't storm the Bastille without me."

He grinned.

I took off.

"Hey, Ellie!" he called after me. "When's your lab?"

I yelled over my shoulder. "Tomorrow at one."

Did his grin just grow?

The computer science building housed all of technical services as well as comp sci. It was located in the mall just down the hill next to the SUB. As I walked through the front doors and looked for the office of university IT, I should have felt relief from the oppressive afternoon heat outdoors. Instead I felt ice cold, trembling with anticipation and dread. A hundred things could go wrong. Once again, my plan seemed about as smart as playing kickball in the middle of the freeway. But given my current family life—a mother I didn't speak to and three ex-stepfathers, what did I really have to lose? What harm could adding one biological father into the mix possibly do? He was just potentially another parent I didn't talk to.

My mother had terrible taste in men, at least to my way of thinking. She liked the jock type with big egos. Men who didn't treat her right, liked to wander, and walked out when things got the slightest bit dicey. Every one of my stepfathers had the same bad points, and their good points were sometimes hard to find and not plentiful enough to satisfy my mom and save her marriages. Not that she was a peach to live with, either. But then, they'd picked her, too.

Given her appalling taste in men, I had pretty low expectations about what my bio dad would be like. Odds favored him being a first-class douchebag. But just like Dex's naïve optimism in chemistry, I hoped against hope that he was a better man. My rationale may have been skewed, but I kept thinking that she *hadn't* married him. Maybe that was in his favor. Maybe he didn't run to type.

Manning the booth on Saturday, he'd seemed charming. He had that personal magnetism that put people at ease and a sense of humor that students love. Then again, who wouldn't like someone who gave you a free flash drive?

In anticipation of him being a douchebag who denied paternity and needed proof if he ever found out about me, I carried a DNA testing kit wrapped in brown paper in my backpack. I know, odd. But it was like a security blanket.

I steeled myself for the worst, put my game face on, and pressed on, taking the stairs to the second-floor office like I was on my way to another soul-sucking chemistry class.

I'm good at math and science, but I'm no programmer. I got the job in IT because of a recommendation from one of my profs at my old school. He was buds with someone in tech services, someone not my bio dad. He sold me, saying that since I was majoring in management information services, this was a good fit for me.

By the time I found my dad, I'd already decided on MIS for a major, with a minor in biochem. I wanted to work in the medical field, but not practicing medicine. I like computer stuff, but I'm not technical enough to want a comp sci degree. When I found out what my dad did for a living, I was stunned. I'd somehow inherited a bit of his technical talents. It was a connection, however small.

This semester I had chosen my classes carefully. None of them met in the computer science building. I wanted access to my dad in controlled measures and circumstances.

I reached the IT offices, braced myself, and opened the door. An admin sat at the front desk. She raised an eyebrow in question when she saw me. "May I help you?"

"Ellie Martin. I'm starting work here today?"

"Ellie! Of course. Welcome! We were expecting you. I'm Karen." The nameplate on her desk said *Karen White*. The phone rang. "Excuse me. Just a minute. University Information Technology. This is Karen."

As Karen handled the call, I looked around the office. The door to my bio dad's office was closed. I found myself staring at it, mesmerized and terrified. *Jason*

Front. If things had turned out differently, I could have been Ellie Front. Which was a curse in itself. Say it fast and it sounds like elephant. Can you imagine the ribbing? Maybe Jason wouldn't have allowed Mom to name me Ellie. Maybe I'd be a whole different person.

"Sorry about that." Karen stood. "First day of class things are crazy around here. This AV doesn't work. We have an emergency in the Culver Aud. Their internet connection is down. It's one thing after another. You haven't arrived a minute too soon. We need reinforcements!" She came around to the front of the desk.

Great. I'd arrived in the middle of a firestorm. Not the best time to introduce myself to my father. Maybe even worse than at the booth in a crowd of faces.

"Let me just take you back to Jason. He'll give you your assignment. This way." She hitched her thumb at his office door. "His door's closed, which means he's up to his eyeballs in emergencies. Generally, he has an open-door policy. You should never be afraid of talking to him. He's very helpful and loves all his student assistants and IT experts."

I wondered if he'd love me once he found out the truth. *If* he found out the truth. I had to be exceptionally careful while I decided what to do. I followed Karen to his office with my heart pounding.

She listened at the door, trying to discern if he was on an important call or not. "We're very casual here," she said. "We call everyone by their first names, including Jason. None of that self important Dr. So-and-So junk in this office." She smiled conspiratorially and tapped on the door.

"Come in."

As she turned the knob and pushed the door open, the phones went crazy again. She shook her head and rolled her eyes. "Jason, this is your new assistant, Ellie Martin."

He was preoccupied, staring at the computer on his desk and typing away madly. He didn't look up. I recognized the intense expression of concentration on his face—it was the twin of my own when I was engrossed in something. My heart skipped a beat. I was hit with a deep connection I hadn't expected. And the thrill of a treasure hunter who finds something that's been lost and presumed gone forever.

Karen squeezed my shoulder. "Those darn phones. Gotta run!"

I froze in the doorway, staring at him, overwhelmed with an unfathomable, totally unexpected wash of love that broke me and made me want to cry. This was my *dad* I was finally staring at up close. My flesh and blood.

Most people go to college glad to escape their parents' rules and control. To go out on their own and do their own thing. I was doing it backwards, hoping my father took some kind of interest in my life. Even the tiniest bit. I had to bite my lip to keep it from trembling.

"Come on in." He barely glanced at me, but his tone was friendly as he waved me in. "Don't be scared. I don't bite."

Somehow I made my feet move, fighting my sentimental nature, waiting for him to look up and—what?

Feel the bond I so suddenly felt? Embrace me as his long-lost heir? Cry with me?

"Let me deal with this." His voice was nice, pleasant, not too high, not too deep. Not at all dad-like, just vital and confident. He was obviously stressed, but keeping it under control, not showing it. Such a refreshing change from my stepdads, who bellowed and raged at the slightest provocation.

He hit a key, looked up at me, and smiled warmly, like he was genuinely happy to meet me.

My heart did another odd little flip. I wondered what his smile would have looked like if he were meeting me for the first time the way he should have nineteen years ago, as a newborn placed in his arms. Would he have beamed with pride? What was the story behind me and why *hadn't* he been there?

He stood and extended his hand for me to shake.

As I looked in his eyes, I knew deep in my soul he was the man who'd fathered me. I didn't actually have a DNA report to prove it. But I knew in the way a baby knows its mother from birth, with primal instinct. Up close his eyes were a shade between green and hazel, like mine. But it was more than our eye color that connected us.

"Call me Jason. Everyone does." As he shook my hand in his warm, confident grip, his brow furrowed.

"Ellie Martin."

The furrow deepened. He cocked his head, studying me with an intense gaze. "Have we met before?" He sounded puzzled. "You look familiar."

I felt almost paralyzed with joy and fear. Ecstatic he felt the familiarity and panicked I'd be outed before I was ready. I smiled and shook my head. "No. I don't think so."

His puzzled look remained. "I could swear... You remind me of someone."

As I fought to hide my fear, I didn't help him out or give him any clues. To be honest, I didn't actually know whether I reminded him of Mom or himself, or his great aunt Martha. I kept smiling, feeling the effort as if my mouth was stretched against its will as my heart did a tap dance in my chest. "Maybe you've seen me on campus?"

He didn't look convinced. He shook his head as if shaking some niggling, vague thought away. "Never mind. It'll come to me." He paused. "You come highly recommended, Ellie." He smiled again, but I could tell he was still trying to place me. "And not a moment too soon. We're swamped."

I nodded. "I'm happy to be here."

His office was cluttered with paperwork, cables, university brochures, and all kinds of software. A few university team posters hung on the walls—football, baseball, men's basketball, women's volleyball. No personal pictures. Nothing helpful in my quest to find out more about him. He had a single digital picture frame on his desk. It was turned off.

Foiled again.

"It's too crazy to train you today. We'll get to that later. Your regular assignment will be dispatching and managing our team of IT specialists. Today, I need you

to help Karen with the phones. There's an empty desk
next to hers. Sit there for now. She'll show you the
ropes."

I nodded.

"Good." He glanced at his computer and scowled,
letting out a deep breath. "Great. Another emergency."

So this was our inauspicious first meeting. How I
met my father.

I was just about to leave and find Karen when there
was a motion behind me.

Jason looked up and grinned at someone over my
shoulder. "Logan! Thank God, you're here." His grin
turned to a frown of concern. "What happened to your
eye? Run into a door?"

That was when my heart stopped—like, literally
thudded to a halt for a second. This could not be. Could
not. What were the odds there were two Logans with
black eyes on campus?

My options ran through my mind in a flash. I was
sunk. Short of vaporizing, there was no way to escape
without him seeing me. Maybe, hopefully, he wasn't as
hot as I remembered or as he looked on his Facebook
page. Or as all those other girls thought he was.

I was instantly glad I'd dressed up to meet Jason,
but worried that in the full light of day, without the
influence of a concussion messing with his judgment,
Logan would realize I was ordinary and plain. Just another girl. I took a deep breath and turned around,
feeling like I was moving in slow motion, seeing every
frame of the room as it passed before my eyes.

"This is—" Jason was saying.

And there Logan stood before me, achingly beautiful, even marred with a black eye.

"El!" Logan's face lit up like he'd just won a full-ride scholarship. "It *is* you."

"Logan?" My heart leaped. I couldn't keep the wonder and surprise out of my voice. Hopefully it covered the awe and fluttery, embarrassed way I felt around him. "What do you mean—it *is* you? You mean you didn't recognize me from behind?"

He didn't miss a beat, just grinned wickedly. "I thought it was you. I *hoped* it was you. But I've been disappointed a few times already today. Girls look surprisingly alike from behind. Without seeing your abs I couldn't be certain. How's the piercing?"

Still just as charming. Maybe even *hotter* than I remembered. The eye was still ugly, but it was no longer swollen shut. Around the edges the dark purple was turning yellow-green. Now that the swelling was down, his cheekbones were more prominent and both eyes danced with joy.

I blushed.

Jason interrupted. "You two know each other?" He would have had to be dead not to notice the way the air between us crackled with attraction.

I cursed myself for letting it show. Jason's tone was wary, like he really didn't need an office romance blooming between us. Like he'd hoped it would be a little longer before the new girl fell for Logan.

"What's this about a piercing?" Jason sounded almost dad-like for the first time.

I found it oddly touching. It was hard thinking of him as Jason, but "Dad" seemed even stranger. I was so used to mentally referring to him as *him*.

"We met at Up All Night," I said.

"I held her hand while she got her bellybutton pierced. Show it to him, El." Logan's eyes egged me on.

I shook my head subtly and gave him a look that let him know I'd pay him back for teasing me later.

Logan laughed.

Jason smiled. "That won't be necessary. Well, this makes life easy. No introductions necessary."

No. It made life incredibly complicated. There went my perfect memory. My perfect moment.

"Sorry. I didn't catch your last name when we met." The look in Logan's eyes was victorious. There was no way to refuse him now and he knew it. He could check the records and find out anyway.

I stared back at him with feigned confidence. "Martin. Ellie...Elizabeth Martin. Any other questions?"

His grin was positively triumphant.

Jason interrupted again. "Logan, get Ellie settled on the phones. Then get back in here. I need your debugging skills. Culver Aud is out of internet service. The business department is holding my ass to the fire."

"This way, Ellie Elizabeth *Martin*." Logan led me to the desk next to Karen's and held a chair out for me.

"And a gentleman, too," I said as I took a seat. "Sometimes."

He just grinned as he pulled a chair up next to mine, way too near for comfort.

"Watch your backside, Logan Walker. I'll get you for embarrassing me in front of the boss."

He leaned close as he showed me how the phones worked and brought up the roster of on-call tech support reps. "I'd rather watch yours."

His nearness sent my pulse racing. I could barely think. How would I ever get any work done in this office with both him and my dad here to rattle me?

"How do I know who to call for what?"

"If in doubt, call me." He winked.

I gently bumped his shoulder. "Seriously. I need to know. Do you want me to get fired my first day on the job?"

"I don't want you to get fired, *ever*. The office would be too dull without you."

Karen shot us a look warning us to stop flirting and start working.

Logan caught it and gave me a quick, almost mockingly professional rundown of the techs, their strengths and weaknesses. "If you have any questions, ask Karen." He rolled his eyes and made a face.

I stifled a laugh.

He glanced at the clock. "Shit. Jason will have my ass if I don't get in there." He rolled back in his chair and stood. "What time are you off, El?"

I liked the way he called me El. It was familiar, and maybe a little presumptuous since we just met. But I liked it all the same. "Five."

"Yeah. Me too."

Jason stepped out of his office. "Logan! Are you coming?"

"Be there in a sec, boss." He turned to me. "Get a burger with me after our shift, colleague to colleague?"

Karen was listening from her desk, I was sure of it. As bad of an idea as it was to get involved with a coworker in my bio dad's office, there was no way to politely refuse and not look like a jerk. Unless I pleaded an overload of homework.

It was like he read my mind. He cut me off before I could speak. "I have tons of homework. But we have to eat, right?"

"Sure. After work," I said. "At the SUB?"

"It's a date."

Why did my heart go crazy again?

He grinned and winked. "Good luck."

Karen watched Logan disappear into Jason's office and shut the door. When he was out of sight, she turned to me. "Logan's a great kid, don't get me wrong. He's a favorite of Jason's. He has a lot of charm and charisma. And a *lot* of problems.

"The girls fall all over him." She paused, studying me. I got the feeling she really was trying to be nice. "Just watch yourself around him. He's a player."

I blushed. "We're just acquaintances."

She nodded like she didn't believe me, like her warning was falling on deaf ears. And maybe it was.

The phones started ringing. I picked up. I was on the phone when Logan came out of Jason's office a few minutes later.

"I have to go out on a call," he whispered to me as he leaned over my desk. "I'll meet you back here at five."

I nodded and he took off. The next three hours were lightning busy, storm after storm of technical troubles. I didn't get a chance to ask Karen anything about Jason. I didn't even see him. He was locked in his office dealing with emergencies. And Logan was out in the field.

I was off at five, but hung around, still working until five thirty, waiting too eagerly for Logan, hoping for another word or two with Jason, and trying to be generally helpful and not look like a clock-watcher. Logan didn't show up, text, or call.

Karen gave me a sympathetic look, like she could read my disappointment with Logan as easily as she read her computer screen. "Go home and get some studying done. We could be here all night."

I was crazy disappointed, really let down about being blown off, falling into the abyss after having been so high earlier. I mean, no matter how busy Logan was he could let me know he had to cancel. He was an IT genius, after all. He could find a way.

I gathered my things and headed out, making mental excuses for Logan. Like they say, hope springs eternal. Maybe he'd lost track of time. Or maybe his phone battery had died.

But I was jaded by the way Austin had treated me and my confidence was broken. I wasn't as trusting and forgiving as I used to be. The doubting side of me kept whispering *Only a douchebag begs a girl to have a burger with him and then forgets about it. He doesn't care. He's just a terrible flirt. A player. Listen to Karen—forget him.*

I had thought Logan was different, sweet and
thoughtful. An irrational anger welled up in me. He'd
wrecked my perfect memory.

I didn't like hanging on any guy's string. I'd had
enough of that with Austin. I wouldn't be like my mom,
making up all kinds of excuses for why her various
husbands weren't where they were supposed to be or
why they missed events that were important to her.
Priorities, it all came down to priorities. And I was
suddenly feeling like I had no priority at all with Logan.

I was halfway to the SUB, lost in hurt, angry, self-
doubting thoughts, when I heard someone calling my
name. Down the street that ran perpendicular to the
mall, Logan jogged toward me, his backpack swinging
from his shoulder as he waved to get my attention. "El!
Ellie!"

I could have kept walking. Acted like I hadn't seen
him. Dinner with him was such a bad idea. I never
should have agreed to it in the first place, the sensible,
cautious part of me warned.

But blatantly blowing people off wasn't me. The
contrite, worried look on his face stopped me. I was,
quite simply, a sucker for him.

Logan was out of breath when he reached me. "Hey.
I thought I'd missed you. I tried to call the office to tell
you I was running late, but the phones were constantly
busy. I didn't have your number to text you. I'm sorry
as hell, El."

He caught my arm. "You're upset with me. It's my
fault. I should have been prepared. Sent up a smoke

signal. Something. Anything." From his tone, it was clear he was trying to tease me out of being irritated with him. "I've blown it already."

"I think fires are illegal in the business building." I smiled at him.

He grinned back.

"You can make it up to me by filling me in on office politics." I was way too blatantly relieved and happy that he hadn't blown me off.

"Over dinner. I'm starving and hate eating alone." He led the way into the SUB and then to the grill and cafe on the second floor.

I could use my dining hall account at the grill, which I was grateful for. Money was tight. Mom was punishing me by withholding funds. I had enough to get by, but I had to be careful. And I wasn't going to let him pay.

To my relief, he didn't try. We got our burgers and fries and headed to our table.

"Logan!" A leggy brunette spotted him and ran over to give him a hug and coo her sympathy over his black eye. "What happened to you?"

"Dangerous game of pool. Never play with Collin when he's drunk."

She laughed. "I'll remember that." She looked right past me like I wasn't even there. "Coming to Collin's party Friday night?"

"Wouldn't miss it."

"Good. I'll see you there." There was way too much innuendo and promise in her simple "see you there."

I couldn't believe I was jealous.

She glanced at his burger, right past me again. "You better eat before that gets cold. See you Friday." She strolled off in the confident way girls who know they're attractive have.

"Friend of yours?"

Logan looked at me. "Yeah." He didn't elaborate and it was really none of my business. As he led the way to a table by the windows with a view of the practice football field below, he attracted more than his share of female attention. He was just that way. He walked confidently and was filled with infectious charm. Even if he hadn't been tall and handsome, my guess was that girls would love him anyway. Charisma can be as sexy as hot looks.

We slid into chairs across from each other with the windows off to the side. Although it was comfortable and cool in the SUB, I was anything but at ease.

Logan picked up his burger and peeled the wrapping back. "How was your first day in the office? Do you love it?"

"Love it? You *are* a crazy optimist." I grabbed a bottle of ketchup and poured a puddle of it into the basket next to my fries. "It was hectic and confusing—"

"And wonderful because I showed up." He had a smile in his eyes as he took a bite of his burger.

I rolled my eyes. "Yeah, that's it—wonderful. How was your day, honey?"

He laughed and winked me. "Cute." He grabbed the ketchup bottle and made a crisscross pattern of ketchup across his fries. "Mine was hectic, and wonderful because I ran into you, Ellie Elizabeth Martin."

He was either an incredibly sweet guy, or, more likely, a player like Karen suggested. To hide my obvious pleasure from him, I looked at his fries and winced.

"What?" He followed my line of sight.

"Your fries are going to get soggy." I made a point of shuddering.

He looked at mine and spoke in a sexy voice. "Maybe I like soggy." He winked while I tried not to blush. "You're obviously a dipper."

I sighed dramatically. "Irreconcilable differences. I suppose as just coworkers we'll have to put our differences aside for the sake of office peace."

He grinned as I realized that came out *all* wrong. It sounded like I was hinting for more, practically begging him to ask me out. I was sure he was used to girls who falling all over him. But in my case, nothing could be further from the truth. I was trying to subtly let him know how things stood between us—just coworkers, nothing else. Period. Jason and Karen had already made it clear office romances were frowned on. And the last thing I needed was to alienate my father before I got to know him. Or lose my job.

I cursed fate for putting me in the path of this gorgeous, adorably sweet guy, dangling him in front of me to heal my broken heart, and then snatching him away in a cruel twist. He was Jason's favorite, way too close with him for me to trust. What if I gave myself away? What if he reported back to Jason that I was asking too many questions about him?

I was delirious that Logan was flirting with me and balancing precariously on the edge of the abyss of certain future unhappiness.

Logan made a show of eating a handful of ketchup-sogged fries. "Seriously, work was crazy. I had to battle one fire after another. Dr. Hall was an absolute shit about being without internet during his lecture. I had to bite my tongue so I wouldn't tell him that being without internet access, maybe some of the students actually listened to his dull lecture."

"You're awful. But I do admire a man with self-control." I took a bite of burger and tried not to stare too hard at him. He was way too easy on my eyes.

"Things in the office will calm down soon. You're going to love working with us. Jason is an awesome boss."

Logan had just given me the opening I was looking for. "Tell me about Jason."

"Tell you what?"

"All the important political stuff—how to get on his good side. What pitfalls to avoid. Who his enemies are. Who his friends are. Which profs and departments should get priority attention. You know, the basics."

"Why are you asking me?" He pulled an onion out of his burger and set it aside.

"Because you're obviously his favorite. Even Karen says so."

"She does?" His eyes danced and he wore an innocent look, pretending like he had no idea when he knew full well he was.

"Seriously, anything you'd like to warn me about?"

"Just do your job. If you have any problems or questions, bring them to Jason before things get out of hand."

"That's it? That's all the wisdom you're going to impart?"

"He's a straightforward kind of guy. His office is always open." He paused. "If you insist on getting brownie points, he's a sucker for *homemade* brownies. And chocolate donuts from Daylight Donuts at the bottom of the hill on Grand."

"No wife to bake him brownies?" My heart pounded.

"She's not much of a cook."

So he was married. I had a stepmom. I tried not to let either excitement or shock show as I wondered what she was like.

"She's a prof and pretty busy with her job and their baby girl," Logan said. "No time for baking."

My heart went into free fall. My dad had a baby girl. I had a sister, a baby sister. I swallowed hard, trying to stay composed while an emotional storm waged within me. "Just one kid?" My voice came out more as a squeak than anything else. I cleared my throat to cover.

"Yeah."

"Is she cute?"

He looked at me funny and I realized I'd pressed too far. "Yeah, real cute. Four months old. Why?"

Of course she was cute. All babies were cute, especially in their parents' eyes. How was a nineteen, almost twenty-year-old, like me going to compete with a baby? Not that I was intending to compete, but this seemed like both a wonderful revelation and a setback all at the same. Suddenly I just knew I had to find a way to meet my sister, too.

"No reason," I said, trying to sound casual while my heart beat out of control. "Just curious. He's a good-looking guy, of course his baby's cute." That was a little vain of me, but Logan couldn't know that.

"Don't get a crush on the boss," he said, with a touch of jealousy in his tone.

I laughed nervously and shook my head vigorously. "Don't be ridiculous! He's old enough to be my dad." And, in fact, he was.

Logan relaxed. "Enough office chitchat. Tell me everything about yourself."

"Everything? No way. It's best to keep a little mystery in a relationship." I tried to sound flippant. But in truth, I couldn't afford to tell Logan much about myself for fear I'd let something slip that might tip off my relationship to Jason.

"I hold your hand during one piercing and we're in a relationship? You move fast. Most guys would be scared off by that." He was obviously teasing. "Good thing I'm not most guys."

Even so, my pulse raced. "You're deliberately misinterpreting me. Of course we're in a relationship. We're colleagues, aren't we?"

"Sure, officemate. Of course we are. Now, spill some deets about yourself. At least give me the basics."

"You already know my name," I said. "And my rank in the office—peon. Will you settle for my student ID number in lieu of a serial number?"

"Safety precaution tip—don't put out your student ID for anyone, El. No matter how handsome he is. In the wrong hands, someone could do irreparable damage with it. If you insist on giving me digits, I want your phone number."

"Wow," I said. "That has to be the most creative way a guy has asked for my number yet."

He shrugged, totally adorably, and pulled his cell phone from his pocket. "I'm a creative guy. Smooth with the ladies."

"Right. Keep talking and I'll have to come up with an equally creative way of shutting you down."

"Come on, El. We're working together. We don't want another almost mishap when we've scheduled one of these after-work socials. We should definitely exchange numbers."

He had a point. And I was totally weak-minded around him. I whipped out my phone and exchanged numbers. As I was slipping it back in my pocket, he put his phone away, too.

He took another a bite of burger and washed it down with a big gulp of pop, somehow managing to eat while stay intently focused on me. "So. What's your major?"

"You get my number and then revert to basic party small talk?" I asked.

"Yeah. I believe in getting the awkward basics out of the way early on. It makes for better office camaraderie."

"Management information services with a bio chem minor. You?"

He whistled. "Interesting combination of major and minor. A bachelor of arts combined with a science minor."

"What can I say?" I mimicked him. "I'm an interesting girl." I laughed, hardly able to believe I was having such a good time with him. "But seriously, I'd like to work in the medical or biotech industries."

"Makes sense." He nodded. "I'm computer science and engineering."

I nodded back. "The way Jason fawned over you, I figured you might be. But, if you don't mind me saying so, you don't look like your typical engineer."

He laughed. "I'll take that as a compliment."

"Good. Because it was."

His face lit up and I realized my mistake. I couldn't believe I was actually sort of flirting with him.

"And you're a...freshman?"

"Transfer student. It's my second year out of high school, but I have junior standing."

He looked relieved that I wasn't a full-on baby freshman. "I'm a senior."

I nodded like an idiot.

"What did you think of your first day of classes here?"

I gave him a quick rundown. "But Chem 202 with Dr. Rhonda Rogers is going to be a bitch. That woman has arrogance and ice running through her veins."

It may have been my imagination but I thought Logan paled at the mention of her name.

He balled up the empty wrapper from his burger and tossed it into the red plastic basket in front of him with enough force to indicate venom. "Get out of her class, Ellie. Get out *now*."

"I take it you've taken a class from her. Her vile reputation precedes her." I sighed. "I'd get out if I could. Believe me. But it's the only section offered and I need it before I can take any other classes in my minor. I have to take it. I have no choice. Don't worry—I have a study group and a survival plan. Anything to protect the GPA and my academic scholarship."

His Adam's apple bobbed. "Be careful, El. She's a vindictive bitch."

CHAPTER FIVE

Even though I protested, Logan walked me back to my dorm. It may have been simply a ploy to find out where I lived, but it made me way happier than it should have. Just like everything about him did.

I paused at the foot of the front steps. "I think I can make it in safely from here. Thanks for walking me back."

"Yeah, sure." He stuffed his hands in his pockets and hesitated.

I had to make it clear we couldn't be more than friends. I started up the stairs. "I'll see you Wednesday."

"El?"

I halted and turned to look back at him over my shoulder.

"Why did you run out on me without giving me your last name at Up All Night?" His tone was neutral—not accusing, but curious. I was sure he wasn't used to girls running out on him.

I froze. I'd been hoping that question wouldn't come up. I took a deep breath and tried to sound light. "Would you believe I have a Cinderella complex? She was always my favorite princess."

He stared at me and nodded. "You want a prince who will do anything to find you? Or your clothes were going to turn into rags at midnight?"

I turned to face him. "I was wearing a crop top and shorts." I laughed. "Every girl wants a prince." My tone became serious. "I'm just not sure I believe in them."

He took a minute to digest that. "Fair enough. My friend Collin's having a party on Friday. You should come."

"Maybe."

"You have other plans?"

"Maybe."

"It's casual. Just drop by. Bring a few of your girl-friends. Collin won't mind. He'll be thrilled."

"We'll see." I started up the stairs again.

"We'll discuss it Wednesday."

"Goodbye, Logan."

Tuesday I had chem lab with Dex. Since we were study buddies, it made sense to be lab partners, too. Which was fine with me. I didn't know anyone else and he seemed to know his way around a Bunsen burner well enough. It was a match made in academic heaven.

Our lab TA was a skinny, nerdy graduate student named Byron who had an acne problem and the scars to prove it—psychologically as well as physically or I missed my guess. Dex sized Byron up with the intensity of a commander looking to exploit his enemy's weakness. Dex made no bones about being a warrior when it came to maintaining his GPA.

"Here's the deal," he whispered to me on the sly as we opened our lab notebooks and set up the experiment. "If we run into trouble, or need help or supplies, you're our go-to girl. Byron's been watching you. He blushes every time he looks this way. I'd be willing to bet he doesn't get much attention from the ladies, certainly not from hot ones."

I probably should have taken being lumped into the "hot girl" category as a compliment, but Dex continued without a pause.

"On the other hand, he looks right through me and the other guys in the class. It's clear he's looking for a girl. And right now, we're in luck—you've caught his eye."

I rolled my eyes. Yeah that was real lucky.

"He'll give you more than our share of attention. Play things right and you'll have him wrapped around your little finger. You'll be his favorite." Dex's gaze swept over my cargo capris and T-shirt.

I was slumming it for chem lab. Why take the chance of ruining something cute?

"Next week wear something sexier."

"Hey! Are you totally sexist or what?"

Dex shrugged and locked a test tube into a clamp stand. "Realistic, baby. I came into this lab willing to do my part to play up to the TA, pimp myself out if necessary. Invite the guy out for a beer and pick up the tab. But it's clear you're our best shot." He grinned. "You don't think I picked you for your brains?"

"Shut up!" I made narrow, angry eyes at him, even though he was clearly ribbing me and trying to get a rise out of me. "I'm here on a full-tuition regents' academic scholarship, wiseass."

He laughed. "I'm here on a full-ride academic scholarship—tuition, books, housing. I have so much in scholarships, they're paying me to attend. I'm making a nice profit out of this deal. I refuse to lose a single penny because of a douchebag lady prof with a stick up her ass." He paused.

I wasn't backing down. You can't take crap from guys like him. They lose all respect if you don't fire back. "Had a lot of financial need, huh?"

He full-out smiled. "Nice try. I didn't qualify for a dime. My dad's loaded." He glanced across the room to where Byron was helping two girls weigh their chemical compound. "Woof. You can outdo those two. Easy. If you put a little effort in. They're clearly trying to make inroads first. Now—do you want to pass chemistry? Or am I going to have to partner with those two?" He gave a mock shudder.

I actually laughed. "All right, I'm in. But only for a little in-class flirting."

"Why? Do you have a big, jealous boyfriend?"

My turn to shrug. "Maybe." Like I told Logan, it's always good to keep some mystery in a relationship, especially if it gives you a measure of power.

Dex stared at me like he could get the truth, or at least more information, out of me. Good luck with that, buddy.

Finally, he gave up. "Our lab grade counts for twenty-five percent of our total class grade. We have to make sure it's one hundred percent to balance out what are sure to be less-than-fantastic test scores."

"I thought you're the great brain," I said.

"I am. I'd be completely confident if life, and Dr. Rogers, were fair.

"Last semester, Dr. Rogers gave one A- out of five hundred students. No A's. A couple of B+'s, a sea of C's and D's, and quite a few fails. Not exactly your normal Gaussian distribution and grade bell curve. This semester Dr. Rogers is even more of a dirty wildcard than usual. She always likes to stick it to students and see them sweat, but now she's on a regular vendetta."

He leaned in even closer and whispered directly in my ear. "I did a little more digging. She's getting too many student complaints for the administration to continue to ignore. Her ass is in the sling now. She's out to make a point."

"Doesn't she have tenure?" I asked, which would protect her no matter what she'd done.

"Are you kidding?" Dex said. "If she had tenure she would have thrown it in our faces with all the rest of the 'stellar' credentials she threw in our faces yesterday. But it doesn't matter whether she does or doesn't.

"First rule of surviving the cutthroat world of business—there are always ways to put people out to pasture. Even tenured professors, if the university wants to badly enough.

"I heard she's in danger of losing a chunk of her funding. Several big donor alums are unhappy. She's giving the department a bad rep." He nodded sagely. "Which makes her like a mama bear protecting her cub. Her research projects are her babies. Without them, she's nothing. That makes her even more unpredictable this semester. She's not the type to back down."

I gave him a wide-eyed, *I can't believe our bad luck* look.

"Yeah. She's dangerous. We're going to play this like world-class chess match—thinking several steps ahead.

"Right now, our first move is to ace this lab. Besides boosting our class GPA, doing well in here where she's not directly in charge will show that it's not the subject matter or our IQ that's the problem. It's the instructor. With luck, we'll be the class to put the final nail in her coffin."

Dex fiddled with the test tube he'd fastened into the clamp. Before I could stop it, it "accidentally" slipped free, rolled across the lab bench, and crashed to the floor, shattering and getting everyone's attention, including Byron's.

"Take that, bitches. Compete with that and my girl Ellie." Dex made a point of staring at the broken glass with decently convincing feigned horror. Beneath his breath, he whispered. "Smile prettily when you ask Byron for a broom and a new test tube. He's on his way now."

I scowled at Dex. "That comes out of your lab deposit."

"My pleasure. Do your job and it will be worth every penny."

The two hours of lab passed in a blur of chemicals and frustration as Dex ordered me around. I've never been good at precise measurements and titrating, or taking orders. Dex, however, was a natural at all of it. He could tell by looking at the gunk in our test tube what elements it contained, what color it would change to, and how bad it would smell when he heated it up. I had chosen wisely when I agreed to bake for him.

"What I don't know, we can dry lab," Dex said. "I'm damn good at that, too."

And I was a decent flirt when I tried, particularly if I wasn't interested in the guy. Having no fear of rejection or dashed hopes took the pressure off me. I took it easy on Byron because I sympathized with him. I just wanted help with chemistry and a good lab grade. I had no desire to mess him up and break his heart like mine was. It was a delicate balance to strike. A normal guy would have seen what I was up to and simply enjoyed the attention and fun. But blushing Byron was a wildcard.

"Tomorrow. Study group. The science library at eight," Dex said as we walked out of the chem building. "We'll group and plan our strategy."

"And study."

"Yeah, that too." Dex paused and cleared his throat. "That was some damn fine flirting in there."

"Thank you."

"Keep it up and do your research. Look Byron up on Facebook and see what winds his clock."

"You never stop, do you?" I shook my head. "I'm not going to Facebook stalk Byron."

"Don't act indignant. Everyone does it."

My backpack was sliding off my shoulder. I hoisted it back up. "Leave the flirting to me. A guy like Byron is easily scared off. We have to proceed with caution."

"You're so wrong about guys, Ellie. A nerd like Byron will lap up any attention you give him and eat out of your hand if you let him. It's not possible to scare him off."

I got the feeling Dex was speaking from experience.

"You're not helping. I'm not into breaking guys' hearts."

"Don't go soft on me, Ellie. Believe me, nerdy guys fight to be TAs precisely because of the female attention they expect from girls that are way out of their league. Let him have his day and his fantasies."

Dex winked and ran off to his next class as I headed back to the dorm for lunch. As I walked, I checked my phone. I don't know what I was expecting. Oh, wait! I lied. I knew exactly what I was irrationally hoping for—a text from Logan. He'd seemed so into me and then he didn't have the courtesy to text me? What was up with that? He was sending incredibly confusing signals and I was direly insecure about everything from my looks to my ability to attract a guy like him. I'd inadvertently laid down the gauntlet with that "prince" comment. I'd been hoping against reason he was the kind of guy who didn't back down from a challenge.

When my phone buzzed in my hand, I jumped and smiled. Until I read who the text was from. *Austin.*

The phone trembled in my hand. I brushed a tear away, hating that he still had the power to shake me up. *Give yourself a year, El. Treat yourself nice; don't beat yourself up. Don't let him kill your self-esteem.* I repeated these mantras whenever I felt panicked that I'd cave and talk to him, or the gut-wrenching anxiety welled up, blaming me for being stupid and naïve. If I'd been hot enough, funny enough, engaging enough, would he have cheated in the first place?

I deleted the text unread, wishing there as a way to block his number for good. Why couldn't he just leave me alone?

I believe in forgiveness. I really do. But in my book, forgiving doesn't erase the consequences of the other person's action. Austin cheated on me, in the worst possible way. I wasn't going to give him another shot at my heart. *Ever.* Which meant I had to harden it against him or I'd do something stupid, like blame just *her* for the whole thing and give him a pass. And talk myself into something destructive like taking him back so I could throw it in her face.

So, no, I was nowhere near forgiving anybody. I needed more time. Forgiveness wasn't something I could fake or force. Not if it was going to be genuine.

When I got back to the dorm, I got a text from my mom. *How was your first day of class?*

Were those two colluding to ruin my day? Of course, a decent mother would have asked me that yesterday, on my actual first day of class. At least she was smart enough not to call me. I texted back a single word— *Fine.* I wanted her off my back.

I knew she was hurting. Going through her third divorce, hurting was expected. I was her support system for the first two, but this time, she'd crossed the line. This divorce was *her* fault. She'd screwed everything up with me and my stepdad Doug.

Was I hacked off at her for blowing things again? Oh, hell yes. My third stepfather wasn't the greatest guy, maybe, but he tried at times. Like me, he was the victim of Mom's bad behavior. We'd both been cheated on. I would have to be dead not to sympathize with him.

I dumped my stuff off in my room and headed to the dining hall in the basement where I met Taylor. She was just coming off shift.

Smiling, she handed me a plate with a crumbled, brownie-looking pastry on it. It was covered in chocolate and marshmallows. "You have to try this! It's heaven on earth. It flies out of here the minute we put it out. Serious. I am not exaggerating.

"I managed to save you this only because it was the crumbled remains in the pan and I hid it in the fridge behind the broccoli. We're the only dining hall on campus that makes it. It's legendary. But the cook only makes it when she's in the mood because it's a real pain."

Taylor watched me take a bite with an eager expression.

"Wow! This *is* heavenly." I closed my eyes and savored the richness. It had a crumbly crust, but the topping literally melted in my mouth. "Is that cream cheese in the frosting?" I licked my lips. "What's it called?"

She beamed. "Cobblestone bars."

I had new secret weapon—exactly what I needed to bribe Byron and placate Dex. Cobblestone bars were like the platinum of pastry. But I planned to hold it in reserve for when it became absolutely necessary to take extreme measures. I didn't see any reason to lead with my heavy guns. No need to move beyond sliced sugar cookies and basic chocolate chip for now. "Any chance we can get this recipe?"

Later that night I looked Byron up on Facebook. He listed brownies and cookies as two of his favorite foods. Good for me. Then, thinking like Dex, I prepared for battle, and the Wednesday night study group, by doing some online snooping, trying to get the dirt on Dr. Rogers. My experience tracking down Jason had taught me a lot. But evidently, not quite enough. I came up empty.

Wednesday was another boring chem lecture. I had so much homework in my other classes, I wished I'd been able to skip it. Dr. Rogers was in fine form, spewing insults, calling her students stupid, lazy asses, lecturing from packed slides, and working equations on a smart board so quickly it was impossible to keep up with her, even on steroids. Dex recorded it all on a small portable recorder.

"Document everything," he said when I asked him if he was recording it to listen to again later.

That afternoon I went to work full of anticipation at seeing Logan and Jason. But Jason worked in his office with the door closed the entire three hours I was there.

Logan was out in the field on an important assignment for Jason. I had orders not to dispatch him to any other job, no matter how urgent. Logan didn't text me, at work or otherwise. He didn't ask to hang out after our shift for a burger. After all the trouble he'd gone to to get my number, I was totally confused and bewildered. I had to resist the urge to text him. But I didn't want to look desperate and pathetic. My imagination was particularly vivid and kept bringing up images of him and that girl from the SUB.

After work, I ran back to the dorm, bought a refrigerated tube of cookie dough from the Market—the convenience store located in a room adjacent to the dining hall—sliced and baked them, and ran off to study group. There were four of us—Dex, two other guys and me. No wonder I was the one who had to bring the cookies. Dex played things close to his chest. The first session was basically a meet-and-greet. Then we worked through our homework problems. I was pleased I could keep up with the rest of the group.

Dex pulled out his secret treasure—the first-week quiz from last semester, ten questions complete with the key. I don't know how he got it. I didn't ask. Dex wouldn't part with it or let any of us snap a picture of it for fear word would get out. But we went over it and discussed it.

"Are you sure this is from the same class?" I asked. "Did they even use the same book or curriculum? There's nothing on here that we've remotely been over."

"And neither had they," Dex said. "Pay particular attention to question six. See how she rearranged a molecule structure so that at first glance it appears like the right answer? Guess again. The correct answer is none of the above. She likes to pull crap like that."

I did my best to memorize the quiz.

When we left, Dex walked out with me. "What happened to our strategic planning?" I asked.

"That was strategic. I was assessing who we could trust and what tasks each is best suited for," Dex said.

"And?"

"If anyone leaks that quiz, they're out."

"Yeah, but how would you know? If you got hold of it, someone else theoretically could."

"Good point. I have my methods. I'm not too worried. I think you're all keepers."

At least I was still in. "I did some digging on Dr. Rogers on my own. I couldn't find a thing on her. The unhappy alum donors are keeping things quiet."

Dex smiled at me. "Now you're beginning to think like someone who's destined to graduate magna cum laude."

"Only with great honor? I think not. You mean summa cum laude." With highest honors.

He laughed. "Don't get cocky, baby. You still have a way to go." We reached a crossroad. Our dorms were in opposite directions.

"I'm this way," I said.

"See you Friday. And bring more cookies next time."

Thursday was another sweltering day. Summer rocked on. It hadn't gotten the memo that school was back in session and it should back off. By the time I got out of class at eleven, it was already nearly ninety. I worked up a sweat walking back from class. When I got back to the dorm, Bre, Taylor, and Nicole were waiting for me in my room, dressed in bikinis and short shorts. Three packed beach bags sat on my bed and a cooler lay on the floor. The room smelled like sunscreen, suntan lotion, and a cocktail of Bre, Nic, and Tay's perfumes.

"Good! You're back. Hurry and change. We're going cliff diving!" Nic was French braiding Taylor's hair as she sat on Bre's bed. Her own hair was already intricately braided.

"What are you talking about?" I dumped my backpack next to my desk, lifted my hair off my neck, and stood in front of the fan.

"We're going to the cliffs." Bre was applying pink-tinted lip balm in front of the mirror over our sink. "Dan and Jake and a few of their buddies invited us along. Get into your suit and pack a bag. They'll be here soon."

I hesitated. The few times I'd seen Jake and Dan hadn't exactly been roaring successes. "I don't get a say?"

"Come on, Ellie," Nicole said. "Don't be a stick-in-the-mud. It'll be fun. Better than roasting here, anyway. The cliffs are legendary. Everyone's going. It'll be a big party. We packed a picnic lunch. The guys are bringing beer. Change into your suit and I'll braid your hair after I'm done with Tay's."

The cliffs were on the river. I'd heard plenty of wild stories about them since moving in. "Can't we go to the dunes?"

The dunes were also on the river. Going to the dunes meant playing beer pong and wading in the river, not risking a major water wedgie from failing to execute a proper pencil dive from forty feet up.

"I snagged the last of the day-old cookies from the dining hall," Taylor said. "We'll have a feast."

"Any cobblestone bars?" I pulled my white bikini out of a drawer.

"No. Sorry. But I'm buttering up the cook in preparation for asking for the recipe."

Fifteen minutes later we were packed into two cars with Dan and his buddies, sandwiched in so tightly that even with the air conditioning going full blast we stuck to each other. Dan drove, speeding out along the roads that wound out of town through rolling golden wheat fields toward the river. Combines combed the fields, kicking up dust and making patterns in the wheat. Dan turned off the main road and headed south, driving

along the crooked roads and taking curves so fast I decided he was trying to make us sick.

The wheat fields gave way to barren sage land and
rimrock hills dotted sparsely with patches of green
scrub brush. Forty minutes after we left, we pulled into
a packed parking lot. The girls had been right—music
blared, the air smelled of beer and coconut oil, and the
rocks were covered with guys in swim trunks and girls
in bikinis. We piled out of the car and grabbed our
towels, coolers, and bags.

Dan muscled his way ahead of us through the crowd,
looking for a bare patch of rock to spread our towels. I
liked to people watch and found the crowd fascinating.
College drama played out before my eyes. Guys hitting
on girls. Girls making plays for guys. Some people totally ignored. Rough housing. Jealous fits. Drunken
antics. And flesh everywhere.

Nic leaned over and whispered to Taylor and me,
"Have you ever seen so many gorgeous guys in one
spot?"

No I hadn't. Just then I was feeling insecure, particularly next to Taylor with her strawberry blond hair,
tiny waist, and toned abs. And Nic with her light co-
coa-colored skin, dark hair and eyes, and absolutely
gorgeously round booty. She had a shapely ass to rival
any ass on the planet. I had a flat little butt and felt
plain next to them. But what did I care? I wasn't looking for a guy. And my bellybutton ring sparkled in the
sun, signaling I was finally cool.

Dan found a spot next to the rimrock cliffs and
waved to us before spreading out our beach blanket. As

we made our way toward him, my heart plummeted. I caught a glimpse of someone it was impossible for me to miss in a crowd. He drew my gaze like a magnet. Logan lounged on his side, propped on one elbow on a blanket at the edge of the cliffs next to the girl from the SUB, casually drinking a beer and laughing as he talked to her.

Shirtless, he was hotter even than my imagination had dared conjure. His abs were washboard, his biceps sculpted, and his shoulders broad and taut, oiled with suntan lotion that emphasized his every stroke of definition. My hands itched to slide over him and be the one slathering him in lotion. A tattoo coiled over his left shoulder, subtle, yet sexy, against his tanned skin.

Next to him, the girl was so perfectly tanned it had to come from a tanning booth. Her hot pink bikini showed it off brilliantly. When she smiled, her teeth were perfect and white. They were joking and laughing intimately while Logan's two friends from Up All Night tossed a football next to them.

I swallowed hard and tried to force my gaze away from him. So that was why he hadn't texted. I felt foolish for hoping a guy like him would really be interested in me. Especially when he made such a gorgeous couple with her.

I wasn't fast enough. Logan looked up. Our eyes met. He looked surprised. I looked away guiltily and pretended not to see him. My party mood slipped away.

Nic picked up on my mood. "What's the matter?"

For the second time, I wasn't quick enough. Her gaze followed mine. "Whoa! Who is that? He's *hot*."

"No one. Just a guy I work with."

"Who? Where?" Taylor looked around. It wasn't hard for her to spot Logan. "You mean the hot, built guy with the dark hair at the edge of the cliff?"

"The one with the pink bikini goddess. Yeah, him. He's an RTA, a resident tech assistant." I refused to look at him again.

"Wow! As soon as we get back to the dorm, I'm going to develop technical difficulties if I have to pull my Ethernet cable out of the wall with my teeth." Tay shook her head. "He is fine."

"He smiled at you," Nic said as we dropped our beach blanket and sat. "You just dissed him."

"Did not. I was giving him his privacy. Leaving him alone on his date." I adjusted my sunglasses.

"Did too. That was just rude." Nic pulled a bottle of suntan lotion from her bag and began slathering it on her legs.

I pulled a bottle of spray-on sunscreen from my bag and handed it to Tay as I lifted up my braid so she could spray my back. I flinched and sucked in my breath. "Cold, cold, cold!"

"I'd say you are." Nic smelled like an afternoon in Hawaii as she lotioned her arms. "Are you going to leave him to the clutches of the pink bikini bitch?"

"I'd say she already has him. She was hanging onto him at the SUB the other day."

The guys broke open the cooler of beer. They handed a couple of cans down to us and went off with Bre to watch the jumpers. I popped mine open.

"What's the story between you two and why are you holding out on us?" Tay popped her can open, too, and took a swig. "When did you see him in the SUB? Are you stalking him?"

"Hah! Right. He begged me to have a burger with him after work on Monday, practically pried my phone number out of me, and then ignored me all week." I took a big drink of my beer. It was cold and tasted good in the heat.

"That's the guy you had the burger with?" Nic's mouth fell open. "You *are* crazy. If that guy looked twice at me, I'd be all over him until he pried me loose."

I held the cold beer can against my cheek, soaking up the cool condensation from it. "His name is Logan. And I told you two. I just came off a bad—no, horribly hideous relationship with a lying, cheating bastard. I'm not ready for another relationship right now. I'm still licking my wounds. I'm certainly not ready to take a further beating by throwing myself at a guy of Logan's caliber."

Austin was pretty hot. I'd always felt like he'd been the settler in our relationship and I was the reacher, grasping for someone out of my class. When he cheated on me, he pretty much destroyed me and cemented my belief that I wasn't worthy. I wasn't going to go there again and shoot for a guy out of my league again.

"So hook up with Logan," Nic said. "And let him lick your wounds."

I shook my head. "I'm not the hooking-up type. Besides, he's way out of my league."

"He is not!" Tay rushed immediately to my defense.

It was sweet of her, but she was my friend and therefore biased. While we finished our beers, I made a point of not looking in Logan's direction.

Bre came running back with Dan. "Come on, you three! It's awesome over there. We're going to jump before lunch and we need everyone."

I frowned, perplexed at why we all needed to be there and jump at the same time as we followed her to the edge of the cliffs. There were two jumping spots into the gentle river current below. One spot was off a ten-foot-high cliff. The other jump was a good forty feet.

As I watched people below climbing out of the water below after their dives and struggling up the slippery rock to the top of the forty-foot jump, I realized jumping was the easy part, assuming you knew how to pencil dive. Climbing back was vicious and required teamwork.

No wonder Bre needed all hands on deck. Groups of friends jumped off one by one into the river and treaded water waiting for the last person in their party. When everyone had jumped, they formed a chain up the cliff and helped each other up, like mountain climbers scaling toward a summit.

As we got in line, I spotted Logan and the girl in the pink bikini waiting in line for their turns in the group in front of us. Why was my eye always drawn to him?

Making the dive required running and jumping off the cliff far enough out so you cleared the cliff walls. One at a time, his two buddies took off at a run and jumped feet first. Then the girl hugged Logan, laughed, and strutted her perfect body to the takeoff point. With the eyes of half the guys around on her, she ran, breasts bouncing, swung her arms, and jumped off, pointing her dainty, manicured feet to show off her long legs. She hit the water with barely a splash to the applause of the guys on the cliffs, who hooted and whistled.

That was when Logan turned and saw me. His face lit up with recognition. He winked at me and mouthed "watch this."

But instead of going to the edge of the running strip, he kneeled and hoisted himself over the edge of the rimrock. I leaned cautiously over the ledge to get a look at him, shaking my head and holding my breath.

He was clinging to the face of the wall in a squat with his back toward the water. The crowd gasped. *Oh, God, he's showing off for me.*

"Logan, no!" I screamed at him.

He didn't hear me. He took a deep breath, pushed off, flexing every muscle in his powerful legs, and did a back flip.

I gasped, watching horrified until his head cleared the rock wall. He righted himself, pointed his feet and hit the water in perfect pencil-dive form, disappearing below the water's surface.

When he popped back up, the crowd erupted in applause and I released the breath I'd been holding. He waved to me, or maybe he was just waving to the crowd. The crowd was evenly split along gender lines over whose dive was better, Logan's or the girl's. Trying to be objective, I gave him difficulty points.

He was the last of his group. The others swam for the shore, but Logan ignored them and treaded water as they called for him to join them. He shook his head and pointed upward while my heart pumped out of control, hoping he was waiting for me and realizing that was seriously insane.

"I'm first. I can tread water forever!" Bre stepped in front of us, ran and dove off.

We clapped and squealed.

Logan kept treading water below while the rest of his group waited for him on a rock just below the surface in the shallow water.

Dan crowded in next.

"What do you think Logan's waiting for?" I asked Nic.

"You, you idiot." She shoved me to the front of the line, but one of the other guys in our party cut me off and took his turn before me.

Logan's group shouted to him and motioned for him. He looked up and began crawl stroking with smooth, even strokes toward shore just as it was finally my turn.

I took a deep breath, ran with all my might, swung my arms and jumped out, away from the rock wall. I pointed my toes, pressed one arm against my body, and held my nose with the other hand. I thought I'd fall so quickly that I wouldn't have time to think. But even as an adrenaline rush pulsed through me, I thought: *Why am I doing this? What have I done?*

Falling, falling, free falling. For a moment I was simply hanging in the air. The next, I hit the cold water with the force of a slap.

Down, down, down into the deep green water of the river, still in free fall until I thought I'd hit the bottom. I kicked and pushed upward, popping back to the surface with water streaming down my face. I brushed it out of my eyes and waved to Taylor to join me, exhilarated.

Just as Taylor tossed herself off the cliff, and all eyes were focused on her, my sides, legs, and arms cramped up so badly I lost control of them. Unable to kick and paddle, I slid beneath the surface, falling deeper and deeper below. As my lungs burned and breath failed me, I thought: *Logan, Logan, Logan. We'll never know what might have been. My dad will never know I existed. And you'll forget me, Logan Walker.*

CHAPTER SIX

Out of nowhere, Logan swam up beside me, his dark hair waving in the water. He grabbed me around the waist with one strong arm. Panicked, I latched onto him like he was a literal lifeline, weighing him down, taking him to the bottom with me. He held me firmly and stroked my face until I calmed enough to stop fighting and went limp in his arm. He pushed off the bottom and kicked, paddling with his one free arm until we broke the surface.

I gasped and coughed. Water streamed over my eyes. My nose ran. My lungs burned.

He was breathing hard, too, as he held me up. "Are you okay?"

I nodded because I couldn't speak.

"Hang on to me while I swim us to shore."

Except for the caw of a crow, the splash Logan made as he swam, and the lapping of the river against the shore, it was eerily silent as people around us realized what had happened. For a moment, all diving stopped and the party buzz died.

Logan pulled me to the rock in the shallows and sat me on it. "Can you stand?"

I wasn't certain I could, but I nodded.

He stood, gave me a hand, and pulled me to my feet as water slid off him and beaded on his chest and arms. His gang was on the shore, making their chain up the cliffs, waiting for Logan and me.

Logan put his arm around me and steadied me against him as we waded to shore, rubbing my arms, trying to warm me up as my teeth chattered. I shivered uncontrollably, unable to get warm, trying to soak up Logan's body heat. He took one of his buddy's hands, pulling me behind him. One by one, they helped us up the cliff.

When we reached the pink bikini girl at the top of the cliff and the chain, she helped me onto the slippery upper rocks with a surprisingly strong, friendly grip. "Are you okay? You're shivering, poor thing. Let's wrap her in our extra blanket."

Logan smiled at her. "Thanks, Kels." He swept me into his arms, pressing me against his warm, hard chest that smelled of coconut oil, sun, and water. It was a re-assuring smell I swore I'd never forget.

Nic ran after us. Bre and Taylor reached the top of the cliffs, helped by Logan's friends, and chased after us. They peppered me with questions.

Logan reassured them. "She's fine. We just have to warm her up."

He reached their blankets, set me down, though I was loath to be out of his arms, and wrapped me in a beach blanket. "God, El, you're blue." Worry was etched on his face.

My nose was running. I was still coughing and trembling. I'm sure I looked horrible. People in the surrounding sites were quiet, staring at me.

The girl in the pink bikini handed me a tissue.

Dan reached us. "We have to get her home," Bre said to him.

"Don't bother," Logan said in a tone that left no room for argument. "I'm taking her to Student Health. Collin, you have room for one more, don't you? You can take Kels home?"

Damn. Logan had brought Kels, the pink bikini girl, with him. Even through my fogged brain I was jealous.

"Yeah, sure, buddy."

"No, you really don't have to. I'm fine." No one listened to my protests.

"Let me get Ellie's stuff for you." Nic ran off to get it while Logan slid a shirt and sandals on and grabbed his towel and keys.

Taylor patted me on the back and spoke to Logan. "Text us when she's seen the doctor." She rattled off her number.

Nic ran back with my bag. Logan tossed it over his shoulder and scooped me in his arms again. He carried me to his truck in the parking lot and helped me into the passenger side while bystanders milled around the truck.

He yelled at them to get out of his way and backed out. Once on the road, I sensed he was driving as fast as he could without losing control around the curves.

"Shit, El, you really scared me out there. What happened?"

"I cramped up, just all of a sudden. I couldn't move my legs. I just sank. It all happened so fast." I shuddered, still cold and coughing intermittently.

Logan must have been sweltering, but he didn't turn the air conditioning on.

"No one else saw me." I swallowed and coughed again. My lungs still burned. I must have aspirated some water, though I didn't remember breathing in underwater. "You saved my life. If you hadn't seen me—"

"Someone else would have." His gaze was fixed on the road, but his jaw was set and his grip on the wheel was firm, like he was trying not to think of what-ifs.

"Thank you," I said. It was feeble and lame, but there was no way to express how grateful I was.

He nodded.

We drove the rest of the way to the emergency room at Student Health in silence. When Logan explained that I had nearly drowned, I was shown right in to the examining room. Logan had to wait in the waiting room.

A nurse took my temperature. The doctor came in and listened to my heart and lungs. He examined my head and neck, explaining he was looking for injuries.

He was gentle and kind. He asked how it happened. I told him how Logan had saved me.

"You're lucky he saw you," the doctor said. "And acted quickly. He really did save your life. I think you're going to be fine. But I have to keep you here under observation for at least six hours. Pulmonary edema can develop as late as four hours after the incident. I don't anticipate a problem, but I don't want to take a chance."

I nodded. "Can I see Logan and tell him? He's waiting for me in the lobby."

The doctor didn't see why not. A few minutes later, Logan walked in. He sat by my bed, took my hand, and squeezed it.

I smiled at him. "I'm making a habit of needing you to hold my hand. I have to stay here for another few hours."

Logan nodded. "The nurse told me. I texted the others."

"Good."

"Do you want me to get you your phone so you can call your mom?"

"No!" I must have looked wild-eyed, because he covered my hand in both of his. "No, no, no!"

"It's okay. It was just a suggestion, an offer."

I took a deep breath. The last thing I needed was for my mom to come flying to campus and run into Jason. Then I'd really never get to know my father.

"You really don't get along with your mom."

"I really don't."

"Someday you'll tell me why?"

"Maybe. It's not a pretty story."

He nodded like he understood. I didn't want him to know the truth, afraid it would color how he thought about me.

I squeezed Logan's hand back and swallowed hard. "Hey, thank you. I owe you one."

"No," he said. "I believe you now owe me *two*."

I don't know how he made me smile so easily. "Keeping score now?"

"Never know when I'll need to call in a debt. Or two." His gorgeous eyes twinkled.

"Okay, I owe you two. I'm beginning to think you're my guardian angel."

"I'm no angel, El, really."

"I'm going to be here at least six hours. You don't have to stay. I'm sure you have stuff to do. I already ruined your day. I'm a real party killer."

"Ruined my day? What do you mean? I've always wanted to save a life. It's on my bucket list. You just made my dream come true."

"Glad I could be of service." I yawned, worn out and very tired.

"Rest." He reached for the TV controller. "I'll be here when you wake up. Mind if I watch TV?"

I smiled sleepily at him. "Be my guest."

He spent the entire six hours with me. The nurses were kind enough to feed us each a light lunch when I woke up. Logan told me that Bre, Nic, and Taylor had stopped by while I was resting. Logan and I watched TV, cracking jokes, making comments about characters and plots and the crazy people on reality shows until they let me leave. He drove me back to the dorm after they discharged me, and insisted on carrying my bag to the front door.

He was quiet in a comfortable, companionable way.

I lightly touched his arm. "Thank you, Logan."

He leaned close. Our gazes locked. He tilted his head. I angled my lips toward his and tightened my grip on his hard, wonderful bicep. My breath caught. Our lips were mere inches apart. His eyes were dilated and wide in the sunlight. I could have sworn I saw desire reflected in them. I closed my eyes.

He leaned past my lips and whispered in my ear, "You're welcome, Ellie Martin."

My eyes flew open, unbelieving.

He handed me my bag. "See you at work tomorrow."

I stumbled to my room, wondering what had just happened. Or, rather, not happened. I should have been grateful Logan had saved me from myself, but I was embarrassed and baffled and incredibly disappointed. Bre, Taylor, and Nic waited for me. They each hugged me.

"Sit! Sit," Taylor said.

A bouquet of flowers from the grocery store sat in a vase on my desk. Seeing it brought tears to my eyes.

"Hey, it's all right." Bre sat beside me and put her arm around me.

"Ellie, you were holding out on us about Logan. He is hot. Even so, nearly drowning to get his attention is over the top." Nic shook her head in mock disapproval.

"You think?" I said, and we all laughed. But in the back of my mind, I wondered what made Logan tick.

He was so kind and attentive and funny, and then he stops short of kissing me? He was giving me an insecurity complex.

Friday morning I had my first quiz in chemistry. Wow, even though I'd studied for it by going over that old quiz from last semester with Dex and the gang, this quiz was brutal and nothing like the one we'd studied. I walked out of class certain I'd failed it. Dex swore revenge on Dr. Rogers.

"Are you sure you weren't duped and got a fake quiz from last year?" I hated to ask him, but it seemed like a reasonable question. Even having nearly died the day before, I should have done better on the quiz than subzero.

"It's authentic," he said. "Trust me. This is just Dr. Rogers being pissy. And now it's all out war."

"I thought it was *already* war?"

"Yeah, but now it's nuclear, apocalyptic war. That bitch will *not* defeat me."

The rest of the day passed quickly, considering I couldn't wait until work. I know, weird, right? You're supposed to dread work, but I was looking forward to it as the best part of my day. I was drawn to spending time with my dad and Logan. Call me an eternal optimist, but I believed I'd been saved from certain death by Logan for a reason. And it was all tied up getting to know my dad before I died and finding out the mystery of Logan.

My heart fluttered and my pulse raced every time I thought of him. He made me smile and feel like no guy ever had before. Even Austin had only stirred mild tremors of the feelings I was developing for Logan. I'd be lying if I said I wasn't totally terrified by the intensity of everything Logan. I was heading down a path I knew better than to travel, but I couldn't stop myself from tumbling forward anyway.

I arrived at the office expecting to find chaos. Instead, I found amazing, jovial calm. Jason was standing by Karen's desk, laughing and joking with her. My heart caught at the sight of him, wondering for the zillionth time just how much I was like him and how much I'd missed not growing up with him. Would I be a different person today if he'd parented me instead of Mom?

It's an odd sensation to meet your dad when you're already grown and off at college, at a time when you should be pulling away from your parents and finding yourself, not bonding with your dad.

There was no shared history. And in my case, no *known* history. My mom had never once talked about my biological dad. She had never told me how I was conceived, only that he never knew I existed. I know how babies are conceived, obviously. What I mean is— was I conceived in the backseat of a car, on the beach, as the result of a brief summer fling? What was the story of me and how I came to be? She hadn't kept a single picture of him that I could find. Not a pressed corsage or movie ticket stub from a date night with him. I seemed to be the single memento from their time together.

There was just one mention of him in an old diary of hers I found locked in a box in her closet along with a DNA report. I had to piece together the story—Mom thought another guy was my dad. She wanted him to pay child support. He refused and the court ordered a DNA report, which proved he wasn't the culprit. I found one terse note in my mom's things. *It must be Jason Front, then. He's the only other guy I've ever slept with.*

I had no idea why she didn't go after Jason, and I couldn't ask either of them without tipping my hand. I also just had to hope Mom was telling the truth—that Jason was the only other one.

I didn't know, I really didn't, whether Jason was a good guy or the villain who somehow warped my mom for good. Was she protecting him? Me? Sometimes my mind goes to dark places. I hoped I wasn't the result of a date rape. Why didn't Mom want to remember?

That was another reason I was treading carefully and hoping to get some kind of handle on who my dad really was before revealing myself. If I revealed myself. But for now, when I saw him, I had no "dad voice" to shudder at. No sense of rebellion. And no happy memories of him teaching me how to ride a bike or coming to a dance recital or helping me with my calculus. Looking at him now was like looking in a funhouse mirror where the distorted reflection changed at will—what was I going to see reflected there, beauty or evil?

Jason saw me and smiled. "Ellie! Glad you're here. Now that things have calmed down, I'd like to meet with you in my office."

"Things have calmed down?" I asked, though it was pretty obvious.

Karen let out a sigh of relief. "We're finally getting back to normal after the usual start-of-the-semester madness."

Jason did a drum roll on Karen's desk and extended his arm toward his office. "Shall we?"

I followed him in. He closed the door after me and offered me a chair across from his desk while my heart raced. The electronic picture frame on his desk was still off.

"Don't be worried. I'm not going to chew your head off or anything. You've been doing a great job, especially without any training. I just want to get to know you a little better and outline what your job responsibilities are, maybe get your thoughts on how the job's going."

I shrugged. "It's going fine, I guess. I don't have much experience to talk about. I like dispatching, but I'm hoping to get more experience that applies to my MIS degree."

He liked that topic. It got him started explaining things. His passion for IT was obvious and lit up his face. He was a born teacher, explaining technical issues in a way that made sense.

When I told him he should be a professor, he laughed. "I prefer to do, not teach." He outlined how he saw my job and what projects he hoped to get me involved in. He noticed I kept looking at that dead picture frame. "Something wrong?"

"You seem like a really technically savvy guy who loves gadgets. So why do you have a picture frame that you never turn on?" Of course, I had ulterior motives. I wanted to see a picture of my baby sister and my dad's wife. I wanted to see a bit of his history so I could piece together his life story. I wondered if he'd have pictures of his parents, my grandparents, on that thing.

He laughed. "It's broken. I knocked it off the desk just before the semester started. I've been meaning to fix it when I get time."

And that was that. I hoped he hadn't knocked it off in a fit of anger, and that he fixed it soon. Curiosity was killing this student.

He finished giving me instructions. I rose to leave.

"I'm taking the office out for pizza and beer at five. My treat. You're invited."

"I'm in." I wasn't going to miss a perfect opportunity to have dinner with him—and hopefully Logan, too.

Back at my desk, I got right to work. Even though it was calmer, we still had plenty to do. To my relief, Logan strolled in from the field just before five.

"Hey, beautiful," he said.

"Why thank you, Logan." Karen did a fake hair-primp, that motion where you bounce your hair like an old-time movie star. "But you know I'm married." She winked at him like he knew he hadn't been talking to her.

"Hey, El. You look like you've recovered."

"Recovered from what?" Karen perked up, her curiosity obviously piqued.

Jason came out of his office. "Time to button things up for the weekend. Shut everything down, people. Let's go get pizza. Karen, are you coming?"

"Not this time, boss. My son's the backup quarterback for the high school team. Fingers crossed he's playing tonight." She began shutting down her desktop computer. "I'm surprised you're not needed at home."

Her comment made me wonder if Jason was henpecked. Was his wife a bitch?

He laughed. "The wife and baby are out of town visiting the in-laws. I'm playing bachelor tonight."

"I'm in," Logan said. "I was hoping it was pizza night. I'm always up for a free meal." He turned to me. "Do you need a ride, El?"

I did, so I took him up on it. A couple of other RTAs showed up. We divvied up into two cars and met at a popular pizza joint in the heart of town down the hill from the university.

Jason bought pitchers of pop and beer for the ten or so of us around the table. I was out with the boss and not legal, so I behaved myself and poured myself a glass of pop. Logan sat next to me and poured himself a beer.

Jason noticed my chaste choice. "Not a drinker? Designated driver?"

"Not driving and not old enough," I said.

"An honest employee. I chose well." Jason grabbed his glass of beer and raised it for a toast. "To a stellar first week. Thank you, everyone!"

We clinked glasses all around and then a general mayhem of conversation broke out. I watched Jason closely. The more I watched him, the more I liked him.

The way he treated his employees—like he really cared about them and they were friends—impressed me. I was the only girl present, which made things a bit awkward.

The guys razzed each other and rattled on about a lot of technical stuff, telling stories of their adventures in the field and about this professor and that, who they liked, which were complete arrogant bastards. Logan was as boisterous and opinionated as the rest of the guys. Mostly, I listened. Until Dr. Rhonda Rogers came up.

"That bitch reamed me, claiming her Ethernet connection in her precious lab was too slow," an RTA named Gary said. "Well, damn it, buy some faster cables with all that research money you're raking in, bitch. We can only do so much. With the kind of data she's running, she needs better than university-issue gear. And she can afford it."

The other guys nodded in sympathy and added their own run-ins with her. Everyone but Logan, who'd gone surprisingly silent. It was clear no one liked Dr. Rogers. But Logan was particularly uncomfortable.

"I have her for Chem 202 this semester," I said, trying to join in and bond with the guys. "This morning she gave us our first quiz. Brutal! It's like she pulled the questions out of thin air. I'm not even sure they were about chemistry. Maybe on a doctoral level. But it was nothing we'd ever seen. And me and my friends had studied thoroughly for it."

"Get out of there," five or six of the guys said in unison.

I laughed. "Wow! Warnings in surround sound."

"Never had her myself. But a couple of my engineering and pharmacy buddies have. That's standard MO for that bitch," Gary said. "She only teaches the one class and yet she does crap for it."

I took a sip of pop. "I wish I could get out, because believe me, I would." Then I explained why I couldn't. And how some of the students, who would remain nameless—but I meant Dex—had a plan to document her ineptness and take it to the department chair.

Gary looked at me with sympathy. "Good luck with that! Students have been trying to get her canned for the last five years, that I know of, since my older brother was here.

"You're up against insurmountable odds. She's the chem department's top fundraiser, which means she's their darling. There's no way they'll kill the golden calf.

"Because she raises so much money from alums and businesses, it follows that the head of the chem department believes it's the students who are off base with their complaints. No matter how much evidence they present to the contrary. The powers that be use faulty logic to defend their position—if the alums and donors like her, she has to be great."

I frowned, keeping it quiet that at least some of the alums weren't as happy as they had been, at least if Dex was to be believed. "Really? But why give her an important class that's required for so many of us? Why not pasture her in some stupid elective? Or let her out of teaching altogether? If she's such a genius and a great fundraiser, play to her strengths and keep her away from us."

"Because she wants that class for her own nefarious reasons, obviously," Gary said. "And what she wants, she gets. I have a theory she's subtly releasing noxious chemicals into her audience and studying the effects."

I thought Jason would refuse to weigh in, or at least change the topic. But he spoke up. "This is just between us, but she's not well liked by the staff or the other professors. You're smart to document everything she does. And then your best bet is to carefully follow procedure before you go up the chain with your complaints."

He outlined a plan to first ask Dr. Rogers for help. "If she doesn't respond, or gives an inadequate or offensive answer, then you proceed to take your complaints to the chair of the department, and so on up the chain until you get satisfaction."

I protested. "That could all take months! Maybe years. I could be graduated by the time we go through the process."

"It's that or nothing," Jason said. "The university won't respond to your complaints unless you follow protocol." He turned to Logan. "You got a pretty good grade out of Chem 202, didn't you, Logan? If you run into trouble, you should ask Logan for help, Ellie."

Beside me, Logan tensed. "I did all right."

I couldn't stand his discomfort. "I'm only going to Logan as a last resort," I said. "I'm over my head in debt to him already. He saved my life yesterday, and that's not just hyperbole. He really did." My voice broke. I was still emotional about it, and there was now a bond between us whether we wanted it or not.

"It was nothing." He bumped me playfully with his shoulder.

"Saving my life was nothing! It was to *me*!" I bumped him back and launched into the story, talking with my hands as much as with my mouth as I told them how brave he was. "So, you see—he's my hero." I squeezed his arm and leaned my head on his shoulder like the heroine in a melodrama as I batted my eyes at him.

It got him to laugh. Questions flew. The guys ribbed him good-naturedly. I grabbed a pitcher and poured another round of beer for the guys around me and lifted my glass of pop. "To Logan for saving my life. Otherwise, you'd all have to find someone else to dispatch you so sweetly to jobs."

"Sweetly? Is that what you call it?" Logan said.

They drank and laughed until Jason cut in. "That's really something, Logan. You deserve a commendation. I'll recommend you for—"

"No!" The force of Logan's response shut everyone up. He shook his head. "No, please. I don't want a big deal made of it. Anyone would have done the same. Let's keep this between us. Ellie's alive and that's enough reward for me." His voice cracked.

I was so touched, I almost cried.

"Live well, El," Logan said to me.

The pizzas arrived. Jason's cell phone buzzed. "Dig in, crew!" He pulled the phone from his pocket and read a text. "Oh, look! A message from my lovely Lyssa."

The guys groaned. This was obviously some kind of inside joke.

My heart stopped. *Melissa?* My mom's face swam before me. "Melissa?" I repeated, numbly.

"Lyssa," he corrected. "Sorry, I forgot you're new. My wife. Brace yourself for a proud papa moment. Lyssa just sent a picture of my little girl Mia getting her first feel of grass on her bare feet." He was grinning ear to ear with that gooey new-daddy expression as he flipped the phone around so we could all get a look.

I felt a pang that he'd never looked that way about me.

I was too far away to get a really good look at baby Mia, but my body reacted anyway. My mouth went dry. My hands trembled so badly I clasped them in my lap.

"The guys think I go overboard bragging about the baby," Jason said to me. He didn't sound at all embarrassed. "I waited a long time to become a dad and I'm going to enjoy every minute of it."

No, you didn't, I wanted to say. *You were a dad nineteen years ago, when you were younger than we are now. You just didn't know it.*

Jason beamed. "Someday the rest of you will understand."

"Yeah, and we're going to text you pictures of our kids sixteen times a day to show you how much," Logan said.

"Oh, she's cute!" I said while the boys rolled their eyes. "Can I have a closer look?"

As Jason handed the phone to me, I willed the hand I stretched out for it not to tremble.

"Be sure to scroll through. Lyssa sent several."

No one seemed to notice as they filled their plates with pizza, but I felt pale as I stared at the first picture of my baby sister and her mother.

Lyssa bore a striking similarity to my mom, only she looked fresher and not as conniving. Seeing the resemblance, I feared Jason had a type. I hoped it was only a physical type. But the romantic side of me wondered— maybe he'd never gotten over Mom? Could she have been the love of his life? Was he replacing her with a lookalike with a similar name?

Mom could be such a witch sometimes, that I felt a wave of anxiety for Jason's marriage. I hoped Lyssa was a whole lot more loyal than Mom had ever been to any of her husbands or lovers.

It was hard to tell exactly who Mia looked like in the first picture. Her mom was bending over her, letting her baby fingers hold her hands as Mia looked up at her and Lyssa stared at the camera. Little Mia's face was scrunched up, as if she wasn't sure whether she liked the grass tickling her toes.

I liked the feel of grass on my bare feet, but I wondered how I had felt the first time. The sense of wonder on the baby's face made me long for her innocence.

I scrolled to the next picture, a full-on shot of baby Mia staring into the camera, eyes wide and a huge smile lighting her tiny face. If I'd been pale before, now I went totally stone cold. Overcome with emotion, I blinked back tears—Mia was the spitting image of *me* as a baby.

I stared, heart racing. If there had been any doubt in my mind about Jason being my dad, there was none now. This baby was my sister, and maybe my clone. For a minute I felt exposed and vulnerable, expecting everyone to make the connection. But no one did. No one knew the baby me but me.

I realized Jason was staring at me and forced myself to pull it together. "She's beautiful!" I sounded over-exuberant, like I was trying too hard. "Super cute."

"That she is!" He nodded as I handed his phone back. He stared at me and frowned, tilting his head as if something had just occurred to him and he was puzzled. "I still swear you look so familiar. I must have seen you before. Damn if I still can't place you."

I panicked again, thinking I'd just been outed; that my father had recognized me as his offspring. Terror. Excitement. I felt like I was about to throw up. Until I realized he was simply mentally cataloguing former students, looking for a one who fit the bill.

My mouth was so dry, it was hard to speak. I had to force myself to smile. "No. Like I told you before, I'm sure of it." Which was the absolute truth.

He was still frowning. He shook his head. "You remind me of *someone*." As my heart literally froze in my chest, he squinted, deep in thought. "I just can't think who." He took a deep breath and frowned. "It doesn't matter. It'll come to me. Probably when I least expect it."

After pizza, Logan drove me home. He dropped the other guys off before running me to the dorm. He was quiet, and not comfortably so. I couldn't figure out what I'd done.

"Is something wrong?" I asked him as he pulled to a stop.

"Maybe I'm the only one who noticed, but you seemed really into Jason." He sounded almost jealous. "And don't give me any of that crap about wanting to please the boss. You stared at Mia's picture a long time."

Damn. Logan *would* notice. I'd have to be even more careful. Logan read me like no other person ever had, even my mom.

"It's not what you think," I said, thinking on my feet. "My second stepdad just had a baby girl with his new wife. The baby's about the same age. I don't even know her. I wonder, sometimes, what it would be like to have a sister. Or a brother. And a dad who dotes over you like that. That's all."

Logan seemed to buy my explanation. He even looked relieved. "A friendly reminder—Collin's party is tomorrow. He twisted my arm to reissue his invitation and express his strongest desire for you to attend. Collin likes to know the people whose lives he helped save. And brag about his heroism before crowds." Logan grinned. "He's dying to show you off. Bring your friends, the more the merrier. Will you come?"

"What about you?" I bit my lip. "I thought you wanted to keep your heroics on the down-low."

"Only from the press and the university. Among my friends, I want their undying admiration."

"I see," I said, but I really didn't. "Are you going to let him take all the credit?"

"Don't worry. Zave won't let him. Besides, half the guests Collin's expecting were at the cliffs and saw the events with their own eyes. They'll keep him honest. They all want to get to know you better."

"I don't want to be a trophy, or an oddity."

"I'll be there. I won't let that happen, I promise. They're really just excited. They want to know you're okay and celebrate doing something good." He paused. "Please, El."

"Are you calling in a debt?"

He laughed. "Not yet, El. I'm saving those for when I really need them. I'm just asking you as a friend to hang out at a friend's party. Meet some new people. They're an awesome group. You'll like them."

Maybe it was only me being optimistic again, but I got the strong feeling he was asking for himself. He wanted me to meet his friends. My heart danced with delight. What girl wouldn't be thrilled by that? "Only if you guarantee you'll be there when I show up. And you won't take offense if I bail out early."

"It's a deal. I'll text you the address."

CHAPTER SEVEN

Bre had a date with Dan, but Taylor and Nic were game to go to Collin's party with me and bask in the sparkle of my celebrity. And, as a hopeful byproduct, meet some of Logan's hot friends.

The party was in an off-campus apartment, a brand new building at the very edge of town where the rolling wheat fields met civilization. Nic drove because she was the only one with a car.

"Wow!" Taylor said as we pulled into the parking lot. "This is absolutely gorgeous. Tell me again why we're living at that dump we call a dorm?"

I looked at the complex and sighed. "Because this place costs big bucks and some of us aren't exactly flush with cash."

"Yeah, that's the reason. Thanks for keeping me grounded. I think I'm going to have to hit on Collin," Nic said as we walked past the clubhouse and the swimming pool in the courtyard. "Or at least become *very* good friends."

The complex was alive with parties that spilled one into another around the pool and into the halls. Music pulsed in the air and the smell of beer and hot, eager bodies overwhelmed the scent of dust and grain from the fields.

It was a clear night after a hot day, but the temperature was mercifully falling. We found Collin's apartment on the second floor. It faced the courtyard and the pool and had a balcony with a view of both.

I took a deep breath and in we went. Inside, the apartment was a packed mass of bodies. I panicked when I didn't see Logan anywhere.

"There she is! There's our girl!" An average-height guy, stocky and not bad-looking—but he paled in comparison to Logan—came forward and put his arm around my shoulder. "Come on in and meet everybody."

He was one of the guys from the SUB. I took it he was Collin. I realized I'd been in shock at the cliffs. I remembered Logan clearly and every minute detail as he rescued me. But not much else. I must have focused almost exclusively on him.

I had only a vague recollection, almost a knowledge rather than a memory, of others helping me up the cliff. The only other person I remembered distinctly was the girl in the pink bikini, Kels. "You must be Collin."

"That's me."

"These are my friends." I introduced Nic and Taylor.

"What do you ladies want to drink?" He led us to the kitchen, where they'd tapped a keg. "We have beer and an assortment of pop, mixers, and the hard stuff."

The apartment was crowded and messy with the results of party madness, but it was also fabulous. They had a leather couch and chair, a huge TV, and impressive speakers. I envied anyone who lived there.

As Collin walked us to the kitchen past one of the bedrooms, I caught a glimpse inside. I saw Logan's backpack. One of his shirts I recognized. A picture of him with a family that must have been his. I realized with a start that Logan lived here, too. He and Collin were roommates. Why hadn't he mentioned it?

"You remember, Ellie, the girl we saved," Collin said to anyone who'd listen. "Yes, she looks different with her hair down." He whispered in my ear as loudly as he could over the music. "They're impressed."

I nodded and smiled and looked around wildly for Logan. Collin introduced us to Zave, the third roommate. Word of who I was spread. I felt everyone's eyes on me. As Collin poured us each a beer, Logan appeared from the balcony.

I smiled at him, weak with relief, as he came toward us. "I was beginning to think you'd lied to me." I had to yell over the music.

"Sorry!" He nodded toward the balcony. "I didn't see you come in." He spotted Nic and Taylor and welcomed them. I could tell they were drooling over him. Logan took my arm and offered to introduce us around.

"I think Collin's introduced us to almost everyone who would listen already," I yelled back.

"What?" Collin said. He was already acting tipsy. "You can't take my girl away. I'm not done showing her off."

Logan slapped Collin on the back. "You're done for now, buddy." He took us around the party. Nic and Taylor found two guys to their liking and started dancing with them.

I stood to the side with Logan like a wallflower, feeling out of place. I wasn't good at parties and small talk. Logan didn't seem inclined to ask me to dance.

"You're bored," he said. "We can't talk here. Hang on. I'll be right back." He went to his room and returned with a pair of binoculars around his neck, his iPad, and a folding chair. "Are you game for going outside?"

I was game for anything that meant going someplace with Logan. I nodded and caught Taylor's eye to let her and Nic know I was going to the pool with Logan. He led me through the crowded hall and outside, but not to the courtyard and the pool. Instead, he took me to the backside of the complex that faced the wheat fields.

"We're just past the height of the Perseid meteor showers, but maybe we'll get lucky. There's less light pollution out here." He set down his beer and his iPad and set up the folding beach chair. It was the kind that reclined and sat low to the ground.

"You entice me to a party and then you con me into stargazing with you instead?"

"Yeah, I'm diabolical. Collin and Zave think I'm crazy, but I like watching the stars. It keeps me grounded and puts things in perspective. Looking out at the universe, my problems seem insignificant in the grand scheme. We can go back to the party if you'd rather."

"No way. Falling stars are lucky. I could use a few." I grinned and shook my head. "You only brought one chair."

"I only have one chair. You can sit on my lap."

I hesitated.

"Or I can sit on yours if you prefer."

"How much did you say you weigh?"

"I didn't." He laughed, fell into the chair, took my hand, and pulled me into the chair against him with his legs straddling me.

"Careful! You're sloshing my beer," I said to cover my nerves and excitement from being so close to him. I could feel his body heat and smell his cologne. My body reacted. There was something about Logan I couldn't resist.

"There's plenty more beer where that came from. Collin never skimps."

"Yeah, but we'd have to go back into the party to get it." I sat awkwardly between his legs, stiff and prim. I was in uncharted territory, not sure whether this was a just-friends moment or something more and not wanting to overstep the boundaries. Most girls would have taken full advantage and cuddled into him, hoping and angling for more.

I wasn't most girls. I had too much to lose if I got too close. "How come you didn't tell me you live with Collin and Zave? And why do you keep saying this is Collin's party when it's clearly yours and Zave's, too?"

I may be slow, but I had realized by now that Logan had money, too. Or his family did. I'd assumed since he was working, he was as strapped as the rest of us, but I guess I was wrong. Or maybe he was asserting his independence from the wealthy father he was on the outs with. I respected that.

"Collin is our party planner. He runs all of our joint social events. We've gotten in the habit of calling them *his* parties, but they're our parties. Our friends know the deal. If we ever called the parties anything but Collin's, they'd get the wrong idea and wonder what happened and why we were fighting with Collin. As for being roommates, it never came up."

I remained in my awkward perch.

He reached over the side of his chair and grabbed his iPad. "What's this being stiff and distant around me, El," he whispered in my ear. "I'm your hand-holding guy. Relax! Stargazing is not for the tense. It's supposed to relieve stress."

I was outed for being nervous. How could he be so calm?

"Tense? Who, me? No way. I'm just afraid of tangling with those vicious killer binoculars around your neck. A girl could give herself a concussion by leaning against those."

"These?" He stared down at them.

Or maybe he was staring down my blouse. It was hard to tell from my angle, but the thought was thrilling.

"These aren't even my most lethal star-watching equipment. You should see my telescope. It's mind blowing." His voice was laced with innuendo as he leaned and whispered so closely it was like he was blowing in my ear.

Shivers ran down my body. What were we really talking about? "I'd love to see your lethal telescope."

I could almost feel him smiling.

"Another time. It's back at the apartment. But I concede your point—my binoculars aren't pillowy soft and comfortable to lean against." He took the binoculars off, set them on the grass next to us, and pulled me against his chest, wrapping his arms around me, holding his iPad in front of us. He wasn't exactly soft to lean against, either, but being next to him was thrilling and so pleasurable I felt like I could rest my head against him forever. It just felt right.

I leaned against the hard contours of his chest and swore I could feel the thumping of his heart. I just couldn't tell if his heart was reacting as wildly as mine in reaction to being so near each other. All I knew for sure was that I didn't want to be anywhere else.

He held his iPad in front of us, turned it on, and brought up an app. "Star Walk," he said. "So I can impress you by naming the constellations." He held the iPad up toward the sky.

"Impressive? You're basically using a crib sheet," I said.

"I get points for buying an app to impress the girls."

"You give yourself points easily."

He laughed and pointed the iPad at the sky. The constellation Sagittarius lit up onscreen. "There it is, the archer."

I squinted at the sky, trying to find the stars that were on the iPad screen, diagramed with lines connecting them, which still looked nothing like a centaur archer. "How can anyone see a half man, half beast god of war in that mess of stars? Even the description says it looks more like a teacup than anything else."

He put his face next to mine and pointed to the sky. "Use your imagination. See that patch of the Milky Way? Imagine what ancient man felt like when he stared at the sky and saw that. How did he explain it? Why wasn't it there during daylight?

"He had to make up stories to explain it. Astronomers were the storytellers and forecasters of their day and the sky was their internet and like TV for the masses. They could watch it for hours as the planets and moon moved across it. Like we are." Logan adjusted the iPad. "Picture the archer standing with his bow aimed at the heart of Scorpius, the scorpion. Legend says he was placed in the heavens to guide the Argonauts in their travels."

"So the heavens were both entertainment and a satellite missile defense system."

"You could look at it that way. Even if the constellation doesn't look like a centaur, in astronomy terms, Sagittarius is impressive—more Messier objects than any other constellation in the sky, including seven globular clusters, four open star clusters, three nebulae, and a patch of the Milky Way."

"That knowledge would be even more impressive if you weren't reading it from an app."

He laughed. "See, off to the right of the body of the constellation? That's the Lagoon Nebula." He reached for his binoculars. "We can see it better with—"

"Look!" A falling star blazed across the sky in front of us. "Did you see it?"

I felt him nodding.

"Awesome. I hope you made a wish." He put the binoculars to his eyes and stared at the sky. Then he handed them to me and helped me locate the Lagoon Nebula. He brought it up on the app and showed me what it would look like if we could see it with something like the Hubble telescope.

We took turns gazing at globular clusters, nebulae, and even the Milky Way, looking them up on Star Walk and debating over which one was most impressive.

"This is no good," he said at last. "Our focus is too narrow. We're missing too many meteors."

"The Milky Way galaxy is too narrow a focus?" I said.

He laughed and settled me closer against him. "Yeah. When there's a whole universe before us."

The way he said it made me think he was referring to more than stars and skies. It felt like the beginning of something big, or maybe the natural continuation of what had started at Up All Night. I wondered why I hadn't met him first, before Austin. I tried to remember what it felt like before I became jaded, when I was naïve enough that "I love you" meant "I love you and only you." And "I'm not going to cheat on you." When I believed it when a guy said he'd wait until I was ready. When I believed love was forever and not just a line.

I wish I'd met Logan then, at that time before I was guarded and afraid of everything, including losing my heart. I could wish on star after star, but it wasn't going to change the situation. It didn't stop me from trying. I wished I'd met Logan at a time when I wasn't trying to connect with my dad and life wasn't so complicated.

A huge meteor flashed across the sky. Its tail stayed lit for a second afterward, burning brightly. And then I wished, really wished on it, that Logan and I could have a chance. If not now, *someday*.

He set the binoculars in the grass next to our chair and reclined fully back until he was lying nearly flat on his back and I was lying against him with my head on his shoulder, my hair spilling around us. For an instant, it felt like my wish had been granted.

The sky lit up with meteor after meteor. We gasped in awe as the biggest ones coursed across the heavens. We pointed and laughed at the small ones. Poked fun at each other for missing one and marveled at the display. I was in complete awe at feeling so completely right with Logan.

"What are you wishing for?" he asked.

"If you tell what you wished for, my wish won't come true."

"We've seen over thirty shooting stars. You can't blow one wish to satisfy my curiosity?"

"No, not one." I couldn't tell him most of the wishes were for the same thing and telling one would be telling all.

"I wished this evening would never end," he said.

I shivered from the force of his sentiment and how closely it matched mine, but pretended I shivered from the falling dew and rapidly cooling night.

He wrapped his arms tightly around me. "You're cold."

I was happy. Happier than I could ever remember being. "You just wasted a wish."

"It couldn't come true anyway." His tone was at once light and full of longing.

"Then why did you wish it?"

"Wishes don't have to be possible."

There was something different and deep about Logan. He was holding something back and suffering like I was. I knew enough about pain and secrets to recognize them in another person for the insidious creatures they were. I wanted to ask him what it was that tormented him, what he was hiding from me and everyone. I bit my tongue. It wasn't fair to ask him. Not when I couldn't, and wouldn't, share either my demons or my secrets.

"Who says it can't come true?" I said, neatly nullifying my own theory about not telling wishes or they wouldn't come true. "We'll hold it in our memories forever." My words tumbled out with so much force it

surprised me. I looked up at him to see if I'd mis-
stepped.

He was staring at the sky, but he snorted softly and
smiled. "I like that. We'll thwart fate and all that shit
about wishes revealed not coming true.

"You should be in the stars, El. The goddess of
tempting fate with her arrow pointed directly at man's
heart." He sounded both almost defiantly angry and
somehow amused at the same time.

I almost told him that I'd wished I'd met him sooner.

We lapsed into silence. Staring at the sky, I saw
what he meant. I felt lame and small in the vastness of
the universe and eternity spreading out before me. But
somehow, it was comforting to think how small and
insignificant my mistakes were and how infinite the
possibilities were.

"I was waiting for you in the water below the cliffs,"
he said out of nowhere. "Why didn't you jump sooner?"

I could have said it was because people kept crowd-
ing in front of me. But I didn't. I said what was even
truer. "I wanted to be sure I wasn't imagining that you
were."

I think he liked that answer. "You almost waited too
long."

"Maybe. But the minute I realized you wouldn't wait
forever, I jumped in, hoping you wouldn't go. You did-
n't stop. You just kept going."

"God, El, I did stop. That's why I saw you go under.
Because I stopped on the rock just off shore and turned
to go back."

I swallowed hard, overcome by the emotion in his voice and pulsing through me. "Thank you."

We both knew what would have happened if he hadn't.

He slid his warm hand beneath my tank top and rested it on my abdomen. My breath caught at the simple touch.

He ran his fingers through my hair. I stroked his arm. The biggest falling star of the night flashed overhead and I made a desperate wish.

He lifted the hair off my neck and nibbled my neck softly, moving slowly to my ear, my cheek, tantalizing and teasing the edges of my lips. His simple kisses, his hot mouth on my skin against the cool of the night, rose pleasure like waves pulsing through me. His hand remained still on my stomach, but I ached for his touch, full of longing I hadn't ever felt.

I rolled over on top of him and stared into his eyes, almost pleading with him to make another memory that would never be ruined. The moonlight was reflected in his deep brown eyes. He cupped my face and pulled it to his. And then he kissed me like I'd never been kissed before: leisurely, gently, and without tongues, as if we had forever to build to something more.

I swung my legs around him, straddling him and pressing myself against him. He arched up into me. I felt him hard against me through his shorts.

He sucked my lower lip and gently parted my lips and kissed me open-mouthed so skillfully it took my breath away.

His hands slid to my waist. He hiked my shirt up and ran his hands over my back until I shivered beneath his touch and wanted more. So much more.

I don't know how long we kissed. Wrapped in his arms, with his mouth on mine, I lost all track of time. The way we kissed was so comfortable and natural, it was like we were two halves that had always been together. There was no awkwardness. No turning our heads the wrong direction. No false stops or starts. No bumping of noses.

When he finally pulled away, he was breathing hard. "I've wanted to do that, and so much more, since I met you, El."

"But?" I knew there was more.

He looked at me with admiration and regret shining with the moonlight in his eyes. "You're too damn intuitive, El." He paused like he was searching for words. Finally, he sighed, like he was giving up. Like there was no good way to say it. "I like you. You're special, El. Really special. But I'm sorry. I'm dealing with a bunch of shit right now, and I can't..."

He trailed off like he couldn't, or didn't want to, finish the thought.

I bit my lip. I knew what he was going to say. We couldn't be together. And he was right. I couldn't be with him, either.

I stroked his cheek, blinking back tears. "No, me either, Logan. I can't."

His brow furrowed. I'd surprised him. For a second it looked to me like he was wondering whether I was saving face or giving him an easy out. I got the feeling lots of girls gave him a pass. They'd do anything for him, take whatever kind of relationship he was willing to give them. I was different. I meant what I said—I couldn't have a relationship with him any more than he could with me.

He frowned. "You can't either?"

"I can't either," I whispered back.

He stared at me. In the dark, his black eye was less evident and his gaze penetrating. He opened his mouth and hesitated. "No." He shook his head. "I can't ask you why any more than I can give you my reasons." He paused. "You'd tell me if you could?"

I nodded. "Absolutely."

"I'm not feeding you bullshit or some kind of line." His Adam's apple bobbed. "You believe me?"

"I do, and I understand. And I won't question."

"Shit, El." He took a deep breath. "I don't believe this. I finally meet a girl—" He cut himself off and let out a heavy sigh. "I can't ask you to wait until I'm ready. I don't know when, or if, I'll ever be ready."

I nodded because I understood too well. I was afraid to ask the question, but I had to. I needed some kind of definition I could hang our relationship on. Was he saying this was it for us, the end of everything?

"What if I need someone to hold my hand?" I took a deep breath, hoping I didn't sound pitiful. "Are we still friends?"

"Always, El. I'll hold your hand anytime, any day." His voice broke as he held me tight.

"You know what I wished?" My voice was full of longing.

He stared at me and cupped my cheek. "You're really going to blow another wish?"

I tried to smile. "It doesn't matter. It's impossible, anyway." I paused. "I wished we'd met before." I didn't have to say before when.

"Me too, El. God, me too." He pulled my head to his chest and held it there, running his fingers through my hair as his lips brushed the top of my head.

I listened to the reassuring thump of his heart, blinked back a tear, and wished with all my being that things were different. That things *could* be different in the future. And that we'd never lose the longing we felt for each other. Even if we lived to be ninety and married other people, I never wanted to lose this feeling.

CHAPTER EIGHT

All day Sunday, Bre, Taylor, and Nic played interrogator, questioning me over and over again about Logan.

"But why?" Nic asked. "Things were going so well. You disappeared with him forever. That black eye makes him hot, gives him a bad boy edge and drags up sympathy, let-me-take-care-of-you points.

"He takes you out to on some lame-ass excuse to look at the stars. Which was obviously code for wanting to make out. And then tells you you'll only be friends? It makes no sense."

"It does to me," I said. "He's dealing with something and needs time. We barely know each other. It's not like he owes it to me to spill all his personal details to me.

"Besides, I don't want a boyfriend, either. I've told you, I'm still rebounding. It's going to take some time.

"Logan's too special to be a rebound guy. I'd rather have him as a long-term friend than a short-lived, failed fling. Anyway, a relationship's not going to happen."

Taylor shrugged as if the solution was obvious. "Then you need to find someone in between. Find your rebound guy and get it out of your system. Who knows? You might find someone you like better. There's a whole campus full of hot men out there."

There was one monumental problem—I didn't want anyone but Logan.

"His friend Collin is hot, too," Nic said. "Do you think he'd go for me?" She sighed heavily, like she was ruing the complications of her life. "Black guys like my shitty dad want pale white girls like my mom. White guys want white girls. It's really crappy luck."

I stared at Nic, almost startled. Why would any guy not want her? She was so gorgeous and funny, I had to fight my envy nearly every time I looked at her. "He'd be crazy not to."

Sunday night, our chem quiz scores were posted online. I got a five out of ten and felt sick. Unlike most profs, Dr. Rogers didn't post the class average or the curve.

Dex called me and ranted. "I got a six."

"Then you did better than I did."

"Yeah, I did better than everyone I know. But that doesn't mean jack. You need to see Byron. Visit him during his office hours. Bring him cookies. Find out the scoop."

Monday in class, Dr. Rogers refused to go over the quiz, saying anyone who didn't understand was ignorant and didn't belong in her class. A ripple of anger and frustration rode through the lecture hall. Despite more questioning, she refused to post the grade distribution.

Dex buzzed with his electronic buzzer. Dr. Rogers called on him. "Having some old quizzes and tests to study would help us out. Will you be posting any?"

"Absolutely not." Dr. Rogers looked almost gleeful and a lot like Hannibal Lecter after a good meal. "They wouldn't do you any good if I did."

I thought the crowd might mutiny. Dex was fuming. If Dr. Rogers was trying to incite a riot, she was certainly going about it the right way.

"This is absolute bullshit," Dex said as we walked out. "Last semester she pulled heavily from quizzes from the semester before. Without any study aids, we're fucked."

Before work I went to see Byron during his office hours. "Office" was a misnomer. He had a desk in a single-man cubicle at the back of a chem lab on the second floor of the chem building. At least he had a window, but it looked out on the second floor of the parking garage next to the chem building. Better than a view of garbage bins, I supposed. If I were him, I would have put up a curtain.

His desk was cluttered with lab notebooks he was grading and the cloth walls of his cubicle held a *Big*

Bang Theory calendar, a periodic table, and some inspirational quotes by famous chemists. It was nothing to write home about.

Byron sat across his battered desk from me, looking nerdy and nervous. Like Byron's hands, the desk was covered with chemical stains. He blushed.

"But we studied so hard for the quiz," I explained. "A whole group of us got together and went over the material and worked problems. But we were blindsided."

Byron looked around as if his tiny cubicle was bugged. "That's Dr. Rogers for you. She likes to mix things up."

"But she won't go over the quizzes. She won't even pass them back so we can study them and see what we did wrong. It's like she's *trying* to fail us. And she's not fighting fair."

Despite Dex's urging, I didn't want to lead poor Byron on. But it was hot and I'd worn short shorts. He was admiring my legs.

I hated myself for doing it, but I played the damsel-in-distress card. "I'm on academic scholarship. I need this class for my minor. If I fail it, I'll lose my scholarship. What can I do?" I crossed my legs and gave him my helpless look.

"Let me take a look at your grade." He brought the grades up on his laptop.

I wished I could see the spreadsheet, but I couldn't see his screen from where I sat.

"You got a five. That's very good. That puts you in the top ten percent." He flashed me a weak smile.

I let out a sigh of relief. "That gives me an A, then?"

He shook his head. "Dr. Rogers doesn't curve." He leaned across the desk and whispered to me. "There's never a good semester to take her class, or to be her TA, but this is probably the worst semester ever. She's in trouble over something with the department.

"Last semester, she added two hundred points to everyone's grades at the last minute. Her way of curving. If she hadn't, over seventy-five percent of the class would have failed and the dean would have been livid. We don't have the staff or the funds to have students retaking chemistry again and again. And we can't afford to anger the alums and donors any more than necessary. Many of these students' parents are both."

He lowered his voice even more, so low I had to lean across the desk to hear him. "When the dean found out what she did, he gave her hell and told her not to try that stunt again." He paused. "She won't be giving anyone extra points this semester."

"What can I do?" I was still leaning forward, feeling like we were a couple of conspirators who could be dragged off to prison at any moment.

He pulled open a drawer. "I'm not supposed to do this. Don't tell anyone. But I'm going over the quiz with anyone who comes in for help. If word gets out. I'm going to have to stop."

I pulled out a notebook and nodded. "Your secret's safe with me." I was keeping a lot of them lately. "Byron?"

"Yeah?"

"What kind of cookies do you like?"

At work, Jason was frazzled. "The baby's teething."

My baby sister was teething. My daddy had stayed up with her. I felt a stab of jealousy. At the same time, I kept wondering if there was any way to get closer to Jason. I had to become something more than a student who worked in the office. I wondered if there was any way I could get him to mentor me like he did Logan. Maybe then I'd be able to determine what kind of man he really was and what had happened between him and my mother.

Logan texted me that he wouldn't be in the office, but he'd like to meet for burgers after work. I wasn't going to turn him down. I hadn't seen him since Saturday night. It seemed important to see how things stood now that we had agreed to be just friends. Would it work?

He was waiting for me outside the SUB wearing a big grin. He pointed to his watch. "I'm right on time this week."

"Yeah, I can see. Gotta love a punctual man. No fire drills today?"

"Calm and quiet."

"Don't sound so pleased," I said as he held the door open for me and followed me into the SUB. "If things stay too calm, you'll be out of a job."

He laughed. "How were things at the office?"

"Karen was in a jovial mood. Her son got to play a full half in the football game. Jason was tired and bleary-eyed from being up all night with Mia, who is apparently teething."

"He's a great guy and he sure dotes on his kid." Logan extended his arm, indicating I should get in line first.

Yeah, I thought. *One of them, anyway.*

We got our burgers and sat at the same table as the week before.

"I think this is becoming our table," I said.

"I like the view from here." He wasn't looking at the football field below. He was staring at me.

I was totally confused. I smiled back, ignoring any implications he may, or may not, have intended. "How are classes?"

"All right. I'm a senior," he said, slathering his fries with a crisscross of ketchup again, grinning as he did. "They cut us some slack. By now, they've given up trying to flunk us out. Their new MO for getting us out of here is to graduate us."

"Must be the life," I said.

"After a hellacious sophomore and junior year, I think I've earned it."

I shook my head and smiled at him.

"You?"

"MIS 301 is cool. So is BA 315. But Chem 202? Let's just say we're already on the verge of rioting and planning insurrection. I've never done so relatively well and still failed.

"We got our chem quiz scores yesterday. Mine was in the top ten percent and I still failed because I got fifty percent and the esteemed, arrogant bitch Dr. Rogers will not curve." I ranted a bit more, listing my grievances until I realized Logan wasn't sympathizing and laughing with me. He wasn't sharing any of his war stories from that class, either. He was staring at his fries and silently chewing his burger with as little enthusiasm as if he was chewing cardboard. And it may have been my imagination again, but I thought he looked pale. "Everything okay?"

He shrugged. "Yeah, fine."

"Jason said you did okay in her class—"

"I can't help you, Ellie. I blanked it all out as soon as it was over."

I tried to lighten the mood. "A big chemistry fan, I take it." I poked his burger basket.

He remained stonily silent.

I took a deep breath. "Okay, I get it. You hate chemistry. I don't expect you to remember it and help me solve problems or anything. I have Dex and Byron and my study group for that.

"But if you could just give us some hints on how to study, how her devious mind works, anything that would help—"

"No!"

My eyes went wide. He looked really pale now and almost angry. It was a mood I hadn't seen before and it scared me. I should have backed off, but I didn't understand his attitude. I wasn't asking for much. "Okay, way to be a friend."

I felt those perfect memories crumbling. If he was going to be crazy and moody, he wasn't the man I thought he was. He saved my life, but he wouldn't give me chemistry tips? It didn't make any sense, but it did hurt my feelings.

He didn't respond so I dropped it. We ate in uncomfortable silence. I lost my appetite and shoved my burger and fries away. I reached for my backpack. "I have to get going. Nic is taking me to the store so I can buy ingredients to make cookies so I can bribe my chem TA. Right now, his help is the only prayer we have of passing that class." I slid back, ready to rise and leave.

"Don't do it, El." His voice was definitely shaking now. "Don't throw yourself at Byron to get a good grade." His voice was low and angry.

"Jerk." I stood. "I'm only baking him cookies." I turned and walked off.

"Ellie!"

I ignored him and kept walking. My experience with Austin had taught me not to trust guys. It made me jumpy and easily spooked. Logan had just thrown up great big red flag. I blinked back tears as I heard a chair scrape along the floor behind me.

"El! Ellie!" Logan came after me. He caught my arm from behind and swung me around to face him.

My face flamed. I felt the eyes of everyone in the cafeteria watching us like we were having a lovers' tiff.

"I'm sorry." He raked his hand through his hair. "I was being an ass. Don't leave. I'll take you shopping. You can bake your cookies at my place. You can't bake in the dorm. Their ovens are crap and if you turn your back for a minute, someone will steal your cookies." His tone was pleading. He was trying to smile, but it looked forced.

And I was pathetic because I really couldn't hold my anger or even my hurt. With his yellowing black eye and the apologetic look on his face, he was handsome and heart-wrenchingly vulnerable at the same time.

I stared at him. It would take a harder woman than I was to reject and walk away from him. Staring at him, I was struck by a realization. "That chemistry class is wrapped up in whatever you're dealing with." I paused. "I'm sorry. I didn't know it was a trigger. From now on, talking about it is off limits between us."

He clenched his fists at his side and a look of relief passed across his face. "Thank you, El. That was a horrible semester. I've been trying to forget what I remember of it ever since."

"You're not making any sense," I said.

"I am if you know what I'm talking about." He grabbed the straps of my backpack. "Let me carry that to my car for you. Let's go bake cookies."

"Are you sure? It's still hot out and it will heat up your apartment."

He grinned. "We have air conditioning."

I gave him a playful shove in the arm, mostly because I couldn't resist the urge to touch him. My hurt and anger had washed away and been replaced with empathy. "Why didn't I notice that at the party?"

"Too many hot bodies heating the place up."

When I agreed to let Logan take me shopping, I hadn't thought about my reduced financial circumstances. And how my relative poverty and frugal ways might embarrass me. With most of my crowd, no one expected a big spender. Frugality ruled. One of the most popular shopping days of the semester was University Day at Shopper's Co. when everything was half price. They held it just before the semester started. The metro bus service ran shuttles from the university to Shopper's Co. because there was never enough parking and you were lucky to get into the place. Dollar pounder beer at happy hour was another popular favorite.

But when I tried to buy the cheap, value-brand chocolate chips and imitation vanilla, Logan stopped me. "My mom is renowned for her baking. Everyone asks for her recipes, which she gives out freely. But she's been accused, more than once, of sabotaging them. She uses top ingredients and that's the key. Use crap ingredients, you get a crap product."

"Thanks for that visual," I said.

He threw the premium chocolate chips and the real vanilla in my basket. "Mom says you can't skimp when you want quality."

I took them out and put them back on the shelf. "You can if you don't have a coupon and your bank account is running low."

He pulled them off the shelf and put them back in my basket. "On me. It's the least I can do for your grade. Even though you are baking for another guy."

I could tell it was his way of making amends, so I let him do it. I made a point of counting on my fingers. "Four other guys, to be accurate."

"Four?"

"Well, there's Byron and Dex and—"

He grabbed my hand. "I get the picture."

"Do you have a cookie sheet and cooling rack?" I asked him, crossing my fingers.

"Babe, we have everything."

"You didn't have vanilla."

"I meant, I have excellent equipment."

Guys and their innuendo! I raised a brow and ran my gaze down him. "I'm sure you do. Let's check out."

"I thought you were going to say 'check it out.'"

"I thought I just did."

His apartment was mercifully cool and quiet, and surprisingly clean, especially given the party they'd recently thrown. "Who's the maid?" I asked.

"Zave and me. Collin plans and shops. We do clean-up."

"Hmmmm. You do good work." I sniffed. "And it smells good in here, too."

"Air freshener. Zave's mom buys them for us to cover the smell of stale beer and ripe laundry." He grinned.

"You actually listen to a mom?"

"Never know when a girl we want to impress might pop by. It pays to be prepared."

Why my heart should trill at that, I had no idea. We were supposed to be just friends.

The roomies were out. Logan dumped our backpacks in the living room while I carried our groceries to the kitchen.

"Help yourself in there," he said, and began calling out directions to where things were while I washed up.

I could make chocolate chip cookies by memory in my sleep. In no time I had a batch in the oven and the apartment smelled like cookies. Logan hung over my shoulder, distracting me as I bent over and checked the first batch for doneness.

"Not crispy enough yet," I said, about to close the oven door. "A few more minutes."

"They look done to me." He was standing so close behind me that if I took even the tiniest step backwards, I would be pressed up against his dick.

It was tempting. If we weren't trying to be just friends. "The dough is still white and barely warm."

"I like my cookies soft and chewy." He was so completely adorable the way he said it, almost pleading and begging for me to please him.

"I suppose that's the way your mother makes them?"

"She does for me."

"And I'm guessing there's an oven fee I can pay off in cookies?"

He was still hanging over my shoulder. "Now that you mention it..."

"Stand back." Against my better judgment, I took the cookies out and slid another batch in. "Another irreconcilable difference—I like crispy cookies and you like warmed-up dough."

"Is that a deal-breaker?" He was eying the cookies.

"It's not as major as the dark chocolate versus milk chocolate chip gap."

He smiled. "You mean some people like milk chocolate chips?"

"See what I mean?"

We settled in to study while I baked. I texted Dex that I was in the middle of baking a bribe for Byron. Then we started instant messaging while we solved chem problems. I should say while I solved chem problems on the sly and Logan worked on his engineering homework. I didn't have a prayer of understanding Logan's homework, so I didn't ask about it.

"Who are you talking to?" Logan asked me after I laughed out loud at one of Dex's snide remarks.

"Dex, my lab partner for the class that henceforth shall not be named."

"So that's why you keep covering your notes and laptop with your arm? Because you promised not to mention that class?"

I nodded. "Sorry. But I'm still in it and I still have a pile of crappy homework to do for it."

"That's a relief. I thought you were carrying on a clandestine relationship right across the table from me."

I smiled in my most enigmatic way. "Who says I'm not?"

"You don't have to hide your class that shall not be named homework."

"That's a relief. I was getting writer's cramp in this position." I picked up my notebook and waved it in front of him, teasing him.

"I didn't say flaunt it."

I set the notebook down and stretched with my arms up and my elbows back. When I looked up, Logan was staring at my chest. He looked away quickly, but from his expression I thought he was having as bad a time dealing with the friendship only thing as I was.

"We're going to have to come up with a shorter name for that class. But even as an acronym it's seven letters and we don't have any vowels to make something awesome and funny out of it."

"I think 'hell' has a nice ring to it." He grinned at me. He was trying, really trying, I could tell.

"I wonder if it has a synonym?" I looked it up on my laptop. "This isn't going to work. All the synonyms have to do with the attraction between two people. They're all way too positive."

"'Hell' it is," he said.

The stove timer dinged. I took out a batch of cookies and stuck the last batch in. Then I had to use the bathroom. I popped up.

"Where are you going?" he asked.

"Um, to the bathroom. I was trying to be delicate and just sneak out quietly."

He smiled. "And I'm trying to save you from being grossed out. Use the one in my bedroom. You don't want to go anywhere near the main bathroom right now. It's Zave's and he isn't the most fastidious, if you know what I mean. You know which room's mine?"

I nodded. This was an open invitation to snoop. I really did have to pee—too much pop while baking cookies—so I ducked into the bathroom without noticing much more about his room than it was pretty neat for a guy's room. His bathroom was pretty tidy, too, and smelled like him—a heavenly concoction of his toothpaste, soap, shampoo, and cologne. I could have lingered in there just soaking in the scent of him.

Once I was finished in the bathroom, I gently opened the bathroom door that led into the bedroom, hoping to give myself a few seconds to take in his private space before he got suspicious and wondered what was taking me so long.

I paused and smiled as I looked around. There's a stage when you want to know everything about the new guy in your life. I was so deep into that stage that I couldn't see a way out. Even though we were supposed to be just friends, every new revelation about him was thrilling, even down to the fact he used soft two-ply toilet paper that was much better than the dorm's. See what I mean? I may have said he was just a friend, but the way I felt was something much more.

"Hey."

I jumped and grabbed my heart. Logan lounged in the shadow of the doorway from the bedroom to the main living space. He was grinning like he knew he'd caught me in the act.

"What do you think?" He took a step in.

I tried to play it cool. "You're neat. Which is a bit freaky in a guy, but admirable."

He laughed. "That's it?"

I looked around. His walls were covered in baseball posters. A signed and framed Chicago Cubs baseball jersey with the last name Walker hung on the wall over his bed.

"You like baseball. That's awesome. I do too. I could argue with your taste in teams, though. The Chicago

Cubs? Really? When was the last time they won a pennant?"

He was supposed to smile or laugh or something. Instead, he shook his head. "And you prefer?"

"The Mariners, of course. They may not be all that much better. But at least they're the hometown team. For the whole state, you traitor." Washington only had one Major League Baseball team and the Seattle Mariners were it.

I walked over to the Cubs jersey. It was signed. "Caleb Walker," I read. "Nice coincidence. Kind of awesome to have an MLB jersey with your last name on it. It's, like, every guy's dream to play major league ball and see his name on a jersey. How'd you swing that?"

Logan stared at me a minute. "He's my brother," he said so deadpan that for a moment I thought he was joking.

"No? Your brother plays major league baseball." I pulled my phone out of my pocket and immediately looked him up.

Logan walked over and pulled my phone from my hand. "There's no need to look him up. Don't believe me?" He took my hand and led me to his desk in the corner. He grabbed a picture frame and handed it to me. "There we are—the happy family. Dad, Mom, Caleb, and me."

His dad was a distinguished older man who looked like he'd been an athlete in his day. His mom was thin and pretty, also athletic looking, like someone who probably rode horses or played tennis at a club. Logan looked so handsome he was hard not to stare at and his brother could have been his twin.

"This proves nothing except you have a brother. A twin?" I said, thrilled by the possibility.

He sighed. "Baby brother. Eleven months younger than I am. It's a common misperception." He picked up another picture. This one was of Caleb in a Cubbies' catcher uniform, squatting, mitt out ready to catch a ball.

"Wow!" I said, trying not to sound as impressed as I felt. As proud as Logan sounded, I sensed there was more to this story and it wasn't all happy. "He's a year younger than you are and he's already actually playing for the Cubs?"

Logan nodded. "He was drafted right out of high school. First round. Only the fortieth player from Washington state since 1965 to be drafted right out of high school and the first first-round catcher drafted at all since 2000." His voice was filled with pride, but his moods were mercurial. Just as quickly, his tone slid into sneering. "My dad's pride and joy. All of his dreams come true in one son."

I was still staring at the picture. I turned to Logan, hoping I didn't see scarring, deforming jealousy there. I set the picture back on the desk, which was when I noticed a picture of Logan with his arms around Kelsie like she was his girlfriend, both of them smiling into the camera, looking happily like two people in love. This was not going well—for either of us.

I was wrong—not every new revelation was beautifully shiny and a new wonder to behold about Logan.

I took a deep breath, pointed to the picture of Caleb, and stumbled forward. "That's the problem with your dad? You think he loves your brother more? You think he's prouder of him?"

"I know he's prouder of him." Logan took a few steps backward and fell into a seated position on his bed.

I sat cautiously next to him, dying to hear his side and not wanting my illusions about him to shatter. We're all human, but whether I'd wanted to or not, I'd put Logan on a pedestal. Kind of hard not to do when he'd been so sweet and saved my life, too. "I'm sorry." I didn't know what to say.

"Don't be. It's not your fault." He leaned back against the wall. "I don't want you to get the wrong idea. I love my brother. I'm thrilled for him. Proud as an older brother can be. He's living his dream. And Dad's. He's earning piles of money and the chicks love him. He even has groupies."

"Well, of course there's that. Every guy's dream to have groupies," I said, teasing.

Logan ignored my comment. "Caleb was born to play ball. He is a seriously intuitive player. He knows things you can't teach, like how to read what a player on base will do. He's gifted. A baseball genius.

"Way better than I ever was, or ever would be. I don't have the intuitive feel for the game he does. He worked fucking hard. He deserves his success."

"You played, too?" I had a terrible sense of where this was headed.

Logan nodded. "Yeah, I played." He snorted. "I was Dad's pride and joy for about three seconds when I was four. Until Caleb picked up a ball at my t-ball practice and that was it.

"From then on Dad pitted Caleb and me against each other in a sick kind of competition, even though neither of us felt compelled to compete against the other. We were actually each other's biggest support.

"Dad did his damnedest to make it impossible for us each to accomplish at our own level and be happy with what we achieved. One of us always has to best the other. Dad brags about the victor and belittles the loser." He paused. "The reigning champ has always been Caleb.

"Nothing I've done has mattered as much to Dad as what Caleb does. My talents don't impress him and never will. I could start the next Microsoft or Google or Facebook and Dad wouldn't care."

I put my arm around Logan's shoulder. My heart went out to him. I didn't have either a father or a brother. But I had a mom who drove the wedge of competition between us, so I understood.

"That's real crappy of your dad." I leaned my head on his shoulder. "But it's his problem, Logan. Not yours."

"Easy to say," he said. "Maybe I could even have dealt if that was it." He stared at the desk across from us. "I was a pitcher, the prestige position. All my life, Caleb and I played on the same teams. Me pitching. Him catching. We were the dynamic Walker brothers, an inseparable, unbeatable team because we could read each other like twins. Baseball stars. We went to the Little League World Series together and won the championship. We played on all-star teams together.

"My freshman year here I played on scholarship."

I squeezed his shoulder. I had no idea. "But..." I was confused. "Where is all your memorabilia? And why—"

"Did I quit?" His laugh was cynical. "I didn't love baseball as much as Caleb and Dad. But I played to please them. My freshman year, Dad came to exactly one game. It was the only one that didn't conflict with Caleb's. That was the excuse.

"He came to the last game of the season, and I think it was only because Mom guilted him into it. It was a bear of a game and we were hurting because we'd had so many injuries. I was a relief pitcher. I rarely pitched more than an inning or two. But our two first-string pitchers were injured."

He took a deep breath. "I pitched the whole fucking game. To impress my dad. And because Dad cajoled the coach and encouraged him to keep me in. And there was no one else." He was silent a minute.

I waited for the rest of what I was certain was a story that ended badly.

"A pitcher should never pitch when they're fatigued. I threw an impressive game—a no-hitter. Until the last inning. I threw a curveball and threw out my shoulder at the same time.

"I collapsed in pain on the mound. Everyone thought I'd dislocated my shoulder. But it was much worse—I tore the labrum in my pitching shoulder."

I gasped, because even I knew what that meant. That was a career-ending injury for a pitcher.

"Yeah," he said. "Only about three percent of pitchers ever come back from that. Half a dozen surgeries later, I was part of the ninety-seven percent. I lost my scholarship. I couldn't play anymore.

"Dad blamed me. Said if I hadn't been hotdogging..." He choked up. "If it hadn't been for Jason Front...

"I don't know what I would have done. I was depressed. I didn't go to class. I was failing out and I didn't give a shit. I drank too much. I totaled my car and banged myself up pretty badly. Subconsciously, maybe I was trying to end it all. I don't know.

"Jason pulled me through. Gave me a job as an RTA, encouraged my love of computers and engineering. He's the best guy around and one of my closest friends. He's like a big brother to me. He's the most awesome dad to Mia. If I'd had a dad like him... Mia's lucky."

Tears welled up in my eyes and my pulse pounded in my temples. This was all too much to take in. The ramifications of what Logan was telling me were overwhelming. My heart was breaking for him and us and everything.

He stripped his shirt off and pointed to the tattoo on his shoulder. "This covers the scars. To new beginnings. It was Jason's gift to me."

I hesitantly touched it and leaned over to inspect it. The scar was so expertly woven in the tattoo, that unless you knew it was there, you'd never see it.

Logan looked vulnerable and handsome, in need of comfort. And I was aching to touch him. I slid onto his lap and straddled him. I leaned over and gently kissed his scar. "You'll always be my favorite baseball player, even though I never saw you play."

He caught my waist and held it tightly as I kissed his shoulder and his neck, and finally pulled back to look him in the eye. He slid his hands beneath my T-shirt and pulled it off over my head.

He pressed a kiss between my breasts, licking the valley between them until I shuddered with pleasure. Then he slowly worked his way up my neck, nibbling and trailing hot, insistent kisses until he found my mouth and possessed it.

He was hard between my legs. I wanted him. I wanted him so badly I ached with the need of it. But not like this. Not when I was just a means of mindless comfort. When he reached to unlatch my front-hook bra, I pulled out of his kiss and grabbed his hands to stop him.

We stared at each other a minute.

"We're supposed to be just friends." My voice was shaky. "I'm not a friends-with-benefits kind of girl." It was the truth. I was all or nothing. I never wanted to be halfway, half anything.

"I'm sorry, El." He was breathing hard. "I can't help myself when I'm around you."

Just then I got a whiff of something burning as the fire alarm squealed.

"The last batch of cookies!" I pulled my T-shirt on, climbed off Logan, and ran for the kitchen. When I

pulled the cookies out, they were burnt black and ruined. Kind of like Logan and me.

I had known it was foolhardy to get too close to Logan, knowing he worked for my dad, and then discov-
ering he was my dad's favorite. But the revelations of
the last few minutes had been too much. It was no
longer foolhardy. It was suicidal. Not to mention we
couldn't keep our hands off each other.

CHAPTER NINE

I left Logan a dozen cookies, tossed the burnt ones, and wrapped up the rest. He drove me home mostly in silence.

He apologized again when he dropped me off. "I'm sorry, El. I didn't mean for things to get out of hand. It won't happen again."

I leaned over and kissed his cheek. "It's okay. It was my fault, too."

Back in my room, I fell into a horribly blue funk. I should have been elated—a reliable character witness with absolutely no agenda and no prompting had just told me what a great bio dad I had. On the other hand, even though I'd known Logan less than two weeks, it was becoming increasingly difficult to keep my secret from him. And I felt an odd combination of emotions—

joy that my bio dad was a good guy. Jealousy that Logan and he were so close. And real terror at what Logan would think if he ever found out the connection between me and Jason. Would he hate me? Feel betrayed? Or like I was using him to get information?

It was all a complicated, horrible mess. I couldn't let what I felt for Logan screw up my plans. I had to feel free to reveal myself to Jason if I felt the need. And the more I learned about him, the more I wanted him to know I was his daughter. I just needed a little more time to think it through and weigh all the ramifications. A little more time without how I felt about Logan making me back off.

As they say, blood is thicker than water—right? A relationship with my dad was more important than a friendship, or whatever it was, with Logan. I had to break it off with Logan. I couldn't see him. I couldn't even be his friend. But if I did, I was going to look like the biggest douchebag who ever walked the face of the planet. How would I ever explain? I couldn't.

On Tuesday, I ignored a text from Logan. And felt like crap. My heart was broken. I couldn't treat him this way. He didn't deserve it. I had to face him and tell him in person that I couldn't even be his friend. But I was a coward.

I felt so meek and beaten down that I cried when I went to Byron's office for chem help that afternoon and gave him the cookies I'd made at Logan's.

Byron was so startled that he awkwardly put his arm around me and swore to play hero.

I put my head on his shoulder and bawled.

He stiffly patted my back like he was burping a baby. "Don't cry. I'll make sure you pass chemistry. It will be all right. We'll make a standing tutoring appointment for every Tuesday after lab. I'll be all yours for that hour. How does that sound?"

I nodded and dabbed at my eyes with a tissue he handed me. I swear his chest puffed out. Logan had saved my life and Byron was determined to save my chemistry grade. Since when had I become so needy?

I texted Logan the ominous *We need to talk.* As everyone knows, "we need to talk" is code for "this may be the last time we ever do."

Logan met me in the mall outside the SUB. His black eye was healing really well. He grew handsomer every day as his face returned to normal, a normal that was new to me. He wore a somber expression when he joined me on a bench in the shade of a large maple tree. Its leaves blew gently in a breeze that finally had a touch of cool to it. Usually I found the sound calming. Today it only sounded sad.

"Hey." Logan sat next to me.

"Hey." I couldn't meet his eye.

"You want to tell me what this is about?" His voice was ragged, like he already knew.

I screwed up my courage before I lost it completely, and spoke softly, trying not to break down. "I can't do it, Logan. It's not working. I can't be your friend. And I can't explain exactly why. It's too complicated and it's all tied up in what I'm dealing with." I dabbed at my eyes. "And then there's the fact that I can't keep my hands off you."

He put a hand on my shoulder. "Yeah, you're an animal."

I tried to laugh.

"What are you saying, El?"

"You know what I'm saying—I can't be your friend and I can't be more. Not right now. Not until I've sorted a lot of crap out. Does that sound familiar? But it's true. And maybe when everything is out, you won't want to be my friend anyway. Or you'll still be dealing with yours and not ready, either."

"I'll always be your friend, El."

He didn't know what he was promising.

"After what you shared with me last night, I feel like the biggest jerk in the world." I finally did look at him, but tears blurred my vision. "It has nothing to do with that. You'll always be my favorite baseball player."

He nodded and remained silent, looking almost as miserable as I was.

"And I still owe you two. If you ever need me, anytime, anyplace, I'll come running. Promise. But just now, we have to be coworkers and that's it." I nearly choked on the words.

"You're right, El." His voice was tender and sympathetic. "I was up most of the night thinking about it. I came to the same conclusion. We both have our shit to deal with, and until we do, we're not free. I agree and think it's best if we don't hang out with each other."

"It's going to be tough. What are the ground rules? Are office gatherings off limits? No more office pizza dinners?" I asked.

"Office pizza and anytime we're in public in a crowd should be okay." He gave me a sad half-smile. "If we behave ourselves."

I nodded, feeling more miserable than after I ended it with Austin.

Logan gave me a hug that lasted too long to be casual. It was definitely a goodbye hug, and poignant because of it. When he released me, he stood to go. "See you around, El. Take care."

I listened to him walk away. I couldn't bear to watch him. And then I broke down and cried.

August melted into September. I stayed on campus for the long Labor Day weekend. There was no way I was going home, maybe not even for Thanksgiving or Christmas if I could help it. Campus was quiet. Bre, Taylor, and Nic all went home. I moped around and did stupid stuff, like trying to piece together Logan's life, even though I knew I should just forget about him.

I looked up his brother and followed the Cubs' games and Caleb's stats. I tried to figure out exactly when Logan had taken Chem 202 and if it had somehow corresponded with his horrible accident or one of the surgeries. I looked up everything I could on labrum injuries, hoping there was a cure.

I baked cookies in the small kitchen in the dorm basement that was for student use and studied with Dex. He tried to get me to come with him to the dunes and play beer pong, but I was too despondent to go anywhere. So I locked myself in the dorm and read romance novels for study breaks and cried because I couldn't imagine romance ever working out for me.

My depression was so deep that Dex couldn't stand it. On Sunday afternoon, he took me out for coffee—his treat—pried the story out of me, and tried to cheer me up. "He's not worth it, Ellie, even if he did save your life. You don't need to get mixed up with someone with problems. Mysterious problems. Find some guy with his head screwed on straight and move on."

I sighed heavily. "But his dreams were shattered and it has something to do with Chem 202. If I could piece it together, I could help him."

Dex gave me his trademarked skeptical look. "Guys don't like to talk about stuff like girls do. If he wanted you to know, he'd tell you. You promised not to pry."

"I'm not. I'm not prying with him. If only I knew what semester he had Chem 202, then maybe I could piece it together."

"You're going to drive yourself crazy, Ellie," Dex said, but he gave me a hug.

Just when it felt like the weekend would never end, Tuesday came. I brought Byron cookies and studied with him in his office. Then I spent the evening repeating everything to Dex and the guys and studying some more. Dex walked me out of the library.

When we reached the usual this-is-where-we-part fork in the road, he pulled a blue folder out of his backpack and handed it to me.

I took it from him, puzzled. "What's this?"

"You wanted to know about Logan Walker's schedule since he's been here. There you go—his complete transcript."

My eyes went wide. "But how—"

"Contact in the registrar's office. Don't ask for details. I never reveal my sources. Just promise me you'll try to move on."

I took the folder back to my dorm room, locked myself in, and guiltily read the contents of the folder. Before the accident, Logan had been a four-point student on the dean's list. His second semester freshman year, his grades started sliding. I figured that by the time of the accident, his grades were already high enough to float him a decent GPA that semester. And maybe he was still hopeful of recovering.

In the fall of his sophomore year, his grades took a nosedive. By then he must have realized he wasn't going to get his throwing arm back. As I read grade after grade in class after class, I realized he'd told me the truth. He'd almost flunked out, just barely passing each class with a C-. I wondered how much pull Jason had used to keep Logan in school.

The last class on the list was Chem 202. He'd taken it that semester. No wonder he had bad memories from it and didn't want to talk about it. Jason had said Logan had done well in chem. I clearly remembered Logan shrugging it off, saying he'd done all right. I was totally unprepared for what I saw on the report. This couldn't be right. Logan got an A out of Chem 202 from Dr. Rogers? I gasped.

Dr. Rogers only gave one A a semester, and that was usually an A-. How could Logan have gotten that A when he was in such a tailspin? But there it was in black and white. Chem was the only thing that kept his GPA high enough that semester to prevent him from being put on probation. It didn't make any sense. None at all. If he'd gotten an A, he'd have to have studied his butt off. There was no way he would have forgotten it all unless he'd gotten a concussion.

My head swam because it didn't make any sense. Maybe Dex was right—I was only driving myself crazy. I had to move on and forget Logan.

On Wednesday and Friday, and every Monday, Wednesday, and Friday afterward, Logan tried to make forgetting him easy on me by avoiding the office. We didn't meet for burgers again, and on the rare occasions I saw him, he nodded almost curtly and moved on without speaking to me.

Is it possible to fall in love with someone in such a short time? Or was I only romanticizing Logan and our brief time together? I rationalized it was hard to forget someone who'd saved your life.

To everyone's surprise, Bre and Dan became a thing. She hung out with him so much we rarely saw her. Nic and Taylor dragged me along to party after party, but I had no enthusiasm for them. Guys hit on me. But none of them were Logan and none of them took me out to wish on falling stars.

I buried myself in my studies, work, and football games. I baked more and more creative cookies, experimenting with using rum flavoring instead of vanilla.

And cherry chips I found at a little specialty shop downtown instead of chocolate chips.

I realized Byron was probably getting the wrong idea, thinking I was baking to impress him. He was easily pleased and surprisingly, just as easy to talk to.

"Have you ever had your heart broken?" I asked him after one of our tutoring sessions while we ate cookies together.

"I get my heart broken every day. Girls aren't into me."

"That's just stupid," I said, vehemently and honestly. I believed there was a girl out there for him. There had to be. There was a mate for everyone, except me. "Girls can be so blind and superficial. A man with brains is hot."

He blushed.

I realized I'd just stepped in it. And if Byron ever got a look at Logan and Austin, he'd peg me as just as superficial as the rest of my sex.

Taylor buttered up the cook, getting on her good side in preparation for asking for the cobblestone bar recipe, which Taylor quickly discovered was her specialty and a closely guarded secret. In the meantime, Tay grabbed a bar from every batch she could. We tasted and experimented, trying to recreate the recipe.

I'd been holding cobblestone bars out as a secret weapon, until I got tired of wasting so many attempts and tossing them in the garbage. I figured out that Byron would eat about anything and still stayed skinny and scrawny. He seemed genetically programmed to be unable to build muscle mass.

I finally let him in on our campaign and brought him a bar from the dining hall for comparison. He ate a lot of failed batches with good grace, rating our attempts as faithfully as he graded my chem quizzes. Once, he surprised me with a chemical analysis he'd run on it.

"It has 240 kilojoules per—"

I cut him off, laughing. "Don't tell me how many calories or kilojoules it has. That will ruin it."

"Okay, can I tell you it contains salt, baking soda, chocolate, flour, and sugar?"

"You may." I gave him a quick hug. "But we already knew that. You're sweet to try, though."

When he blushed, his cheeks turned patchy with bright red splotches, highlighting his acne scars. He looked cute in a really sweet, nerdy way probably only a mother and a girl he was helping with chemistry could love. And by love, I mean in the platonic sense.

Taylor sneaked in to watch whenever Cook was baking them. She came off shift with tidbits like "It has cream cheese in the frosting." And "She puts the marshmallows on while it's hot." Then I would head to the kitchen to try again.

Time after time, we gave it our best shot, but as October rolled around, Byron still hadn't given us a perfect ten. Byron graded my chem quizzes and lab reports. I was still failing the chem quizzes, but my scores now suspiciously matched Dex's as the highest in the class and I didn't think they were due to my superior intellect.

Every time I failed another chem quiz along with five hundred odd other students, I wondered how Logan had managed to ace them.

I was regularly getting one hundred percent on my lab reports. Again, I pretty much knew who the culprit was and his name was Byron. I suspected he went easy on me, padding my scores by an extra point or two.

I liked to earn my grades. I wasn't a cheater by nature. I wanted to ask him to stop. Maybe I would have if Dr. Rogers hadn't been such a bitch and I could think of a kind way to ask him without getting him in trouble or hurting his feelings. But the bitch Rogers wasn't playing fair, so why should I?

Dex was livid the first time I outscored him on a lab report. After that, I casually mentioned to Byron how Dex was my lab partner and shouldn't we be getting the same scores? Then Dex's lab scores became perfect, too. He nearly threw his shoulder out patting himself on the back for the genius of his plan.

"I bet if you slept with Byron, you could get him to steal the midterm for us," Dex said to me after one particularly grueling study session.

I didn't dignify that with a response.

"Oh, come on! What do you have to lose? A few minutes of your time?"

Fortunately for him, I could tell he was teasing. "My integrity, my self-respect." My virginity, I could have added. "Just drop it, Dex. I'm not sleeping with him. I won't prostitute myself for a grade."

I'd done everything but with Austin. But I hadn't lost it. The thought of actual sex scared me to death.

Being the consequence of failed birth control, I lived in fear of repeating my mother's mistake. I don't think my mom was stupid. And I knew she was careful—through three husbands and numerous lovers, she never gave me a little brother or sister. But somehow there was me and I refused to end up like she had—alone and desperate.

As the semester rolled along, I became friends with Karen in the office. I even went to one of her son's football games. She told me stories about the office staff and the RTAs. I learned a lot about Jason from her—best boss ever. Great dad. Wonderful mentor. Supportive friend. Didn't anyone have a bad thing to say about him?

I got to know Jason better, too. Guessing who I reminded him of became a running joke between us. At first it made me nervous, but after a while, I realized he had no idea and was just teasing.

He took me on as a mentee and gave me a project in the management information systems arena, coaching me at every step and helping me clarify my analysis and thinking. Sometimes, I pretended he knew he was my dad and he was doing the dad thing for real. He even said he'd talk to the business department about getting me internship credit for my project. Everything I saw about him, I liked, especially his calm, reassuring manner. He seemed like he could shoulder the weight of anything life threw at him. Anything, maybe, but me?

Daily, I was tormented by what I should do. Keeping my secret was eating me up inside. At times I felt like a fraud. But was it right to upset his perfect life? Was I only a liability? Had too much time passed? Would he forgive me for deceiving him and not revealing myself immediately? If I never revealed myself, could I ever be with Logan?

Except for Logan and me avoiding each other, I loved my job and made friends with many of the RTAs. As I got to know them, I became aware of their particular likes and strengths and tried the best I was able to dispatch them to jobs they were most suited for. I think they appreciated my effort. I got a lot of thank-yous and kudos for being a better dispatcher than last year's.

Jason put me in charge of scheduling and I tried to schedule everyone around exams and big projects they had on their plate. I took care of everyone but Logan. Jason alone was in control of his schedule and assignments. He and Jason were so close I was jealous on both sides—I wanted to be close to my dad and Logan.

Though my group studied, we failed weekly chem quiz after quiz. My other classes were stressful and gave tons of homework, but they were nothing compared to chemistry. Dr. Rogers refused to help. She blew off her office hours. She called us idiots while devising more and more diabolical, off-the-wall quizzes. I wasn't being paranoid when I thought she had a vendetta against us. The class grew more and more belligerent.

Dex organized the first salvo in our campaign against her. He got nearly half the class, over two hundred students, to email her for help on the same day.

In less than twelve hours she sent all of us a non-response response that was just helpful and innocuous enough that she stymied us with a single chess move. It was like she had it written up and on file ready to send. If we took her quick-response email to the department chair, he'd shut us down for being whiners. To his eyes, our complaint looked completely invalid.

"She's a worthy adversary," Dex said. "She's savvy enough to keep us from moving to the next step. She responded to over two hundred emails within twenty-four hours and gave just enough help to be totally unhelpful and keep herself out of hot water.

"As I suspected we would, we're going to have to take another approach. Going through university channels and using approved procedure will not work. But when the shit hits the fan at least we can say we tried." Dex got an evil gleam in his eyes.

I was afraid to question him further.

We hit our first round of midterms. The Chem 202 class begged Dr. Rogers for an old test to study. She refused. We studied our asses off. I aced four of my five midterms. I failed chemistry with one of the highest grades in the class, just below Dex's. I only knew where I ranked because Byron texted me so I wouldn't slit my wrists.

I texted Dex the news as soon as Byron texted me. Of course, Rogers posted the exam grades late Friday afternoon so she could blow us all off and hide out from us while ruining our weekend. A true win-win for her.

Dex texted me back that he was calling an emergency strategy meeting and the pizza was on him. He said he'd swing by to pick me up. Bre was out with Dan and probably staying over. Taylor and Nic were both out on dates. I had nothing better to do on a Friday night than study and plot revenge.

Dex picked me up around nine. He had the two other guys from our group with him. Dex took us to Spiro's, the same pizza place Jason had taken us the first week of class. The parking lot was packed, but Dex got lucky and got a spot just as someone pulled out. We piled into Spiro's and had to wait fifteen minutes to be seated. The waitress led us to a U-shaped booth against the back wall. Just what I needed. We had a fantastic view of the entire crowd that was at Spiro's—groups of friends and couples on dates.

I slid into the middle of the U next to Dex as the waitress passed out menus and took our drink order.

I opened my menu. "The pepperoni's really good here and they don't skimp." I glanced up just as the waitress walked away to get our beverages.

Sitting almost directly across from me right in my line of sight, Logan was holding hands with a pretty brunette, cuddled close in an intimate way. They were laughing and smiling. She fed him a bite of pizza.

I froze and went totally cold. I had thought my heart was dead before. Now it simply stopped. Logan was dating someone else, the player. He couldn't date me because he had stuff, mysterious stuff, he was dealing with, but he could date someone else?

I knew I was being irrational. I knew I'd told him we had to end it, too. And we did. Because of me. I also knew I had no right to be angry or jealous, but I was.

"Ellie? What's wrong?" Dex followed my line of sight. "Shit!" He covered my icy hand with his. "Ellie, listen to me. Don't look and don't let seeing him upset you. Don't let your emotions show on your face. The last thing he needs is an ego trip."

I swallowed hard and grabbed my purse. I had to escape, but I was boxed in. "Excuse me, boys. Sorry, Dex. I can't stay here and stare at him—"

Dex threw his arm around my shoulder. "Calm down. You're not going anywhere. You're not a coward. Just play along."

It looked like they were getting ready to leave. Logan picked up a pizza box. As the brunette stood, her napkin fell onto the floor. As Logan leaned down to pick it up for her, our eyes met. A look of surprise crossed his face.

Dex gently grabbed my chin, turned my face to his, and rubbed his nose to mine as if we were cutesy, in-love Eskimos.

"Remember—play along." He laughed at a joke I hadn't told. And then he kissed me. And I mean *kissed* me—full throttle, full tongue.

I was too stunned to move.

When he pulled away, he whispered in my ear. "Did he see that? Is he reeling with jealousy yet?"

"Yeah, he's reeling. Any minute he'll come over here and punch your lights out. Not." Logan really did look pained. I couldn't help smiling. "You're a surprisingly good kisser."

Dex smiled back at me. "I'm good at a lot of other things, too. Any chance you want to become study partners with benefits?" Coming from Dex that wasn't a come-on, just a joke.

"No."

Logan took the brunette's elbow and turned his back to me as he walked her toward the exit.

"No?" Dex said.

"Think of the ramifications—what would happen to our chem help if Byron found out?"

"Good point." Dex tucked a lock of hair behind my ear. "Maybe another semester?"

Logan was out of sight, but I was still shaken. "I'll keep you in mind."

Dex really was sweet. Somehow he'd defused the situation. I no longer wanted to run. Dex was right. I'd look like a coward.

The waitress arrived with our beverages. With the danger passed, Dex removed his arm from around my shoulder.

"Danger averted," Dex said. "Now we can get to work."

I'd been so obsessed with Logan, I hadn't even been aware of our other two study partners, Joe and Kirk.

"Was that the ex?" Kirk asked.

I nodded.

"Leave it," Dex said. "Did you two guys look into what I asked?"

It was loud in Spiro's. Dex had to shout over the noise.

"My uncle owns a camera shop," Kirk said. "I can get your supplies."

"Joe?"

"I'll have it in a few days," Joe replied.

Dex nodded, looking as serious as a president about to order a nuclear strike. "You didn't order online? There's no paper trail, no electronic trail? It's not going to be coming through the mail?"

Joe and Kirk assured him there were no trails.

Dex relaxed.

"What's this about?" I asked.

"I'll tell you in the car."

Our pizza arrived. We ate. Chemistry didn't come up again until in the car after Dex dropped Joe and Kirk off.

"This is war," Dex said.

"Yes, I know that. Nuclear war."

"No, after that midterm, this in intergalactic planetary destruction war."

"Okay, intergalactic war," I said. "What are you planning to do?"

"Rattle Dr. Roger's cage." He laughed.

"So why do you sound like Dr. Evil?" I said.

"It's just a prank, Ellie. We have a motto—*Primum non nocere.*"

"Do no harm," I said, translating the Latin. "I thought that was for doctors."

"And pranksters who don't want to be expelled if they're caught," Dex said. "Don't worry. We're being careful. That's why we're not leaving a trail. And in the extremely remote possibility we are caught, my dad gives big to this university. If he threatens to pull his support, the administration will look the other way."

"For you, maybe."

"For all of us." Dex smiled again. "Are you in?"

"I like to know what I'm getting into before I agree," I said.

"All right, but I'm only telling you because if we're caught, you'll be implicated because you're part of our study group. If you decide not to join in, you'll have to swear that I never told you anything."

"Agreed."

"You know that ancient overhead projector with the rolling transparency paper that Dr. Rogers uses to scribble equations on so fast we can't keep up?"

I nodded.

"They used projectors like that when my dad was in college. He had a prof who everyone hated who used to write too fast, too. Just like us, Dad and his buds got tired of it.

"They made a plan, and one night broke into the prof's classroom and rigged the projector with camera flashcubes and a smoke bomb to 'blow up' when the prof turned the projector on for class. It was brilliant. The prof was nervous about using it the rest of the semester and trembled every time he turned it on. It was legendary."

Dex laughed at the thought of Dr. Rogers being jumpy for the rest of the semester. "I have the old man's plans for it. It's pretty simple, really. And the best part is if the old man ever finds out, he can't give me any shit over pulling his own prank. The apple, as they say, doesn't fall far from the tree."

"Your dad is an evil genius. I now see where you get your talent." I paused. "Was he ever caught?"

"If he was, we wouldn't be using it. Too easy to trace it back to us," Dex said. "It's our good luck that Dr. Rogers and the university haven't completely switched over to smart whiteboards. She should give up that ancient projector when she works equations."

"What's a flashcube and where are you going to get one?" I asked.

"Flashcubes are from like the sixties and seventies when you still had to use film in your cameras and they didn't have electronic flash. One bulb of the flashcube exploded every time you took a flash picture. Camera aficionados still use them for specialty shots. It's retro. Remember what Kirk said? His uncle owns a camera shop."

"Wow! Okay, I'm in. What do you want me to do?"

"The least risky thing—play lookout outside the chem building while we install the prank. That way if we get caught, you can get away."

"But—"

"No buts, Ellie. I can handle more risk than you can. Be ready to move when I call you. We'll strike when the time is right."

CHAPTER TEN

It was just after eleven when Dex dropped me off. Early. Bre, ever conscientious, texted me not to expect her back until tomorrow. Alone in my room I had too much time to think about what Logan was up to with the brunette. Why did it hurt so badly to think he'd moved on so fast?

In a petulant moment, I cursed him, wishing him ugly babies if he ever married the brunette. Which, if I'd been rational, wasn't really fair to the babies. Sins of the fathers. I wondered what my dad had done that I deserved this misery.

I worked on a chem lab report, but finally gave up around one. We had a sink in our room, but the bathroom was two doors down. I brushed my teeth and washed my face, then changed into my PJs and robe. I was just reaching for the doorknob when the rhythmic thumping began in the hall just outside my door.

I froze. It was followed by the unmistakable sounds of sex. "Oh, oh, oh! More! Harder!"

I was trapped in my room by another girl's passion. An unreasonable sense of rage washed over me. I had no date. I couldn't have the man I wanted, not even as a friend. That man, the one I ached for, was out with another girl, maybe banging her at this very minute. I was prone to imagining the worst. It was a character flaw of mine. And ever since Austin, it was all too easy to fall into—along with self-pity.

Enraged at the unfairness of life, I pounded my door. "Hey! I'm here and I hear you. And I have to pee. I'm giving you two minutes to finish and then I'm coming out."

More frantic thumping was followed by a groan.

I started counting. "Ten, nine, eight—"

"Shut up, bitch!" a drunken male voice yelled.

Nice. "Nice name to call your date. Next time get a room," I yelled back.

A fist pounded my door from the hallway so hard the door shuddered. My heart raced. I feared the ass out there was going to break it down. I grabbed my cell and one of Bre's golf clubs.

"Is that the campus police I hear coming?" I had my cell, ready to dial 911.

I heard some scuffling. Then the door at the end of the hall into the stairway slammed.

I took a deep breath and counted to ten slowly before cautiously opening the door. When I looked out, the hall was empty. I made my bathroom run and climbed into bed, emotionally exhausted. I drifted off to sleep, thinking of Logan.

And fell into a beautiful dream. I was on a dock at a beach house on a lake at night. I lay on a beach towel on my back with my hair fanning out around me and the straps of a white bikini untied at my neck. As a full moon rose over the lake, it lit the lake and my bikini, even my pale skin, until they glowed pearlescent and magical.

The lake lapped softly against the dock, gently bouncing me and rocking the boat tethered next to me rhythmically. The air held a tang of lake and falling dew. Overhead the stars came out one by one, creating a constellation before my eyes until Sagittarius sparkled directly overhead. Miraculously, I could see the archer clearly in the pattern of stars, half gorgeous man, half horse, tall and proud with his long hair streaming behind him. His bow was pointed directly at my heart like cupid's arrow.

I heard footsteps coming toward me up the dock from the shore. When they stopped, Logan stood over me, silhouetted in the moon. He stripped off his shirt. His skin glowed, too—only his tattoo remained a dark shadow of design. He eased to his knees over me. As he straddled me, he kissed my nose, my lips, then his lips were hot against my neck.

His kisses traveled down to this rise of my breasts. As he peeled back the strings of my bikini, my breasts budded in the night air, pointing toward the stars, aching for his touch. My breath caught as he bent and gently kissed them, as his mouth opened around them and his tongue circled them, licking until I moaned. Pleasure like I'd never felt before built between my legs with tight, pulsing intensity. I needed his touch. I needed him and arched up against him. Just as he slipped his hands beneath my bikini bottom, I woke with a start to the sounds of rhythmic banging and moaning in the room next to mine and a burning pain in my bellybutton.

I flipped on the light. My bellybutton was red and inflamed, which seemed like a metaphor for everything that was going wrong in my life. I almost ripped the ring out right then.

My hand hovered over it, but I couldn't make myself pull it out.

The office was in chaos when I arrived on Monday. Karen wasn't at her desk. The phones were ringing unanswered. Jason was in his office, and was that a baby crying?

I grabbed the phone and took the call. One of the classrooms in the ag building was having trouble with their sound system. Just as I called up the RTA schedule and dispatched Gary to handle the situation, Jason stepped out of his office with a crying baby on his shoulder. My heart stopped as I realized I was looking at my baby sister for the first time.

She was propped with her back to me over Jason's shoulder as he patted and bounced her. All I could see was a nice, round head with a mass of light hair. She had a set of lungs on her, that was for sure.

"Reinforcements at last." The relief on his face was almost comical.

"Is that the baby?" I walked over to get a look at her.

"The very same. I don't know what's wrong with her. She usually likes this position. I've fed her. Changed her. Burped her. And still she screams." He glanced at his watch. "And I have a meeting in ten minutes." He looked harried. "Lyssa has an important meeting she couldn't miss and the nanny called in sick at the last minute."

"Poor baby." I rubbed my hand on her little back. She seemed to calm some. "Where's Karen?"

"At the dentist. She should be back soon. I was hoping she'd be back sooner." He bounced the baby. "I've been hoping futilely for a lot of things, like for Mia to fall asleep." He sounded really frazzled.

"I'll watch Mia for you while you go to your meeting. I'm good with babies." I held out my arms to take her.

That was when the worried new dad look crossed his face. He was protective of his baby and not sure he could trust me. It cut me to my core. He'd never looked that way over me. He didn't even know he wasn't a new dad, but a dad of long standing. A dad who should have the wisdom of years of parenting. One of those dads who gladly hands the kid off to reliable help. I was jealous and sad at the same time. No dad had ever been protective of me. I'd had to sail through the years when a girl wants to adore her daddy completely empty-handed.

"I worked in my friend's mom's daycare for two years helping out summers when I was in high school.

I'm a certified babysitter. I took the training and have the certificate to prove it."

He looked sheepish, like I'd caught him in his insecurities and doubt. Like he could trust me with the office, but not with the baby. He glanced at his watch again. "This isn't in your job description."

"Don't worry. I won't file a formal complaint." I held my arms out for her again.

He reluctantly handed her over. "Mia, this is Ellie," he cooed to her.

I hadn't expected to be introduced to my sister this way. When I took her in my arms, her face was red and contorted from screaming. She was anything but a beautiful baby just then, but a wave of love for her washed over me. "Aren't you beautiful," I cooed to her, because she was to me. "You're just a gorgeous girl."

I held her in front of me with her head cradled in my hands, bouncing her in my arms. She quieted and looked up at me, tears standing in her eyes and running down her chubby baby cheeks.

For a minute, her little mouth screwed up like she was going to scream again. I smiled at her and made fish lips. Babies love fish lips. To my delight, she smiled back and made a cooing sound.

"We're going to get along just fine." I glanced at Jason.

He looked stunned and relieved. "That's amazing."

"Told you I'm good with babies. Where are her supplies?"

"I'll grab her diaper bag." He disappeared into his office.

I simply stared at Mia, cooing at her as she cooed
back to me in her cute baby voice. It may sound completely stupid and narcissistic, but I think, on some level at least, she recognized me. Recognized me as family
where my father didn't.

Jason reappeared with a diaper bag, a rocking car
seat, and a computer bag. He set the diaper bag and car
seat next to me at my desk, still looking amazed that
Mia was suddenly so happy. "Do you think you can
handle the office *and* Mia until I get back?"

Just then the door to the office swung open and Logan strolled into our warm, familial scene.

Jason let out a breath of relief and smiled in Logan's
direction. "Looks like you won't have to. Reinforcements have arrived."

Logan spotted Mia and me. He flashed me a quick,
uncertain smile and walked over to coo over Mia. "Hey,
baby, hey." He shook her little finger while I wished he
would talk sweet like that to me. I wanted to be his baby.

"Logan, you're on dispatch today until Karen or I
get back. Ellie's on childcare duty." Jason bent and
brushed a kiss on Mia's forehead. "Behave yourself,
Mia." He used that baby talk voice adults use around
babies that sounds ridiculous in any other situation.
"She likes to be rocked in her car seat. If she looks like
she's getting sleepy, strap her in and rock her. It's
about her naptime. I'll be back as soon as I can."

"We'll be fine," I reassured him.

And then he was off and it was just Mia, Logan, me,
and an uncomfortable silence. My heart pounded. I

hadn't been this close to him in nearly two months. And although time supposedly heals all, it hadn't put a damper on the physical pull I felt toward him. I told myself a hundred times a day that pining after Logan was stupid. But my heart didn't listen. And now my body was ignoring me, too.

Logan dropped his backpack next to the desk where I sat with Mia and pulled up Karen's chair. He rolled it next to us. I didn't look at him, but I was keenly aware of him.

"She's a beauty," he said.

"She's perfect." I studied Mia's tiny, perfect hands as she wrapped her baby fingers around one of mine. Her fingers were long and slender—really long like mine were, and slightly crooked like mine, too. Characteristic. For an instant I panicked, thinking the similarity was so obvious anyone could see it. Fearing Logan would realize we were sisters because of our fingers. I told myself that was silly and forced myself to calm down as I jiggled my finger as Mia held on and Logan remained unaware.

Mia kicked and waved her hands. Her bootie flew off, revealing her tiny foot and toes. Her baby toe was short and stubby and curled in just like mine. Another dead giveaway if anyone cared to look. Fortunately, the weather had cooled. I was wearing boots. No one could see my toes.

I hadn't expected to get so emotional on meeting my sister, but I felt this well of pride and love. Tears formed and blurred my vision. Sitting next to Logan admiring my sister, I had a vision of Logan and me doting over our baby. But that would never be.

Logan was staring at me. I'd dropped my guard, forgetting for a second how easily he read me. He leaned over, picked up Mia's bootie, and handed it to me. "You okay? You seem choked up. You must really love babies."

I didn't answer, just took Mia's little foot in my hand, pressed the bottom of it to my lips, and blew a raspberry. She laughed and kicked as I wrangled her bootie on her.

And then in that quicksilver way babies have of going from full-on to off, Mia yawned.

"You are fighting sleep, aren't you, tiny thing?" I turned to Logan. "Put the handle back and pull back the straps so I can put her in her car seat."

He did as I asked. I gently laid and strapped her in. Mia yawned again, making a baby squeak. Sometimes I squeaked, too, when I yawned. I wondered if I was looking too hard for similarities or were squeaky yawns genetically programmed? After being an only child for so long, I couldn't get past the novelty of having a sister. As I leaned over her, gently rocking the seat and smiling and cooing at her some more I noticed her earlobes were attached like mine and Jason's. "There's a good girl. Go to sleep."

As I rocked her gently, her eyes opened and closed like a doll's with each back and forth, getting heavier and heavier, opening less and less far each time. Why do babies fight sleep?

"How've you been?" Logan asked.

Terrible, I thought. *Depressed and lonely without you.* I shrugged. "All right."

"I saw you at Spiro's." His tone was purely conversational, disappointingly so.

I hated the way he masked his emotions with such apparent ease. But I admired his courage. He was a brave man to get the taboo topic out in the open.

I fought to keep my tone casual, like no big deal. "Yeah, I was there with my study group."

"It didn't look like studying to me." There was enough of a tease in his voice that I nearly missed the slight undertone of jealousy.

Or maybe I was just being optimistic.

"We were drowning our sorrows in pizza after getting our midterm results from the class that shall not be named."

"That bad?"

"Worse."

He was silent a minute. "Do you always drown your sorrows by necking with your study partner?" Logan was the rare breed of person to whom charm and charisma were second nature. But this time he was trying too hard to be glib.

I could have said something sassy and snide. But for some unfathomable reason, I didn't. "That was just Dex joking around. He's a surprisingly good kisser."

That aching, frustrated longing from my dream welled up as I got a whiff of Logan's cologne. I concentrated on Mia, smiling at her as I rocked her, wishing I were alone with her so I could tell her who I really was at least once. "How was your date?"

"Fine. Average."

It broke my heart that he didn't bother denying it.

"There was no spark." It was a simple statement of fact.

"Sorry." But I wasn't.

He leaned over and smiled at Mia, but his charm was lost on her. Her eyes were mostly closed now. She'd settled down and was quiet and drowsy, content as I rocked her.

"Are you wearing a different perfume? You smell different."

Part of me was ecstatic he remembered how my perfume smelled. Part of me was confused. "No, just one of my regulars." Then it hit me. "You're smelling the tea tree oil. It's for my bellybutton piercing. To help it heal. It was getting infected."

Nic had taken me to town to the tattoo and piercing parlor on Sunday to buy some.

"It's nice. It smells good."

I laughed. I couldn't help myself.

"What?"

"Cut the BS. Tea tree oil isn't used in perfume for a reason." It doesn't smell bad. Just tangy and a bit medicinal. That's why you don't find it as a key scent in perfumes. There's no woodsy or floral undertone of tea tree oil.

Mia's eyes shut. She let out an adorable little hiccough and snuffle, the kind babies make when they've been crying too long and finally settle down.

"I've missed you, El," Logan whispered.

My heart skipped a beat. "I missed you, too, Logan."

I stared at Mia. It was no good. I had to work out my family situation before I could get involved with Logan. But I also had to know. "But it's no good. I'm still dealing with stuff." I paused, searching for the right words. "You're seeing other girls." I bit my lip. "Does that mean you've worked out your issues?"

"No." He shook his head softly for emphasis. He didn't elaborate.

"Dad's Weekend is less than a month away," he said, changing the subject out of the blue. "The week after Halloween. My dad's coming this year." His snort was full of derision.

"You don't want him to come?" I wish my dad just knew I existed. I'd love for him to come to the football game with me and hang out and do father/daughter stuff.

"Hell no."

I held my finger to my lips. "Shhhh." I pointed to the baby.

Logan lowered his voice. "He's just coming to check up on me. To make sure I'm walking the straight and narrow. Not drinking too much. Keeping my grades up. Dating the right girls."

My curiosity was aroused. "Have you dated the wrong girls in the past?"

"Dating isn't the right word," he said, sounding cagey and evasive. "But yeah. Let's just say Dad wasn't pleased with my behavior and took care of things."

"Wow! Controlling." I didn't like the sound of his dad.

"Not as much as you'd think."

He was speaking in riddles.

"It would really make him happy when he comes if I was dating a nice, sweet girl, the kind he'd approve of. And it would get him off my ass."

"Good luck with that. I hope you find someone." I fought to keep the sadness out of my voice.

"I already have."

I swallowed hard and stared at Mia, wishing I were a baby with a daddy who doted on me. Life would be so much simpler. Babies didn't even know the meaning of heartbreak.

"You," he said.

I turned and stared at him. "But—"

"You owe me two. I'm calling in one now. I need you to pretend to be my girlfriend. Just for Dad's Weekend."

I hesitated. This was such a bad and horribly dangerous idea.

"You promised, El. Whatever I needed, whenever. I *need* this."

I swallowed hard. I had promised, but I'd thought any request would be more of the "my battery died, come pick me up or give me a jump" kind of thing.

Just then the door to the office swung open and Karen breezed in. "That was the longest dentist visit. Never crack a tooth, Ellie. Half my mouth is numb." Which explained why she was talking funny.

In unison, Logan and I held our fingers to our mouths and shhhhed her, pointing to the baby.

"Oh, oh, oh," Karen whispered as she walked over and smiled down at Mia. "What a little angel. Where's Jason?"

"At a meeting," I said as Karen took her coat off. "He'll be back soon."

She nodded just as the phone rang and we all jumped.

As Karen lunged for it, I gently rocked Mia's car seat and turned to Logan. "Okay."

"You'll be convincing?"

I rolled my eyes. "Totally."

He grinned. "I'll be in touch with the details."

"You mean you'll be giving me a list of things your dad does and doesn't approve of?"

His grin deepened.

CHAPTER ELEVEN

I was so stunned I had to talk to someone. After work, I headed directly to Nic and Taylor's room, texting Nic to tell her I had to talk to her. Tay didn't get off shift from the dining hall until six. Nic met me at the door. Their room was the envy of the floor, mostly because Nic's aunt was an interior designer and had furnished the room with sample eighteen-inch carpet squares taped together on the bottom to form really cool wall-to-wall designer carpeting. The rest of us had to make do with area rugs over the ancient, cold linoleum that probably dated to two centuries back.

The equally ancient steam heat was on, banging the pipes and fogging the windows.

"What's up?" Nic closed the door behind us. "Even your text sounded excited."

"More like confused. I'm officially Logan's fake girl-friend." I dumped my backpack and fell into her dish chair as I spilled the details, every minute detail complete with insecure commentary. Except for Mia being my sister—I left that part out. "So he called in a favor and practically demanded that I play his girlfriend for the weekend. What do you think it means?"

"Other than you're crazy?" Nic was sitting on her bed. She shook her head. "Fake girlfriend? Have you never watched a romantic comedy? That way leads to disaster."

"And then a happy ending."

"This is real life," Nic said. "In real life we don't scam dads by pretending to be girlfriends of guys who have issues. Anyway, what's in this for you? And what happened to his mysterious commitment issues?"

"There's nothing in it for me," I said. "I'm keeping my promise."

"Uh-huh."

"And his issues?"

I shrugged. "Still there. We're just friends."

She gave me thin, suspicious eyes. "I thought that was the point—you two can't be friends. You want my opinion?"

She didn't wait for me to answer.

"This way leads to madness. He's stringing you along, keeping you on the hook. And when you go too far afield, he reels you back in. The timing is awfully suspicious, don't you think?

"He sees Dex kiss you and then, suddenly, there Logan is, asking you to pretend to be his girlfriend. As a favor. *Right.*

"First this Austin you told us about and then Logan. I hate to say this, but you have terrible taste in men. I thought you weren't over Austin, anyway. I thought that was the issue."

"Time has passed," I said. "The heart heals."

"This is a bad idea, the worst—"

The door swung open and Tay charged in waving her phone. "I just had the best shift ever!" Her eyes were bright and shining, her cheeks flushed, and she looked like she'd just jogged the two flights of steps from the dining hall to her room.

"Best shift ever, seems like there's some kind of work craziness virus going around." Nic shifted on her bed. "Don't tell me someone asked you to be his fake girlfriend, too?"

Taylor shot us both a confused look. "No. But Jordan, the cute guy who works the grill, was on shift with me!"

Yeah, we all knew all too well who Jordan was. In fact, we pretty much knew his life story. Taylor talked about him non-stop. A shift she worked with him was heaven. A shift without him was hell. We all had our favorite hot dining hall guys. We picked them out for fun the first week of class and argued over their attributes. Nic and I were happy to worship our dining hall guys from afar like eye candy on a shelf, but Tay had actually fallen for hers. Our tastes were wide and varied.

While the three of us agreed Logan was hot, we argued the various merits of our dining hall guy faves. I didn't see what Taylor saw in Jordan, but that was me.

"He made me a heart-shaped grilled cheese!" Taylor swung her phone around so we could see.

"You took a picture of it?" Nic leaned in for a closer look. "Wow! That's a good one."

A heart-shaped grilled cheese sandwich was a real score in dining hall terms. It was made by cutting the sandwich in half diagonally and then flipping one half of the sandwich so that the rounded side made a heart with the other half. It took like an extra second and a half to make. But in a busy dining hall, mostly you were lucky to get your sandwich slapped on your plate so that the cheese didn't ooze over the side. Since the beginning of the semester, when we saw a girl—whom we later learned was a class-one bitch—get one from Nic's hot dining hall guy, Taylor, Nic, and I had all been angling for one. Until now, our flirtatious efforts with the dining hall guys of our choice had yielded exactly zero heart-shaped grilled cheeses.

I squealed with Taylor and gave her a high-five. "You did it! You are the queen. Did he ask for your number?"

"Not yet. But it's only a matter of time." She had a devilish look in her eye. "I haven't told you the best part..."

"It gets better?" I asked.

"Oh, yeah." Taylor pressed the picture of the heart-shaped grilled cheese to her chest, smiled, and brought up another picture. "Today the cook made cobblestone bars. Jordan created a distraction while I snapped this!" She swung her phone around with the dramatic flare of a detective revealing a murderer.

I took the phone from her hand and gasped when I realized what I was looking at. "OMG! The cobblestone bar recipe? No way." I broke into peals of laughter.

Nic grabbed the phone and grinned her diabolically happy grin. I grabbed Tay and hugged her. Then the three of us did our happy dance and squealed.

When we calmed down, I took a better look at the recipe. "Two gallons of eggs, ten pounds of flour, pour into six full-sheet pans—whoa! This is like an industrial-size recipe." My elation started to ebb.

Nic grabbed the phone and took a look. "We'll have to cut it down."

"Yeah, but how?" I squinted over her shoulder at the recipe.

"Online conversions." Nic sounded more confident than I felt.

"Yeah, but how are we going to change gallons of eggs from commercially packaged cartons to the number of eggs needed for a thirteen-by-nine pan? How many eggs are in a carton? How much of a commercial sheet pan is a thirteen by nine?" I frowned in thought. "Dex! If anyone can figure it out, he can. He's the conversion king. Text it to me. I'll forward it to him."

While Tay texted away, Nic prompted me. "Aren't you going to tell Tay about your fabulous news and how you agreed to be Logan's fake girlfriend?"

I made thin eyes at Nic, paying her back for her sarcasm.

"What?" Tay looked up from her phone as she pressed send. "Oh, that explains the fake-girlfriend question. What's this about?"

I explained it again to her.

"What's his game?" Tay's brow furrowed like she was confused. "I thought you two couldn't even be friends? Haven't we spent the last month and a half trying to cheer you up? And now this? It's crazy, Ellie. Logan's an awesome guy and all, totally hot, but he uses that to keep girls on his string."

"Why am I having a déjà vu moment all of a sudden? Are you two in collusion, because you're sounding an awful lot like Nic."

"Great minds think alike," Taylor said. "If you insist on playing girlfriend, proceed with extreme caution, Ellie."

"Yeah, I know. He only asked me because he knows I know the situation. I'm the one girl he can trust not misconstrue things and get the wrong idea."

Nic rolled her eyes. "Yeah, it's real smart to pick a girl who can't keep her hands off him. It does add authenticity to the act, I'll give him that."

"Shut up!" I frowned at her. "I wonder why he asked me so far in advance? It's weeks away. What does that mean?"

Tay and Nic shook their heads in unison, looking like I was being totally pitiful.

"Yeah, he really picked wisely." But beneath Nic's snarky tone lay an undercurrent of sympathy. "Self-delusion is grand, isn't it?"

On Tuesday night, our chem study group met in Kirk's dorm room. He had a single and the topic of the night was top secret, for our ears only. I had to fight my way through a game of assassin to get there and was shot twice with airsoft guns. Both times in the chest, meaning my breasts. *Guys!*

Dex was in an excited mood. He pushed a printout of the cobblestone bar recipe to me. "There you go, darling. Perfect timing. You'll need them to distract Byron. I just emailed a copy to you. Am I a genius or what?"

"Yeah, you're humble. That's what I love about you, Dex." I was barely listening to him brag as I scanned the recipe. "What is this? One whole egg and two tablespoons? You don't measure eggs in tablespoons."

"You do when you convert from gallons. I looked up the volume in cups of a standard large egg, figured out how many would make a gallon, and then sized it for a thirteen-by-nine pan just like you asked. And it came out one full egg and two tablespoons. Just crack an egg and scoop two tablespoons out."

"Of the white part or the yoke?" I was pulling his chain. There was no way I was using two tablespoons of egg. That was just silly. I clicked on the recipe in my email and edited it to two eggs.

"Hey! What are you doing? Recipes are like precise chemical formulas. You can't mess with them."

"Can too. Apparently, I'm our baking expert for good reason. Adding two full eggs will only make the bars slightly cakier, if anything. Chill."

He looked at me skeptically. "You're going to have to make a test recipe and try your theory. And do it soon. We need those bars. Our supplies are in place. We move as soon as we get the last logistic secured."

I eyed the recipe again. "I can't make these in the dorm. Taylor's deathly afraid our cook will find out she pinched the recipe and she'll lose her job." I looked around the group, settling on Kirk. "How are your ovens here?"

"Do we even have ovens?" Kirk shrugged. "We could check, but I haven't seen any. I think it's only those old-fashioned girls' dorms that have them. The new ones, the coed ones, and the old guys' dorm don't."

"Anyone?" I asked.

Blank looks all around.

"Go to Clark Hall across the street from yours," Dex said. "It's the same vintage as yours. It should have an oven."

I shook my head. "Too close. It uses the same dining hall. Word could get out."

"I don't see the problem." Dex looked put out and unenthused about my baking problem. "You've been experimenting all semester in your dorm."

"Yeah, but if we suddenly show up with a recipe in hand and everyone sees we're successful, first of all everyone will want some. Second, word spreads and all the girls will want the recipe. Then the cook finds out." I shook my head. "It's too risky."

"Find someplace," Dex said. "Or find another way to divert Byron. He's key to the plan."

I protested. "Wait a minute! We all agreed to keep Byron out of this."

"That was before we did our recon on the chem building. They lock the doors each day at midnight." Dex pulled out a hand-drawn diagram. He was paranoid about leaving any digital footprint, saying part of his dad's success in not being caught was that nothing had been digital back then. "The janitor moves through this part of the building first and is done by two a.m. That's when we strike." He grinned like he was enjoying the planning way too much.

Like any good sidekick, Joe grinned with him. "I've double and triple checked. We should be clear by then. The parking garage is usually empty then, too. We're golden."

Kirk nodded. "I've been over and over the security system. The building entrances and all first-floor windows are alarmed. The windows on the second floor are not. We can reach them by climbing across the four-foot gap between the parking garage and the chem building. Byron's office is positioned perfectly to make our entrance." He looked at me. "We need you to make sure his window isn't locked."

"That's where the diversion comes in," Dex said. "Distract Byron and unlatch the window."

My heart raced with excitement at the thought. I couldn't wait for Dr. Rogers to get a taste of her own nasty medicine and I was more than happy to dish it out. "I can't guarantee he won't notice and lock it again before you arrive."

"That's a risk we'll have to take," Dex said. "'Tis the season of pranks. We'll strike next Tuesday night. Wednesday morning when she turns the projector on for class." He rubbed his hands together and laughed, turning serious just as quickly. "We can't have anything out of the ordinary. Ellie will show up for her regular help session and make her move. Get the cobblestone bars ready or prepare to throw yourself at Byron, baby. Whatever it takes."

I could have asked any number of different girls in one of my classes if I could bake my cookie bars at one of their dorms or apartments. But the fewer people we involved, no matter how peripherally, the better. That was my reasoning. It may have been faulty. It was definitely needy and self-serving. Because the only other person who knew I baked for Byron was Logan. He had an awesome kitchen, the best I'd found around campus, for baking. And I wanted to see him. Could not keep my mind off him. Had to see him. A month and a half of resisting him out the window. I was back to the achy longing of square one.

So I texted him when I got back from Kirk's. *Desperately seeking kitchen to bake top-secret cookie bars in. Can I use yours? Payment in said cookies. Rates negotiable.*

Then I waited in agony for his reply text. Will he or won't he? Will he reply right away, showing he was near his phone and I'm still a top priority with him? Will he play it cool and ignore my text for a decent interval, even though he got it immediately? Is he really out of reach? There are only a few places, like the shower, to be truly out of reach. And someday soon someone is going to invent a waterproof cell phone and then even the shower won't be off limits.

Five minutes passed, then ten. Fifteen minutes later, he replied. *When?*

I made some mental calculations. I absolutely needed them to be fresh on Tuesday. I could hardly ask to use Logan's kitchen twice. The ice-cube-sized freezer in my mini fridge would hold exactly one bite of cookie bar, and things disappeared from the freezer downstairs. Which left me with one risky option. *Monday after work*, I texted back.

You got it. Need a ride?

Yeah, that would be great.

See you then.

Fall always made me melancholy—the way the sun sat low in the sky and made shadows long, hinting at darker, shorter days to come. On campus, leaves of stunning gold, orange, and red fell from the trees lining the streets of Greek Row and the edge of the old dorms in the quad and along the main mall. They rustled against the blue sky of an absolutely perfect fall as I wondered what kind of crazy I was made of.

I knew I was walking a reckless path, but was powerless to stop myself and so eager for Monday it was ridiculous. I had to hang out with Logan and convince myself what I felt during the first hot weeks of the semester had been just an illusion. That in the interven-

ing time I'd made him into a fantasy man no real guy
could live up to. Maybe then I could let him go.

I went to the student bookstore with Bre to pick out
a Halloween card for Dan and tried not to crack and
cry because I had no one to buy a card for, no one to
prepare Halloween treats for, and no one to take me to
a Halloween party. There was no sexy devil in my future, no hot zombie. I was a solo ghost.

My mom had the audacity to send me a care package. It arrived on Wednesday, a week and a half before
Halloween, five days before I was going to Logan's to
bake cobblestone bars, six days before the caper that
could get me expelled. I tossed it in the garbage uno-
pened with the same ferocity I deleted her texts with,
tore up her letters, and marked her email as spam.
She'd changed her email address six times already trying to fool me. But she hadn't succeeded yet.

Yeah, I know. I seemed harsh, cold-hearted, cruel.
But she'd made the choice to hurt me, not the other
way around. I never in a million years would have done
to her what she did to me. And with the douchebag
guys she'd dated, I've had the chance, too. A Halloween
care package wasn't going to placate me. Honestly, I
didn't know what it would take to fix us.

"Aren't you going to open it?" Bre pulled the white
priority mail box out of our wastebasket, horrified.

"Do I look like I'm going to?" I held my hands out
for it. "My mistake. I should have taken it to the garbage dumpster. Then my intention would have been
clear."

"No." She shook her head and clutched it to her chest. "You can't throw it away without looking at it. There could be something valuable in here."

I laughed bitterly. "Right."

"What if I open it and see?"

I arched a brow and cut her some slack. She was trying to be helpful. "Out of my sight?"

"Of course."

I shrugged. "It's up to you. If there's nothing obviously valuable like gold coins or diamond jewelry or something that clearly already belongs to me, you can have it. Just don't show it to me. Don't tell me what it is. Deal?"

Bre hauled it off. Later in the week, she showed me the sexy witch costume she'd "bought" for Halloween. We both knew where it had come from, but neither of us mentioned it. I wondered if that was how my mom viewed me—in her mind, was I the witch?

CHAPTER TWELVE

Monday arrived both too quickly and inexorably slowly. Logan met me outside the SUB, like old times. He wore a beanie and sweatshirt and an adorable smile. He looked so absolutely hot, the sight of him made my heart contract. It felt like old times again as he led me to his car. A wind kicked up and gray clouds were building against the hills to the west. A storm was brewing, which seemed so appropriate.

"Do you need me to take you shopping?" he asked as we got in.

"Nope. I have all the supplies in my backpack." I'd even kept the cream cheese for the frosting in the office fridge while I worked.

"And you got the good stuff? You didn't skimp?"

"Skimp? For this important mission? No way. Yeah, I got the good stuff."

"You're still baking for Byron?"

I was touched he remembered, and even more pleased he sounded like he was feeling out the situation, ready to be jealous if I was baking for a new guy. "And the guys. Yep."

There are people in this world that you can be away from for months or years and pick right up where you left off when you see them again. People that you don't know well, but feel like one of your best friends. It was that way between Logan and me, only so strong it was frightening. If things were different, he could have been the love of my life. Maybe he was and I was doomed to a solo life, to be an old, lonely spinster. The thought was too depressing. I didn't have any siblings—that knew about me—so I couldn't even end up as someone's old doting auntie.

It was like Logan and I just fell back in together and were right back where we left off, trying to dampen the electricity and chemistry between us. Trying to keep our hands to ourselves when they were like magnets resisting the pull.

It was quiet at his apartment. Collin and Zave were out. I wondered if he had asked them to give us space. The apartment hadn't changed much, except for a fishbowl on the console table.

"You got a pet!" I went over to examine it, bending over to get a good look. "A fighting fish?"

"They're low maintenance." He stood too close behind me. I could feel his body heat. "I haven't been able to kill it yet. We tried goldfish, but we had terrible luck. Went through half a dozen in less than a week. It was too cruel to continue innocently killing them and all those deaths were depressing the hell out of us. We were holding a fish funeral every day. Zave was afraid we were going to plug the toilet from flushing so many. Collin said he felt embarrassed going back to the pet store for more fish. It was getting so they bagged a poor victim up when they saw him coming.

"I blame Zave. He overfed them."

I smiled at the thought of the boys trying to care for a fish so carefully they literally killed it with kindness. "Your betta fish is beautiful. Is it a girl or a boy?"

"Male. That's all the stores generally sell. Only breeders have females. The males are prettier. They sell better." He grinned.

"He's really vibrant." I looked up at Logan. "Does that mean he's angry?"

Logan studied the fish and shook his head. "If he is, he's perpetually angry. He always looks like that."

"It's good to know my presence hasn't upset him," I said. "Some fish are highly territorial." I wished Logan were.

I tore my gaze away from Logan, stood, and nodded toward the kitchen. "I'd better get busy before it gets late. These cookie bars require cooling time between baking and frosting."

Logan followed me, standing right behind me as I set up. "Do I get to watch or will that compromise the security of this top-secret concoction?"

"You're good. Unless you divulge my baking secrets to absolutely anyone else. Then I'll have to kill you." I turned to get the recipe out of my backpack on the table and ploughed directly into him, startling me, at least. As I braced my hands against his hard chest, he grabbed my arms, stroking them gently, like a lover, and smiled.

My eyes popped open wide. "Aha! Using diversionary tactics to get my secrets. Trying to rattle me. Very smart. But I won't crack anything except eggs."

"El—"

I was trapped between the counter behind me and him. It would have been so easy to crumble like the buttery crust I was about to attempt. "We can't keep running into each other like this."

"Why not?"

"You know why not." My voice went soft. I pleaded with him, hoping he understood before forcing myself to smile and sound light. "I need my full concentration for this task. This is a recipe so delicate, so complicated, so fine, that it has never before been attempted in a home kitchen. I only have one shot at getting it right or I fail this mission. And failure is not an option. I'll be banned from the study group."

I pointed to the kitchen table nearby. "You need to take a seat at the table."

He nodded, ran his hands up my arms until I shuddered, and dropped his hands from my arms before taking a seat. I had to reach around him to get my recipe.

Logan was the rare college man who had a kitchen equipped with a heavy-duty standalone Kitchen Aid mixer. Which again pointed to him having money. I was so tired of wimpy handheld mixers that smoked and stalled in heavy dough I could have cried with joy. Especially as I mixed the crust in silence, feeling Logan watching me, and the Kitchen Aid whipped through it like butter.

As I pressed the crust into the pan, my hands covered in buttery dough, I noticed the dark oven. Logan had succeeded in rattling me.

"Turn the oven on to three-fifty, will you?"

"Wow, I'm honored. She's sharing the top-secret baking temp with me." He glanced at the oven. "I have permission to leave the table?"

I grinned. "Just to turn the oven on. Practically everything bakes at three-fifty, wiseass. It's like the default temp of baking."

He turned on the oven.

I microwaved another stick of butter to soften it for the filling just as a gust of wind howled around the building. "If you have homework or something else you need to do... You don't have to babysit me."

"I like watching you work."

The way he said it made my heart race. "Okay, then make yourself useful and tell me about your dad while I work." I added the butter to the filling mixture I was putting together. "How am I supposed to impress him? What does the perfect girl for his son look like?"

"You."

I almost fell over. It was a good thing I was facing the counter, not him, because I was certain my face gave everything I felt away. When I composed myself, I turned slowly to face him. "Are you trying to mess with my concentration again? Do you want me to ruin these cookie bars?"

He grinned. "I'm serious, El. Why do you think I picked you?"

I took a deep breath and studied him. His expression was completely serious. He wasn't joking.

I swallowed hard and tried to veer back to our agreed relationship status by ignoring what I saw and making light of what he'd said. "Because I'm the only one who owes you."

He laughed full out.

"You're crazy."

I turned my attention back to my task. I poured the filling into the pan, set the timer, and popped the cookie bars into the oven. When I was finished, I turned around to face him. "Okay, while they're baking you can distract me."

"Happily." He popped out of his chair and was next to me with his arms around me before I could protest. "I've missed you, El. I've missed you so damned much it hurts."

"Logan—"

"I've been thinking, if we can just hang on through this semester with the way things are, just keep our distance until after finals, them maybe we'll have a shot."

I studied him, letting my puzzlement show. "What's special about next semester? Why then?"

"I can't explain now. Just trust me, El. Please. I'll explain when I can."

I swallowed hard, confused. Whatever his mystery was, it was going to be over. If it was only him...

But what about me? What was I going to do about Jason and Mia? But even with the stakes so high, I couldn't turn him down flat. "I'll think about it."

He smiled. "Promise?"

I nodded, took a step back out of his embrace, and grabbed his hands. "But for now, I'm just your fake girlfriend, okay?"

He grinned. He wouldn't have if he knew how long the odds we faced were.

"Let's sit in the living room." I pulled him toward the sofa. "You can finish briefing me on what your dad expects."

We sat next to each other, thigh touching thigh.

"I wasn't kidding earlier in the kitchen. Just be you. You're perfect—gorgeous but you don't know it." He sounded just a touch sad.

But my pulse raced. "You need to have your eyes examined."

He smiled. "See what I mean?"

"Shut up. What else?"

"You're just fishing for compliments," Logan said. "You like hearing me sing your praises."

"You're awful. I'm just trying to help you. What else?"

"He likes your major because he's really into tech stuff."

"Likes? That sounds like he already knows about me." I frowned.

"Of course he does. I had to prime him. It wouldn't feel authentic if I sprung you on him when he got here. Besides, this way I get brownie points for an extra couple of weeks.

"He's already made dinner reservations for three. But keep the weekend open. He'll probably expect you to sit with us at the game and he mentioned something about getting a third ticket to the comedy show if he can swing it."

My mouth went dry as the reality of meeting his dad and the depths of my deception sank in. "That all sounds like a lot of togetherness, pretty serious stuff. How many other girls have you introduced him to? Is this the way he treats them all?"

Logan shrugged. "I have no idea. I haven't introduced him to anyone I've dated since high school."

I paled. "That's terrible!"

"I thought you'd be pleased."

And I was. More than was good for me. I was also horrified at what I was doing. "What are you going to say when you and me the fake girlfriend break up?"

He looked nonplussed. "That we didn't work out. Breakups happen."

I didn't like the guilt that was welling up in me. "What else have you told him?"

"That you work for Jason, too. He was thrilled. He loves Jason. Jason helped me get my shit together after

I fell apart. He's Dad's hero. I told him you're Jason's second favorite after me."

I looked away. Jason was a delicate subject.

"Did you tell him you saved my life?"

He shook his head. "I left that part out. Dad isn't wild about my cliff-jumping proclivities." He laughed. "Hey, lighten up. That's it. That's the end of the bio I shared with him."

I had to make Logan see that not everything about me was perfect. "What about my family? What if he asks about them?"

"What if?"

"Your parents have been married a long time? Never divorced?"

"Yeah. So?"

I sighed. "So when your dad asks about mine, like where is he? And I say I have no idea. I never knew him. I was born out of wedlock. I don't even know who my dad is. He's going to be okay with that?"

I didn't let him answer. "And when he asks about my mom and I say she's going through her third divorce and I don't speak to her?" I shook my head. "He's not going to like my family."

"Who cares? They aren't you."

I licked my lips. "Okay, I can handle this. I'll avoid mentioning them." I grabbed the TV controller, eager to change the subject. "Want to watch something while the cookie bar bakes?"

A blast of wind and rain hit the sliding glass door off the kitchen. It was like the weather was crying with me. Logan put his arm around me. I leaned my head on his shoulder as he flicked through the channels.

Zave and Collin breezed in, soaked and jovial. They were each loaded down with shopping bags.

"Logan! You missed an awesome shopping run. We've been to the Goodwill and Shopper's Co. We're going to be the hottest zombies in history! We found the most frigging awesome decorations. Our party is going to be the place to be." Collin stopped short, as if just seeing me. "Oh, hello, Ellie. Our little rescue girl has finally decided to pay her old friends a visit, has she?"

"Nice to see you, too, Collin. Zave."

Zave dumped his bags by the sofa. "Something smells delicious." He headed to the kitchen and rubbed his hands together when he saw the cobblestone bars cooling on the counter. "The famous cobblestone bars—whoa!"

"Keep your hands off them," Logan said. "They're El's. And they're not frosted yet. She baked them for her boyfriend."

I rolled my eyes. "I baked them for my lab TA because he's so sweet and gives me extra help."

"I'll give you extra help if you'll bake for me," Collin said.

"She doesn't need your kind of help," Logan said.

Zave dropped into the only chair in the room. Collin plopped onto the sofa next to me. "You are coming to our Halloween party on Saturday?"

"I—"

"It's going to be epic," Collin said.

"Legendary." Zave grinned. "Collin's parties always are."

"Assuming we all graduate as planned, this will be our last college Halloween bash. A Halloweekend to remember. So convenient Halloween is on a Saturday this year. It's a sign! I'm going to outdo even myself and last year's party." Collin turned to Zave. "Our renters' insurance is up to date?"

"Dad took care of it personally."

Collin smiled. "So it's settled. You'll come."

I glanced at Logan.

Collin got the message. "He hasn't invited you? Logan! Where are your manners?" He did a great imitation of a scolding mom.

"Would you like to come to our party, Miss Martin? We would be very happy to have you as our guest." He spoke formally and stiffly on purpose.

I laughed and bumped him with my shoulder. "If I have nothing better to do."

"We'll take that as a yes. There isn't anything better to do." Collin grabbed the TV controller from Logan. "What are we watching?"

"Spartacus! I almost forgot—have you fed him?" Without waiting for an answer, Zave got up and fed the fish. I thought Logan was probably right—Zave was the most likely the culprit in the case of the dying goldfish.

"I hope you're going to put Spartacus away someplace safe for the party," I said. "You don't want him to end up like the goldfish."

"You mean Spartacus One through Six? No, you're right," Zave said.

"You named all the goldfish Spartacus, too?"

Three heads nodded.

"I'll have to keep him in my room," Zave said.

"Or better yet, ask the girls across the hall to take him," Collin said. "No room here will be safe during our legendary Halloweekend party."

It was one a.m. by the time I finished frosting the cobblestone bars and cleaning up. I cut a small plateful and set them out for the guys. Collin got a carton of milk from the fridge, took a sip directly from it, and got four glasses out. "Milk, anyone?"

I politely declined. Logan and Zave got a large glass each and dug into the cobblestone bars I'd left for them.

"These are awesome," Logan said.

Collin spoke with his mouth full. "A worthy bribe for a lab TA, the next best thing to sex."

I rolled my eyes. Outside, a storm raged at full force. After they'd polished off the cookie bar, Collin and Zave wandered off to their rooms. I hinted to Logan. "I should be going."

"Do you have to, El?"

The rain was beating against the window. The wind angrily pounding the building in gusts.

My heart stopped. I stared at him, wondering what he was asking. I let the question shine in my eyes.

"Zave and Collin won't care. I have an extra tooth-brush you can use. I'll drive you to class in the morn-

ing." He looked completely innocent and totally beguil-
ing.

I hesitated and decided to make myself clear while
my heart hammered in my ears. "They won't mind me
sleeping on the couch?"

Logan took a step into me and wrapped his arms
around me. "Why would you sleep there? I'm asking
you to spend the night with me."

I licked my lips. "Logan, I'm not...I don't..."

He kissed my forehead. "I'm not asking you for sex,
El. I just want to sleep cuddled next to you for one
night." His voice was tantalizingly low and tender. He
ran his fingers through my hair and tipped my chin up
so I had to look him in the eye. "I'm not going to force
myself on a fake girlfriend. Promise." He smiled, took
my hand, and led me to his bedroom.

It was hard not to stare at the Cubs jersey and posters and hard not to remember the way his dreams had
crashed.

His bathroom was connected to his room. He led me
to it and handed me a new toothbrush and a clean
washcloth. "Ladies first."

When I came out, he was shirtless, wearing only a
thin pair of cotton lounge pants. I could barely keep
from staring at him. The bed was open and the pillows
fluffed. A T-shirt lay on the bed.

"Choose your side." He pointed to the T-shirt. "A
nightshirt, in case you want one." He disappeared into
the bathroom.

I slid off my shoes, peeled off my top and bra, and
pulled the T-shirt over my head before shimmying out

of my jeans and folding everything neatly. I wished I'd worn my cuter panties. The T-shirt was soft and well worn. Best of all, it smelled clean, but like him—his laundry soap and the smell of his apartment.

I grabbed my phone and texted Bre that I'd be back in the morning. She'd expect it and freak if she didn't hear from me.

I'd just slid into bed when Logan came out of the bathroom, his face rosy like he'd scrubbed it. "You look better in my T-shirt than I do." He flashed me a grin that melted my heart and climbed into bed next to me. "How do you like to sleep? Face to face? Spooning?"

I shrugged. "What do you like?"

"I'm a spooner." He lay down and patted the pillow next to him.

I lay down, keenly aware of him as he wrapped his warm, bare arms around me. When he cuddled close to me, I felt his erection hard against me. My heart raced, nervous, scared, excited.

"Don't worry about that, El," he whispered in my ear. "I'm not going to use it. When I'm near you, I can't help it." He kissed my neck. "Relax. Sleep tight."

I tried, I really did. But I was all too aware of him. I had never slept with someone's arms around me. Wrapped in his embrace, I felt safe, and awkward. I was afraid to move, worrying that I'd disturb him. It took a long time, but at last I drifted off.

When I woke, he was still sleeping, his face relaxed and handsome, peaceful in a way it wasn't when he was awake. It broke my heart a little to think he carried that mysterious burden around with him. I wished he could share it with me, and at the same time, a part of me didn't want it to taint what I knew of him.

I carefully untangled myself from his embrace. I checked my phone. A text from Dex, reminding me in code that it was mission day and to be on my game. I responded that I was bringing my A game and set the phone on the nightstand by the bed. Then I slipped to the bathroom.

When I looked in the mirror, I was puffy-eyed from sleep and I had a sheet print across my cheek. My scar stood out pink and ugly. I was exposed and there was nothing I could do about it. I'd left my makeup at the dorm. I was no beauty in the morning.

I frowned as I ran my fingers through my hair, trying to tame it and brush it around my face to cover the scar at least a little. I brushed my teeth, rinsed my face, and gave up. This was as good as I got. I smelled like Logan and his bed.

In the bedroom, I slid my jeans on.

"Morning, beautiful."

I gasped and jumped and pressed my hand to my heart.

Logan leaned on one elbow, watching me. His hair was tousled almost artfully and the drowsy look in his eyes was simply sexy.

"You scared me." I looked around for my cell phone.

"I didn't mean to." He held my cell phone up. "Looking for this?"

I let out a sigh of relief. "Yes." I lunged for it.

He held it out of my grasp. "Come and get it."

"Just give it back."

He looked at the screen and handed it over. "Nice picture of Mia. I haven't seen her in that outfit before. When did you take it?"

My heart stopped. I didn't have any pictures of Mia on my phone. As I took the phone from him, the baby me smiled back at me. "Were you snooping on my phone?" My hands shook.

"Hey, sorry. Calm down." He took my hands in his. "Sorry. The picture was up when I grabbed it. I only took it so you couldn't sneak out on me." He flashed me a boyish, charming, apologetic smile.

I took a deep breath and forced a smile back, refusing to be a bitch about it. I believed him, but it was a close call. I slid the phone in my jeans and put a tease in my voice. "Would I sneak out on you?"

He looked me over and cocked a brow. "Going somewhere?"

"Not far, unless you take me."

"I promised I'd take you home. Give me a sec." As he slid out of bed, it was hard not to stare at him. He was so well built, firm and buff in all the right places.

I reached for my blouse.

He shook his head. "Don't change. I like the way you look in my shirt. Keep it." He headed to the bathroom.

The storm had blown over. The morning was clear and fresh. He drove me back to the dorm, swinging through a coffee stand drive-through and buying me a mocha and an apple cinnamon scone on the way. I sipped the mocha and picked at the scone on the drive.

When he pulled up to the dorm, there was an awkward moment when I didn't know what to say. I was lame at saying goodbye.

"I'll be in touch about Dad's Weekend plans. Keep the weekend open." He looked at me funny and brushed my lips with a feather-light touch. "Crumbs." He grinned. "See you, El."

I nodded and slid out of Logan's car with the cobblestone bars, not looking back as he drove away. I sneaked into the dorm, hoping no one saw me. Just my luck. Nic was headed to the shower, carrying her towel and shower caddy as she stumbled toward the bathroom. Her eyes lit up when she saw me. "Look who's doing the walk of shame."

"Shut up." I fell in step with her as we walked toward the bathroom and my room.

"And wearing a shacking shirt." She whistled. "Logan's? Nice."

"It's not a shacking shirt."

"Shacker, shacker, shacker. Did you spend the night with him? Judging from the stupid smile on your face, of course you did. That makes it an official shacking shirt. I want all the details."

I held the pan of cobblestone bars out for her to see. "I was making cookies. That's all the details there are."

"Isn't 'making cookies' code for sex?" she said.

We reached the bathroom.

"I have to shower or I'll be late to class. You can fill me in later." She wiggled her eyebrows lecherously.

I had to hurry, too, or I'd miss chem lab. And that would be catastrophic. Dex would kill me. When I let myself into my room, Bre was already up.

"Oooooh!" Her gaze ran up and down me wearing Logan's old rec league baseball T-shirt. "You little shacker, you."

I shook my head. "Not you too."

"Who else has seen you?"

"Nic."

"We're all going to want the details."

"I made cookies. We slept." But I couldn't stop grinning. "Those are all the details, period."

"Shy, are we? We have ways of making you talk." She let loose the witch's cackle she'd been practicing to go with her sexy witch's costume.

CHAPTER THIRTEEN

I barely had time to shower before chem lab, let alone do my hair and makeup. The only extra time I took, I folded my shacker shirt and put it in my drawer with my T-shirts and tanks. The shirt smelled like Logan— his cologne, his soap, his bed—and I vowed never to wash it. I was hoping it would perfume my whole wardrobe with the scent of him forever.

I ran back from lab and fixed up before I went to see Byron—like, extra fixed up. I even put on a half-row of fake eyelashes to give my eyes that sexy siren look. And painted a row of eyeliner that Marilyn Monroe would have envied. And sexy red lips with a dot of light gloss in the middle to make them look lush and full. Having learned from the master, I knew all the tricks. Maybe it was overkill. Maybe I was being too obvious, but I wasn't leaving anything to chance.

I artfully arranged a selection of the best cobblestone bars on a plastic fake silver tray I'd bought at the dollar store. Then I wrapped it in plastic wrap and tied a silver bow around it with curling ribbon. I grabbed the plastic fake silver cake server, also from the dollar store, and put it in a bag. And then it was show time. I headed to the chem building with my heart pounding.

Byron's office was in the middle of the second floor, far enough away from the dean's office and the admins that I reached it without being seen by any of them. I breathed a sigh of relief that the lab surrounding his cubicle was empty. There were often students making up lab experiments they'd missed or other TAs working milling about, working on projects.

I peeked over the wall of his cubicle. Byron was head-down working. I balanced my showy platter of cobblestone bars on one hand like a waiter in a fancy restaurant and held it in the door to the cubicle. "Tada!"

Byron startled and looked up, blushing when he spotted me peeking around the corner. "What's this?"

"I did it!" I slid into the cube, crossing my fingers no one came into the lab, and hoping and looking for an opportunity to get to the window. The windows opened up. Dex had reminded me it had an old-fashioned latch in the center. All I had to do was turn the latch so it didn't catch. If I could I should open it the tiniest bit so he'd have a hold to pry it up.

"I can't wait for you to try them!" I sauntered into the cube and made a show of placing them on the desk before him, pulling the cake server out of the bag with a flourish, along with a matching small silver plastic plate and fork.

"Wow! Fancy."

"Presentation is everything. Isn't that what you tell us about lab write-ups?"

He grinned and his face became blotchy with darker patches of red. "These look fabulous. You're confident you got it right?"

I grinned. "I'd bet a quiz grade on it."

"Whoa! That's a stiff bet."

"Open it, open it, open it!" I bounced on the balls of my feet and clapped my hands softly. I had to remind myself not to overdo it.

I watched as he untied the silver ribbon and pulled the plastic wrap back.

He took a deep sniff. "They smell good."

I came over to his side of the desk. Standing close enough to rattle him, I put my hand on his shoulder as I leaned over him and served him a piece, setting the fork on the plate next to it.

He picked up the fork.

I had to resist the urge to cross my fingers behind me. "Wait!"

He paused.

"I forgot milk. You can't try them without milk." I knew Byron always kept a carton of milk in the lab fridge along with various experiments. It was part of the custom for him to get it to drink with my cobblestone bar experiments.

"You're absolutely right."

I stepped out of the way. He pushed back, jumped up, and dashed into the lab to get his milk.

Was I devious or what?

I grabbed a napkin, looked around nervously, and dashed to the window while Byron's back was turned. Holding the napkin so I wouldn't leave any prints, I tried the latch. It stuck and I panicked. It was clear no one had opened the window in a long time. My palms were sweating as I forced it. It came loose as I heard the refrigerator door fall shut.

I swallowed hard, gave the window a good tug, and sighed with relief when it opened a fraction of an inch without screeching to alert the whole lab. I slid it back down so it was almost imperceptibly open as I hear Byron's footsteps approaching. I swung around and leaned against the windowsill, smiling at him encouragingly as he walked in.

"Got it!" He beamed as he held up the milk.

I pulled his chair out for him like he was a king. And watched with exaggerated anticipation on my face as he dug into the nicely plated cookie bar and took a bite.

"Mmmmmmm. Mmmmmmm. Mmmmmmm. These are delicious!" He made the coveted okay sign. "You did it! These are better than the dining hall's!"

I squealed and leaned over, hugging him from behind. Even his neck was bright red. "Take another bite," I whispered in his ear like Eve.

When I left the lab, I texted Dex the prearranged code. *Had a great chem tutoring session. Eager to share.*

I met Dex, Joe, and Kirk in front of the chem building parking garage just before two a.m. We'd all dressed in black. I was carrying pepper spray in case I ran into trouble.

We didn't speak as we climbed over the security gates and made our way to the second floor. Earlier, Kirk had pinched a ladder from a maintenance closet in his dorm. He delivered and hid it in the garage. They planned to stretch it across the gap to Byron's window. It was my job to pull it out of sight if anyone happened by. After our caper, Kirk would return it to the closet where it had hopefully gone unnoticed as missing.

Fortunately, the glow from a nearby streetlight cast enough illumination around us so we could see, but could still hide in the shadows.

As Kirk and Joe maneuvered the ladder into place, Dex handed me a walkie-talkie. "You left your cell phone at home?"

I nodded. Dex didn't want any evidence we'd been in the garage. Cell phones could be tracked. Paranoid, maybe. But none of us wanted to get in trouble.

"Good." He pointed to the military-grade walkie-talkie. "It's preset to a secure channel." He showed me how to work it and made me take a practice run with it. "Only use it if someone's approaching and we're in trouble. If all goes well, we shouldn't be in there more than twenty minutes to a half-hour."

"And if you don't come back?"

"Thinking of contingency plans." He tapped his head. "Good thinking. If we're not back in an hour, call campus security and report a break-in." He paused. "Let's hope it doesn't come to that."

"The ladder's ready." Joe stood back to let Dex inspect it.

Joe had balanced it on the ledge outside Byron's window and anchored it on our side by tying it to the parking barricade.

Dex made a show of pushing on it to see if it was secure. "Let's go."

I held my breath as Dex climbed across with his backpack slung over both shoulders and tried the window, crossing my fingers no one fell and that the window opened. Wiry Dex climbed across like an acrobat. He was stringy, but strong.

Even so, he cursed as he struggled with the window. "I thought you unlocked this."

I tried not to panic. "I *did*. I even opened it a few millimeters. Maybe he noticed and relocked it."

Just then it gave way and Dex climbed in. The other two guys followed, leaving me as a lonely lookout. It was October and a slow ground fog was building. Dry branches and leaves rattled eerily against the building. I jumped at everything, wishing I was inside and knowing I couldn't leave my post. A car drove by on the road beyond the building, music blaring. I ducked, huddling in the shadows against the wall, imagining all kinds of horrors as time ticked by agonizingly slowly. It gave me way too much time to finally think through the consequences of this insane prank.

At last, I heard whispering and the ladder groaned and scraped against the concrete wall. Joe, then Kirk, appeared and climbed across. Dex came out and shut the window before working his way across the ladder. Joe and Kirk immediately began taking the ladder down.

My heart hammered in my ears. Dex wore a grim expression I could see even in the dim lighting.

"What's wrong?" My heart hammered wildly. This was a better scare than any haunted house I'd ever been to. But I didn't plan on ever repeating it. "What happened? Did something go wrong?"

Joe and Kirk, on the other hand were exuberant.

"Went off without a hitch! Perfect. Tomorrow when that bitch turns on that damn projector, she's going to get the surprise of her life," Joe said.

Kirk nodded.

I turned to Dex and frowned. "You don't agree?"

He looked at me blankly. "Everything went according to plan. Now let's get out of here. Everyone get a good night's sleep. Drink an energy drink before class if you have to, but you're all under orders not to look sleepy in class. We don't want anything giving us away."

I argued with him. "Not looking sleepy will give us away. No one looks perky in chem. I always bring a cup of coffee to keep me awake."

He didn't argue as he waved at us to follow him and Kirk and Joe grabbed the ladder. I didn't understand Dex's mood. But it worried me. If he cracked...

I arrived for the chem lecture full of anticipation and fear. Lately, those two opposite emotions had become my constant companions. I never had one without the other. It was like I was living the first day in a new situation every day. I carried my coffee and took my usual seat next to Dex, yawning for show. I loved my seat. It was right behind a speaker box that made a perfect coffee table. I set my cup on it.

"Late night?" he said, heavy on the sarcasm.

"I had a lot of homework that kept me up." I dropped my backpack at my feet and pulled my notebook out.

Going to the lecture was basically an exercise in futility. You could learn everything you needed to know by studying the notes online. Not that any amount of studying seemed to make a difference in that class. Everyone would have skipped, except Dr. Rogers took attendance and docked points for not being in class.

Using my i>clicker, I logged in as present.

The room filled up. The bell rang. Dr. Rogers took her place at her podium, the projector next to her, ready to be turned on. Usually, she fired it up first thing. Today, however, she turned on her laptop and began lecturing from PowerPoint.

Suddenly, I couldn't breathe. Had she somehow gotten wind of what we'd done? What if she didn't use the projector all lecture? What if it went off for the next professor who used it?

Beside me, Dex sat stiffly, his expression masked. Every time she even glanced at the projector, I braced myself. I almost cracked and left, unable to stand the tension—would she or wouldn't she?

Dr. Rogers flipped through PowerPoint slides at breakneck speed, her voice grating on my already frayed nerves as my heart thudded in my ears. *All that risk for nothing.* Ten minutes passed. Fifteen. Just when I'd given up hope of her working equations on the rolling transparency projector, she reached over and flipped it on so suddenly just the action startled me.

There was a flash of light. A pop and bang. A puff of smoke.

Dr. Rogers screamed and jumped back. The audience, including me, did a collective start, jumping in their seats at the crack of the firecracker. They gasped as one. Some people ducked. Others jumped up and headed for the exits like we were under attack. The rest quickly realized this was nothing more than a prank and started to laugh. Then they grabbed their gear to head out. Lecture was clearly over.

Dr. Rogers waved her hand in front of her, trying to clear the smoke. She screamed into the mic. "I've been sabotaged! Get back in your seats! No one is leaving my lecture until the culprit who devised this Halloweek prank is caught or confesses." She coughed and kept waving at the smoke as she grabbed her cell phone and dialed.

She was usually unattractive. With her face red and pinched with anger and contorted from screaming, she was the perfect picture of a Halloween witch.

We were braced for this reaction based on the reaction Dex's dad's professor had had and our knowledge of the bitch Dr. Rogers. We had a pact—no one confesses. We were sitting in an audience with nearly five hundred equally valid suspects. It was the perfect crime. She couldn't hold us forever. We could hear her talking to campus security over her mic.

Beside me, Dex slowly slid his notebook into his backpack. I took a sip of my coffee. Around us, the auditorium buzzed with speculation and praise for the geniuses behind the prank.

"Who do you think did it?" I asked Dex, keeping up pretenses and blending in.

"I dunno. But who ever they are, they deserve a medal. I'd like to buy them a beer."

As campus security streamed in, Rogers called IT services. I perked up, listening to her scream at Jason, demanding his best tech, demanding Logan. *Now.*

I couldn't hear Jason's side, but it was clear he was negotiating with her.

"Logan and no one else. Now." She hung up.

I felt myself pale. Logan was never assigned to manage the AV equipment for Dr. Rogers and Chem 202. Never. Why was she demanding him now?

My mouth went dry. Campus security took Dr. Rogers' statement and fanned out to interview people in the audience.

And then Logan arrived carrying his tech repair kit. I couldn't understand why Jason had agreed to send him. Logan walked right past the bitch without looking at her or acknowledging her in any way. But she focused right in on him, her eyes lighting up the minute she spotted him.

She watched him like a predator, with a gleam of lust and ownership in her eyes. With a contradictory lovesick puppy look blended in.

My stomach turned. I felt nauseous as I realized why Logan avoided Dr. Rogers and Chem 202—she was obsessed with him.

CHAPTER FOURTEEN

"Ellie! Ellie! You look pale. Are you okay?"

It took me a second to realize Dex was talking to me. "I'm fine."

"Sure?"

I nodded, staring at the bitch Rogers like a gawker at a gruesome crash, unable to look away.

Dex was obviously worried I was about to freak out and break or something. That must have been his main concern.

He followed my line of sight, silent as he took in and processed what he was looking at. "Shit, shit, shit! That's Logan."

"Yes."

Dex put his arm around my shoulders and gave me a squeeze. "That explains the A," he mumbled almost to himself.

We both knew what he meant.

"It's all right, Ellie. It's okay. I'm on it. She's not going to hurt you." His tone was fierce. He was vehement.

That was when I knew he saw what I did.

The bitch leaned over Logan, putting her hand on his shoulder as he bent to inspect the projector. Logan froze, then shook her hand off like he was disgusted.

She was still mic'ed. I swore I could hear her breathing quicken with sexual excitement when she touched him. "How bad is the damage?"

"There is none." Logan pulled the remains of a flashcube and a firecracker from the projector and held them up. "It's just a prank, a Halloweek prank." He did something with a wire and the projector turned on, humming and working like normal.

The bell rang. With verification that it was just a prank, campus security couldn't hold us. I grabbed my backpack and ran out of the auditorium, taking the steps two at a time with Dex rushing to keep up. I couldn't breathe. I needed fresh air before I suffocated. My thoughts swirled so fast, I couldn't grab a rational thought.

Outside, the sun was shining, burning off the last of the fog from the night before. I inhaled deeply. When I exhaled, I could see my breath. I practically ran up the hill away from the chem building, away from everything.

Dex hung with me. At the top of the hill, he grabbed my arm. "Slow down. Breathe slowly before you hyperventilate."

"You saw what I saw."

He led me out of the stream of students making their way to class, pulling me to the dewy grass off the beaten track. "I saw a predatory cougar."

I stared at him.

"I'm not going to have to get a paper bag, am I?"

I stared at him and tried to breathe more slowly.

"Good girl." His voice was surprisingly tender.

"He slept with her. Logan slept with her to get that A." I was still in danger of breathing too fast and my heart pounded like it wanted to escape from my chest.

"That's not the only explanation."

"Isn't it?" I shook my head, feeling jittery, like I needed to pace or something. "Then what is?"

Dex took me by both arms. "It's one-sided, Ellie. Listen to me."

I shook my head and laughed in way that was almost manic. This was twisted, like Austin all over again. Why couldn't older women stay away from the men I loved? "You can't know that—"

"I *do* know that." He shook me gently. "Listen to me, Ellie. Trust me. Right now I have more faith in Logan than you do."

"The why won't he talk about it? Why is it a forbidden subject between us?" I kept shaking my head. "No. Creepy douchebag guys that make my skin crawl have had crushes on me before. They've tried to give me gifts I wouldn't accept. But I can still talk about them."

I gulped in air. "He slept with her for that A. He prosti-tuted himself for it. That's why he can't talk about it."

"Ellie!" Dex shook me harder. "Stop it! Stop it now!"

His words felt like a slap. Tears filled my eyes.

Dex's voice became soft. He relaxed his grip on my arms and pulled me into a hug, pressing me tightly against him as I cried for real. "You're imagining the worst. It's not what it seems. I know I'm being cryptic, but I'm taking care of things, handling them."

I sobbed into his coat while he held me.

"This is bigger than I am. I had to call in help. But it will all be resolved soon, within a few weeks." He hugged me tighter. "In the meantime, promise me you won't confront Logan about this. You won't mention what we saw. You won't accuse him. Stay away from him if you have to. Do whatever it takes. If you con-front him and accuse him of sleeping with Rogers for an A, you'll lose him forever." He held me away from him so he could look me in the eye. "Do you hear me? Do you understand?"

I nodded.

"You promise?"

I nodded.

"Say it. Swear to it."

"I promise."

He let out a breath. "Good."

"Dex?"

"Yeah?"

"You really are a great hugger." I tried to smile through my tears.

"Come here." He pulled me to him again.

I dreaded going to work that afternoon—like, *really* dreaded it with a passion. What could I say to Logan? I had promised Dex I wouldn't make any accusations or confront him in any way. Which ruled out a great conversation starter like *So, you slept with the bitch prof for an A. That's why you can't help me. You don't know any more than I do. It's pretty clear she still really has the hots for you. When were you planning to tell me?*

The thought made me so sick, I could barely think it. But no matter how hard I tried to push it out of my mind, it hung around the periphery, haunting me.

Our prank took on a life all its own. Someone caught it on their phone and posted the video online. In just a few hours, it got thousands of views. This prank was truly going to be legendary. It was the talk of campus, the buzz on everyone's lips. People were congratulating the anonymous pranksters, offering to buy them beers, begging them to out themselves.

Fat chance.

By the time my shift started, the university was promising to catch and punish them and warning would-be copycats to think twice before pulling a similar stunt.

There was no way to avoid talking about it. Not to mention it would look weird and almost point the guilty finger at me if I totally ignored it. If I saw Logan, wouldn't I naturally be dying for up-close details?

Dex warned all of us to keep up the show. To speculate along with everyone else about who the guilty parties were. To be as excited and thrilled and curious as the rest of the class and campus.

So I slunk into the office, hoping Logan wouldn't show, that he would be out on assignment all day or call in sick. To my immediate relief, he wasn't in.

Karen spotted me. "Good! You're here. Jason's out at a meeting. I'm manning this place alone and need to run up to the third floor for a minute. Keep an eye on it for me while I'm gone?"

I nodded and hung up my coat.

"Great! I won't be long." She dashed out.

No sooner had I sat down at my desk than the door swung open. I looked up just as Logan walked in. My heart stopped. My palms went cold. My stomach burned with rage and hurt. I turned the actress on.

"It's the man of the hour!" I forced myself to smile at him and act natural, even though I knew I was prodding the beast. "The guy with the upfront view to the epic prank of the century. I want *all* the details."

I clapped my hands like an excited child. "You should have seen the look on her face when it happened! It was almost worth half a semester of torture. By the time you got there, she was merely apoplectic. But the initial scare? That was awesome!"

Logan stared right through me. "Is Jason in?"

I shook my head. "Out at a meeting." I stood and came around to lean on the front of my desk and look Logan in the eye. "Come on! You can't hold out on me. How did they do it? What did Dr. Rogers say to you? Give me the scoop."

Logan's eyes snapped with anger. "I can't talk about it." His tone warned me off.

I ignored it and spoke in my confidential tone. "You can tell me. I won't tell anyone."

He glared at me. "Shut the fuck up, El! I don't want to talk about it."

He couldn't have hurt me more if he'd struck me. "Hey! No one talks like that to me. I just asked a simple question."

He spun on his heel and reached for the doorknob.

"You can't walk out on me." I was almost screaming at him.

"Watch me." He stormed out, leaving me staring after him.

He's guilty, I thought. *No matter what Dex says.*

My heart broke. I took deep breaths to keep from losing it.

Just then Karen came back, wearing a puzzled look. "What's wrong with Logan? I saw him in the hall."

I shrugged. "No idea."

We didn't text. We didn't call. We were now officially not even friendly colleagues. Somehow I made it through the week without running into Logan, though it was pretty clear that was intentional on both our parts. Bre, Nic, and Tay heard the story and walked softly around me, trying to get me to go shopping and get a costume for Halloweekend. They insisted I come out with them, that it would help heal my broken heart.

I refused. I didn't have the heart for it. Okay, I knew Logan hadn't cheated on me like Austin had. But he wasn't the man I thought he was. I was, rightfully so, jumpy about guys who went for cougars. And sleeping with the bitch Rogers was so awful it colored how I thought about him.

I couldn't bear to open my drawer with Logan's shirt in it. I spent Wednesday night washing the clothes in my laundry hamper so I'd have clean things to wear without dipping in that drawer.

I skipped chemistry on Friday and used the time to work on my MIS 301 paper. If I was going to fail chemistry, I had to get A's in all of the rest of my classes. Dex took my i>clicker and clicked in for me. The university equated that with cheating. But what did I care? After the prank we'd pulled, which trended on Twitter and was the talk of campus all week, what was one more possible expellable offense? We were like major heroes, superheroes whose identity remained a mystery. No one had any clue who had pulled the caper off. They just all wished they'd thought of it.

Dex took notes for me, too. But it didn't matter because the bitch Rogers posted hers online. Dex said I missed quite a show. I should have seen how jittery and nervous she was the entire lecture, especially when she turned the projector on. He took video of it on his phone to show me.

I wanted to call into work sick. I really couldn't face Logan and was dreading Dad's Weekend with a passion, even though I figured I was no longer Logan's fake girlfriend for the weekend. But Karen called me in a panic, saying Logan had called in sick along with half the crew. Yeah, he was definitely avoiding me. She asked if I could come in early.

I suspected, and probably so did she, that most people were blowing off work to start the Halloweekend party early.

When I arrived, Jason was talking to Karen at her desk. "Our sitter for Saturday night just called to cancel. Lyssa's mom is out of town at her sister's and can't fill in. I can't believe the faculty actually scheduled their party on Halloween and expects us to come. My VP will have my butt in a sling if I don't make an appearance.

"Where are we supposed to get a sitter? Every reliable high school and college girl has plans. Lyssa's unhappy, but I may have to go stag."

"I don't." I could hardly believe the words popped out of my mouth. They swiveled and stared at me as I took my coat off and hung it on the rack by the door.

"I don't have any plans. I'll do it. I'll watch Mia."

Jason looked perplexed and uncertain. "Are you sure, Ellie? You still have twenty-four hours. A lot can change in that time. There are hundreds of parties on campus you could drop into. With Halloween actually on a Saturday, this is an epic Halloweekend."

"I'm not in the partying mood this year." I wasn't in the mood for anything. "What time do you need me?"

Friday night the dorm was loud with parties and partiers. I huddled in my room, a hermit, trying to ignore the revelry around me. I texted Collin and told him I couldn't come to his party because I was babysitting Mia for Jason in a pinch. I knew he'd tell Logan. I waited for Logan to text me, but he didn't. So that was the way it was.

The dorm didn't quiet down until after three. Bre and I slept in until noon. Then we both staggered to the showers and got some breakfast in the cafeteria— boo-berry muffins and scary eggs. It was nearly two by the time Bre went to the library to study, leaving me in the room by myself.

There was a knock on the door just after she left. I rolled my eyes. What had she forgotten now? Bre was too lazy to get her key out and I wasn't in any mood to leave the door open. Nic and Tay and everyone else on the floor knew to leave me alone in my black mood. I'd locked myself in on purpose.

I popped up and opened it without thinking. "What do you want now—"

I froze. Austin stood in my doorway. As I reached to slam the door shut, he stuck his foot in the way and held out his arm to block it. There was no point in trying to shut it now.

Two girls from the floor walked by just then. They gave him the once-over and motioned to me behind his back that he was smoking hot. I ignored them. They didn't know him like I did.

"Can I come in?" He looked sheepish. "Please, Ellie."

I don't know what possessed me, but I took a step back. I guess I've always been a sucker. "Suit yourself." I retreated to my desk chair. It seemed the safest place and the easiest way to keep my distance.

He came into the room and closed the door softly behind him. "You look good."

He lied. Without makeup, I looked heartbroken and like crap, which probably gave him the idea I was still into him. I instinctively touched my left cheek and rubbed the tiny scar on my cheekbone, which suddenly ached like it was freshly sliced again.

"What brings you to campus?" I forced myself to remove my hand from the scar and stared at him, measuring his effect on me. Anyone looking at him now would say he was hot. He certainly looked better than the bloody mess he'd been when I'd pulled my third stepfather off him. At the time, I'd thought Doug was going to kill him. Funny how Doug blamed him and I blamed Mom.

Austin was like a handsome stranger to me now. With some relief, I realized he no longer made my heart constrict.

"Schwartz and Bradley are having a party. They've been begging me to come all fall." He sat down on Bre's bed across from my desk and stared at me.

I was relieved he was on her bed, not mine, and that he'd chosen not to come too close to me.

"You wouldn't answer my calls, texts, or emails. I had to come see you. We need to talk."

I pursed my lips and shrugged. "About what?"

"Come on, Ellie. Don't give me that. About everything. I can't leave things the way they were." He made a move that looked like he was going to stand and come to me.

"Don't come near me." Almost subconsciously I grabbed a pair of scissors from the caddy on my desk. I glanced down, surprised I was holding them. I was still angrier than I thought. Anything to protect myself. I set them back down.

"What is there to say, really, Austin? You had *sex* with *my mom*. Before my eyes." I snorted like I was trying to laugh, but it wasn't funny. "Next time I'll remember to call before I make a surprise run home to do laundry."

The images flashed before me again. Pulling up and parking in front of Mom and Doug's house. Doug's car pulling into the driveway right behind me. Getting out of my car. Waving to him as I grabbed my laundry basket from the backseat. Doug waiting in the driveway, holding his briefcase.

"What are you doing here?" Doug asked as I walked up the front walk.

I held up my laundry basket. "I'm out of clean clothes. What are you doing here? I thought you were out of town."

"Caught an earlier flight home so I could surprise Melissa."

His key in the front door. The two of us joking with each other. Freezing in the entryway as we heard the distinctive thumping and moaning of sex. Turning toward the living room. Looking directly at Mom and Austin making the sign of the two-humped whale on the couch. So shocked neither of us could process it. As obvious as it was, it just didn't make sense.

Doug dropping his briefcase. The roar that came out of him as he charged them and pulled Austin, naked from the waist down, off Mom. The sickening thud of his fists hammering Austin again and again while Mom screamed at him to stop. The blood from Austin's nose and lip spattering the cream sofa and the carpet, the wall behind them. Mom reaching for her clothes and phone.

Not thinking, just grabbing Doug's arm, trying to pull him away from Austin before he killed him. Flailing and failing miserably, a mere gnat toying with a raging bull. Wedging myself between them. The searing blow to my head that was meant for Austin. Staggering back into the end table. A lamp crashing to the floor. My ears ringing so loudly I couldn't hear anything but the sound of consciousness fleeing. Someone catching me before I went down.

Doug's bloody fist. His prized class ring gleaming through a coating of blood. Something sticky running down my cheek. Touching my face. My fingers coming away bloody. Stunned, confused, barely hanging on. My lip swelling. The taste of blood and violence.

Doug sobbing, broken. "Ellie, Ellie, I'm sorry."

The cops arriving. Sharing an ambulance with Austin to emergency. The lights. The doctors and nurses. The stitches.

The aftermath. The assault charges Austin filed against Doug. The restraining order Mom filed against him. Going back to school. Only coming back to the house once to get my things, when I knew Mom was out. Finding the note about Jason Front when I searched her private papers looking for answers. Hoping my real dad was a better person than my mom.

Austin stared at the floor. "You saved my life. He was going to kill me. I owe you."

I didn't argue with him. I probably had. Doug was in a murderous rage that afternoon. Crime of passion, I knew firsthand what that meant now. Doug wasn't ordinarily violent. He'd never touched Mom or me, or anyone I knew of, before. If he hadn't accidently hit me when I stepped between them, who knows how badly he would have beaten Austin. Striking me brought him back to his senses. Even though he gave me a hairline fracture on my cheek, and a permanent scar, I would take that blow again in a heartbeat.

"I didn't mean for it to happen." Austin's voice wavered. "I loved you."

I noted he was speaking in the past tense and felt absolutely no sorrow over it, only relief.

"She invited me over for dinner, saying you'd be there. We had a few drinks. She came on to me—"

"So it's all her fault? Or maybe it was the alcohol's? Wearing alcohol goggles, you couldn't tell the difference between my mom and me? Hint—she's the older one."

"Ellie..."

I took a deep breath. "You think I don't know Mom's a slut? Nothing gives her more of a thrill than flirting with my boyfriends. She competes with me for everything, and my men are like her ultimate prize.

That's why I keep them away from her. But, damn it, Austin! All the others resisted her. Why couldn't *you*?"

He had the good grace to look ashamed and not offer another lame excuse.

"I'm sorry. That's what I came to say. I wish I could go back and undo it all. I wish we could go back to the way things were."

"That's not going to happen." I swallowed hard. I was over him, but being betrayed by anyone, especially your own mother, was a wound that didn't easily heal. "I can't be around someone who's slept with my mom. I'm sorry, I just can't."

He looked up at me. "I know you don't want to hear this, but she's sorry, too. She misses you."

My mouth fell open. "You're in touch with her?"

He held up his hands in protest. "No, no! Not like that. She cries and leaves me messages, begging me to tell you she's sorry."

"How touching."

"Are you ever going to forgive her?" He sounded and looked worried, like he really had done something unforgivable by coming between a mother and daughter.

"Not in the foreseeable future."

He hung his head. "There are always two sides to a story, Ellie. What I did was wrong and I'd take it back in a minute. But she's a lonely woman. I'm not excusing her. But in her way, I think she genuinely loves you. She's just horribly insecure and jealous of how together you are. When she looks at you, she sees how she could have been."

He took a deep breath and looked up at me. "Will you at least forgive me?"

I took a breath that matched his. And then I realized something. I was tired of living with the burning anger and hatred I'd been harboring for him. It was only hurting me, not him. I needed to move on. Letting go and forgiving him was the first step, and the best thing for both of us. I finally felt like I could.

"I forgive you, Austin." I said it as sincerely and genuinely as I could, because it was the absolute truth. And as stunning to me as it was to him. "I *really* do."

A look of relief crossed his face. An awkward silence followed.

"I'd better go."

I nodded.

He stood to leave.

I walked him to the door.

He touched the scar on my cheek and rubbed it gently. "You really are beautiful, in all the right ways. Happy Halloween, Ellie."

On impulse I leaned up and kissed him goodbye on the cheek. "Happy Halloweekend. Take care, Austin."

CHAPTER FIFTEEN

News travels fast. Bre, Taylor, and Nic arrived back from the library full of questions about the hot guy that was seen going into my room. I explained what had happened.

"I can't believe the infamous Austin was here and I missed him." Nic shook her head. "You actually forgave him?"

I nodded. "Yeah. It was the right thing to do. But it was as much for me as him." I don't think they really got that. They wouldn't unless they'd been hurt like I had. I knew what they were thinking, too, the corollary—that I should forgive Logan for sleeping with the bitch Dr. Rogers.

That, however, was less about forgiveness and more about disgust and disappointment. He hadn't done anything directly to me that demanded my forgiveness. But he wasn't the man I thought he was. And I couldn't get over that. And the horrible image of him with Dr. Rogers. That was almost as bad as the image of Austin with my mom.

After ending their inquisition of me, Bre, Taylor, and Nic spent the rest of the day getting ready for the big night. I watched them with a sort of amused sadness. The hallway outside our room had been decorated for weeks with orange and black crepe paper, spooky webs, and giant plastic spiders. All of the door decs along the hallway, including ours, were Halloween themed and handmade by our RA, complete with colorful, cute pumpkin stickers.

Bre's mom had sent a metal haunted house candleholder, and two spooky gargoyles to keep watch over us and chase away evil spirits. We lit the tea light in the haunted house and set it on Bre's dresser as soon as it got dark. The gargoyles were positioned as sentries. And we set an orange plastic bowl full of candy by the door.

The hall was filled with laughter and lively spirits and a wild cast of characters as girls got ready to go out and party. Everyone was getting dressed up. The pervading theme running through the costumes was simple—"sexed up." This was the night to go hot and show what you got. Girls dressed as popular bite-sized candies in short, colorful dresses with the appropriate candy logos pinned at their midriffs. Bras and short shorts reigned as costume pieces even though the weather had turned cold.

Bre looked hot in her witch's costume, but I didn't feel the slightest pang of regret for throwing it away. Tay was a sexy bee in a costume her older sister had made her. Nic had gone for the sports costume—a jersey, unbuttoned low to reveal her bra and tied up around her midriff, a cap, short shorts, and knee-high socks. Sports costumes were popular because they were easy, easily sexed up, and could be pulled from almost anyone's wardrobe on the spur of the moment. Inexpensive *and* convenient.

The girls finally convinced me I should dress up, too, though I saw no reason.

"They might want you to answer the door and hand out candy," Bre said, which is what finally convinced me.

"How about a sexy zombie?" Tay held up her tray of Halloween makeup and a tube of fake blood. "Zombies are easy. I can transform you, no problem. And you have that really cute black and white bra. That skirt you accidently tore will be perfect."

I rolled my eyes. "And scare the baby? No way. Plus I can't show up to meet the boss's wife looking like I'm trying to seduce him or waiting to let a guy in the minute they leave."

Tay sighed and set her makeup tray down. "You're no fun."

I had brought my *Hunger Games* District 12 shirt with me from last Halloween, and my plastic bow and quiver. I dragged them out and placated Tay by having her braid my hair in the classic Katniss side braid. A touch of makeup, my mockingjay pin, and I was good to go.

Jason was picking me up early, at seven. The staff party started way earlier than the student parties. I tried not to think about Collin, Zave, and Logan getting ready for theirs, the legendary, epic party of their college career. The rest of my gang wouldn't head out until much later. When Jason texted that he was on his way, they walked me to the dorm door to wait for him and teased me about taking a coat. No one, except for the biggest wet blankets, ruined their costume by putting a coat on over it.

"I can't very well show up with my alcohol blanket on," I said as I grabbed a pair of cotton gloves.

"That's what we'll be wearing." The three of them laughed in unison.

I knew they would, too. They already had their tequila and shot glasses lined up and ready to go. Two shots to keep you warm before you headed out was a pretty standard alcohol blanket. "Eat something with it."

Tay laughed. "Yes, mom."

"I still can't believe you're babysitting for your boss on Halloween!" Nic shook her head. "I bet they'll get back early enough you can still go to Collin's."

I flashed her a skeptical look, knowing I wouldn't. I couldn't explain how badly I wanted to see my baby sister, because no one knew I even had one. This might be the only opportunity I got. And now with my illusions about Logan crushed, there was no party I wanted to be at, especially his.

A car pulled up and Jason—dressed in a dorky tweed jacket, jodhpur riding pants, and old-fashioned boots—got out.

I saluted my friends. "May the odds be ever in your favor!" I ran down the steps to meet him.

"Katniss!" he said when he saw me. "They let you out of the district for the night?"

"Let me out? I thought this was the district." I looked at him and arched a brow. "And you are?"

"That bad?" He laughed. "You'd recognize me with my hat, pipe, and magnifying glass. I left them at the house. We have a theme—intellectuals."

Professors and administrators would have a lame theme like that.

"Any guesses?" he said as we got in his car and he started the ignition.

"You deduced I was Katniss. That's brilliant, Sherlock."

He laughed. "Very good."

"So Lyssa is Watson? That's not very couple-y."

"Watson is a woman this season on *Elementary*."

"Hardly classic. Still not romantic."

"Lyssa would never stand for playing my intellectual second, anyway." He turned off campus and headed toward the prosperous new residential section of town where most of the staff and professors lived.

"I hope she's not Moriarty."

"Not quite."

When we arrived, Lyssa called out to us. "We're in here. I'm feeding Mia or I'd get up." Her tone was happy and content, friendly and feminine.

The house smelled like nutmeg and cinnamon. A bowl of candy sat on the console table near the front door. My heart raced as Jason led the way toward the family room. The house was gorgeous and spacious, and decorated like they'd consulted a designer. Everything was tasteful, even their Halloween decorations— Indian corn and collections of expensive glass pumpkins and gourds set around artistically. Nothing that would scare a baby.

We found Lyssa sitting on the sofa feeding Mia a bottle. The look on her face was pure love as she smiled at her baby. Unlike my mom, Lyssa was beautiful in a way that was classy, and, for lack of a better word, wholesome. Which is to say, there was nothing slutty about her. I couldn't imagine her ever flirting or sleeping with one of Mia's boyfriends.

She was dressed in a purple Victorian gown with a high collar, her hair twisted into a chignon.

I turned to Jason. "Irene Adler."

He laughed. "You're quick."

Lyssa looked up at us and smiled.

"Lyssa, this is Ellie."

She smiled at me. "I finally get to meet the famous Ellie. I hear you're good with Mia. Jason sings the praises of your work all the time, too."

I shrugged, surprisingly embarrassed by the praise. "Babies like me."

"Look at her, Lyssa. Does Ellie remind you of anyone? I've spent all semester trying to think who."

A wave of alarm washed over me—what if Lyssa saw what he'd missed?

Lyssa's answering laugh was melodic. "That's been driving him crazy all semester." She studied me and shook her head. "Katniss Everdeen?"

We all laughed. I hoped neither of them noticed how nervous mine was. No one could see the resemblance to my dad, not even his wife? I wasn't sure whether that was insulting or reassuring. But at least the moment of panic had passed.

She smiled at Jason. "Sorry, babe. I can't help you. I don't know. I don't see it."

"And you were my last hope." Jason winked at her. The love between them was obvious and adorable in a way that almost broke my heart.

This would never be my life.

Jason gave me the tour, showing me where everything was. Answering the door for trick-or-treaters slowed him down. "The bulk of the little trick-or-treaters will be over by eight thirty. Which means it will be the high school and college kids after that. Turn off the porch light then, or before if you like, I don't expect you to answer the door. Just ignore anyone who comes after."

When Mia finished her bottle, Lyssa handed her to Jason and gave me the instructions again, making sure I had their numbers and showing me the babysitter's guidebook they'd made that had all the pertinent information. "There are donuts and munchies on the counter for you. The fridge is stocked with pop and cider. Feel free to use the coffee machine. Mia should settle down for the night about nine thirty."

"Don't worry about us, we'll be fine."

Lyssa finally put her coat on and kissed Mia. Jason grabbed his props. I carried Mia and walked them to the door.

"We'll be fine. I have lots of experience with babies." They finally left just after seven thirty. I watched them pull out of the driveway and answered the door to a bunch of trick-or-treaters with Mia in my arms. It was awkward holding the bowl and Mia. She didn't like the position she was in when I leaned over. Her tiny mouth pursed up like she was going to cry. And the kids grabbed handfuls of candy. At this rate, it wasn't going to last long.

I decided that was it for trick-or-treaters. When they left, I shut off the porch light and all the lights at the front of the house and retreated to the family room, where I played with Mia. She had everything a baby could want—plush toys, including a goofy pumpkin and a cute ghost, teething toys, even an iPad of her own loaded with children's books. I read her stories and played the baby-approved videos Lyssa had said she could watch.

I felt peaceful and happy holding her. I realized how Katniss could not think twice about taking Primrose's place in the lottery. I was about to make a similar sacrifice—letting my dad go so Mia could live a happy, uncomplicated life.

Just like Lyssa said, at around nine thirty, Mia got fussy like she was fighting sleep. I took her to her room and put her on her changing table to change her diaper before putting her to bed. A fancy teddy bear sat on the dresser above it. Her room was a study in shades of pink.

I smiled at her and blew a raspberry on her tummy when she arched up, trying to roll over and get away from me changing her diaper.

When she was changed, I grabbed a bottle and sat in the rocking chair as I rocked and gave her the bottle. Seeing the perfect world Mia and Jason lived in, I realized I couldn't destroy it with the knowledge of me. Now that I was trying to move on and get over Logan, it didn't matter if I kept the secret forever any way.

But I wanted to tell Mia the truth just once.

"Want to hear a bedtime story?" I used my soothing, cooing voice that babies liked. As I rocked, her little eyes fluttered open and closed with the back and forth motion, once again like a doll's. "I'm not just *any* babysitter. I'm your big sister." I kissed her forehead.

"Yeah, I know. Pretty incredible, isn't it? Even our daddy doesn't know who I really am. We're actually only half sisters. We have different mommies." My voice broke.

It took me a minute to compose myself. I lowered my voice to a bare whisper as I told her about the ugliness of my life. "You got the better mommy, believe me. Mine blames me for everything that's wrong in her life. She slept with my boyfriend."

I bit my lip and took a deep breath. "You don't know what that means, but it's bad, like the ultimate betrayal. Now I don't talk to her." Realizing I wasn't telling her the most soothing bedtime tale, I hummed a lullaby.

"Better yet," I said, "you get to live with our daddy and grow up with him. I only get to work with him. He thinks I'm just another student. So take advantage of that. Make him do all the dad stuff like teaching you to ride a bike and drive a car and go to your high school daddy/daughter dance." I paused.

"I never had a dad in my life, let alone one who loves me like Jason loves you. Sometimes, the thought makes me a little jealous. But that's just life, you know." I hummed another lullaby for her.

"No one loves me. I don't even have any other brothers or sisters." I hugged her close and blinked back tears. "Don't take your life for granted. Appreciate it and love your family. Not everyone is as lucky and loved as you."

I kissed her once more as she drifted off to sleep and gave a baby snort. I rocked her for another ten minutes, until I was certain she was soundly asleep.

I laid her in her crib. "May the odds be absolutely always in your favor. And when it's time to find your prince, may he be loyal and true."

On Monday, I skipped chem again. Dex clicked me in. I thought he'd protest and tell me to man up. But he agreed to cover for me without argument. Then he encouraged me to hang in there, making me wonder again what the boy genius was up to. And feeling a wash of sentiment that almost made me cry because he was such a good friend and sounded so sympathetic. I almost thought Dex was missing his calling. Maybe he should have considered grief counseling.

I went to work feeling a sense of relief now that I'd finally decided not to come clean with Jason about being my bio dad. One less thing to worry about. Late on Friday, Jason had told me that Logan was going to be out of the office all this week on special assignment. So I swung into the office feeling pretty good.

Until I saw Karen's face. "Jason wants to see you in his office." Her tone was worried and ominous, like I was in big trouble. Which made no sense.

I glanced at the clock. I was five minutes early. I frowned and was starting to slide my coat off when Jason stepped out. "Ellie, I need to see you. *Now.*"

I slid my coat back over my shoulders and grabbed my backpack as my heart raced. As I walked across the office, I felt like I was taking the walk of shame.

"Close the door." His voice was hard.

I stared at him from just inside the door, refusing to sit and be intimidated. I'd had enough confrontations over the years with Mom's men to know never to put myself in the weak position. I waited for him to speak.

"Ellie, we have a problem." He took a deep breath, looking uncomfortable. "Maybe I should say, *you* have a problem. I'm sympathetic. I'm willing to get you help—"

I frowned. "Get me *help*? *What* are you talking about?"

"Your obsession with Mia and thinking you're her sister—"

"What?" I felt the blood rush to my face and flame, followed by a current of rage both startling and scary in its intensity. Suddenly I knew how Doug felt when he smashed Austin's face.

"Don't deny it. We have a nanny cam. Maybe I should have told you, but I thought you'd assume. Everyone has one." He paused. "I caught it on film—"

"You filmed me? You spied on me? You asshole!"

He looked startled by my outburst. But what did he expect? "Calm down, Ellie. Let's not let this get ugly—"

"Too late." Seriously, I had to fight to keep from throwing something at him. It was a good thing there was nothing handy. I took a deep breath. "I hate to tell you this, Sherlock, but you should have left well enough alone. I was going to be altruistic and keep my secret so I wouldn't mess up your *perfect* life." I whipped my phone out of my pocket and brought up the picture of me as a baby.

"You've been wondering all semester who I remind you of—how come you've never realized I remind you of *you*?" I whipped the phone around so he could see the picture of me.

"Congratulations! It's a girl. Nineteen years ago. Whip out the cigars, daddy. You're my father."

He grabbed the phone and stared at the picture of me. "Why do you have a picture of Mia—"

He cut himself off and went pale as he realized Mia didn't have an outfit like the baby in the picture was wearing. And the room in the background wasn't familiar to him. His mouth fell open. His eyes narrowed. "Who?"

"It's been nearly twenty years, but Mom will be really pissed if she ever finds out you don't remember the time you spent with her. Or were you such a player you honestly have no idea who my mother is? Does the name Melissa Ann Sawyer mean anything to you?"

He slumped and leaned back against his desk, going so pale he was deathly white. "No. It can't be. I don't believe you. It was just once—"

"Hate to tell you, but once is all it takes." I slipped my backpack off my shoulder, set it on the floor and whipped out that DNA test kit of mine. "I kind of expected that would be your response. Mom has terrible taste in men. They always deny accountability. Why should you be any different?"

He jumped when I stormed over and slapped the kit on the desk next to him. "Want to prove it one way or the other?"

Jason froze, staring at the kit.

"It's your call," I said. "But if you refuse, I'll contact my lawyer and sue you for college expenses. The judge will make you prove paternity." I was bluffing, probably. But I was so angry and hurt that maybe I would.

I ripped the brown paper off the kit and tore open the box, pulling out the sealed swabs and envelopes for the child and alleged father. "Two days plus mailing time is all it takes. The results are posted confidentially online."

His Adam's apple bobbed. He stared at it like it was a coiled snake. "Where did you get that?"

"Does it matter? You can buy them just about any-where—Walmart, Walgreens. Check the freshness date if you're worried." I held the box and one of the swabs out to him.

He grabbed the box, read the directions, and tore open the swab's wrapper. "This stays between us."

I nodded. "I was just about to make the same demand. No one else knows, not even Lyssa. Not Logan."

He nodded. "Agreed. Ready?"

We held our swabs like a pair of duelers, eying each other with about as much trust. Together we ran the cotton swabs against the insides of our cheeks and over our gums. We each watched the other as we put the swabs in the appropriate envelopes, filled them out, and stuck them in the large envelope.

He stared at the envelope on the desk and ran his hand through his hair until it stood up on end at odd angles. "How *is* Melissa?" His voice was soft, nearly a whisper.

I didn't like his concerned tone, like he was genuinely curious and maybe had cared about her at one point. Maybe still did. It frightened me. "I don't know."

He stared at me.

"If you really watched that nanny cam video, you know what she did to me and that we don't talk."

He shifted like he was uncomfortable. "The audio wasn't that good, Ellie. There was a point when you were whispering. I didn't catch everything."

I had to disabuse him of any sentimental notion he might have harbored about my mother. "She slept with my boyfriend."

His eyes went wide. He gave me a pitying look. "I'm sorry."

I couldn't tell whether this was the kind of thing he expected of the Melissa he'd known or not. I lifted my chin. I wasn't a pity case. "If you mean how has she been in general these last twenty years?" I shrugged. "She's in the middle of her third divorce."

I narrowed my eyes at him. I could see the curiosity still shining in his. "We made a deal—no one knows. That means you promise not to contact my mom. She doesn't know you're here. If she finds out, she'll raise hell and make both our lives miserable. Got it?"

He nodded.

"One more thing—I need this job." I pointed between him and me. "This thing between us is personal and has nothing to do with my job performance. I don't appreciate being called on the carpet at the job when my record is spotless. That ends here."

He looked sheepish. He should have. He'd overstepped professional bounds and abused his position of power. I think he got my implied threat, too.

"You're right. I'm sorry about that." He stared at the envelope. "What do we do now?"

"We walk it to the post office together and mail it. Then we go back to work and wait."

He grabbed his coat from the rack in the corner. "Let's go."

It was almost impossible to concentrate for the rest of my shift. I had to keep ignoring Karen's questioning looks. Jason ostensibly left for a meeting, but I thought it was cover. I was sure he needed time alone to think. Accusing me of having some sick obsession complex with Mia was probably an intellectual alibi. When confronted with the truth, he couldn't escape it.

I had a moment of panic—what if I was wrong? What if Mom was wrong again and Jason wasn't my dad? It passed. We were going to find out. But deep down I knew.

On the way back to my room I ran through the math. It would take one to three days for the test kit to reach the lab. Then twenty-four to forty-eight hours for the results. That put getting the results back at Thursday at the earliest, but more likely Friday or Monday. The thought made my pulse race and my stomach knot. One way or another, my world was about to change.

The week slunk on at a crawl. Logan and Jason were working on a special, top-secret project together that kept them out of the office. Jason was avoiding me now, too.

The week was annoying and sad in other ways, too. Everyone had a dad who was coming for the weekend and making plans. Even the dorm had several dad/daughter functions planned. Posters advertising campus Dad's Weekend events hung everywhere and reminder notices popped up on my university email account every morning. I got real sick real fast of answering questions about what I was doing with my dad and the looks of pity I received when I said all I had was a single mother.

Bre talked non-stop about her daddy. She was daddy's little girl and had all kinds of fun things planned to do with him and Dan's dad. Too much and too many girlie things, in my opinion. She was so nervous and excited about meeting Dan's dad and his dad meeting hers she was hard to live with. I avoided her whenever possible.

Taylor and Nic were a bit mellower, but just as excited in their own way. All of them invited me to tag along with them, but I thanked them, reminding them I was Logan's fake girlfriend for the weekend—though I was pretty sure that was off, even if Logan had not officially said so. But it made for a good cover so they wouldn't pity me so much and worry about me being alone.

On Friday, I went back to chem class. Waiting for the DNA test results was driving me crazy and making my stomach burn with each passing hour. How many times a day can you check your email? Every time a new message pinged on my phone my heart stopped.

Dex, who'd been so understanding on Monday and Wednesday, insisted with startling vehemence I return on Friday. Even though I argued with him, insisting I needed the time to study for a BA 315 quiz.

"You fucking well better come or I'll never forgive you," he said. "Man up. You have to move on, Ellie."

My heart hammered so loudly as I made my way down the auditorium steps to where Dex was saving my usual seat that I swore the entire class could hear it.

"Good to have you back, Ellie. I was afraid you wouldn't show." Dex handed me a cup of coffee.

As I took it, I forced a shaky smile. "What did I do to deserve this?"

"It takes a brave woman to face her fears. I don't think you'll need that to stay awake today, but just in case." He winked.

What did he know? He was being totally cryptic and seemingly unconcerned that we'd be discovered as the perps in the great projector prank. A week had passed without suspicion. I wondered how long it would take me to calm down. I was under way too much stress. The news had been all over social media that the cops had no suspects and other, more important cases to solve. Halloween had been a banner night for DUIs, minors in possession, drug busts, assaults, and vandalism. In retrospect, pulling the prank just before Halloween had been another of Dex's brilliant strokes, one that I hadn't realized before.

The bell rang. Dr. Rogers walked to the podium.

"Don't look away," Dex whispered to me. "You have to see this. It's the best part of class."

She stared at the projector, obviously nervous, flipped the switch on and jumped back before glaring at us, daring us to laugh.

The class was pin-drop silent. Dex leaned into me and whispered again. "If anyone laughs, she goes on a tirade. It's kind of fun to watch. I have it all on film. But last time she threatened to dock the grade of anyone she caught. *Killjoy*."

I hated her on sight. Really hated her, practically shivering with revulsion. How could anyone *sleep* with her? How could anyone ever touch her cold flesh and kiss her tight-lipped, pinched mouth?

My mouth went dry as I opened my notebook and poised my pencil to take notes. I braced myself, trying to steel myself against the sound of her grating voice, trying not to picture it going silky as she cooed sweet nothings in Logan's ear. Trying to shut all the unbidden images of her touching him from my mind. I felt sick, like I was going to throw up.

This was a bad idea, a very bad idea. I couldn't sit here in her class. I was crazy to think I could. A tidal wave of panic crashed over me. It was too late to drop chem. But there was no way I could finish the semester. I could stop going, take my F, and retake the class next semester, but what would I gain? She was the only prof who ever taught it.

I could barely breathe. My college career was ruined. I had to get out of the class before I passed out or threw up. I grabbed my coffee, notebook, and backpack.

Dex caught my arm and gave it a reassuring squeeze. "Hang in, Ellie." His eyes were full of compassion. "Just a little longer—"

A commotion at the back entrance of the auditorium caught our attention. I turned to look. Two uniformed police officers and another man I assumed was a detective walked down the aisle toward us.

My heart stopped. We were in deep trouble now. They were going to arrest Dex and me, embarrass and humiliate us before our peers and that bitch Dr. Rogers. I could just picture her sick, satisfied smile. *Students really are beneath me.*

My hands trembled so badly I had to set my coffee down and clutch the pop-up desk.

Dex put his hand over my white knuckles. "Breathe," he whispered, his voice reassuring and calm as the cops walked passed us all the way to the podium. "This is going to be legendary."

I collapsed with relief and put my head on my desk.

"Stop that," Dex whispered in a teasing tone. "You look guilty." He laughed.

What was so funny? What did he have to be excited and happy about? There was no doubt he was.

"I don't look guilty. I look sleepy. Stupid nine o'clock classes."

"Dr. Rhonda Rogers?"

Her mic picked up the detective's question.

I popped my head up. What was going on?

"I'm Detective Wright." He flashed his badge. "We'd like a word."

She stared at him and his fellow cops with ice in her eyes. "I'm in the middle of class." She pointed her dry-erase pen at them and then at the door as if she had complete authority to order them out of her classroom like misbehaving students.

"I'd rather do this in private," Detective Wright said.

"Really?" She flung the word like an insult. "Then you can wait for office hours."

Detective Wright didn't flinch. "I think you know why I'm here. The jig is up. Come peacefully. You don't want to make a scene in front of your class." He stared at her.

She glared back at him and bolted for the door. One of the other two cops grabbed and restrained her as she kicked and screamed obscenities.

Detective Wright whipped out a pair of handcuffs and cuffed her. "You have the right to remain silent..."

The crowd gasped as he recited the Miranda warning and it began to sink in that they were arresting her.

I turned to Dex with my eyes wide.

He was smiling.

"You knew about this!" I whispered to him.

"Shhhhh. You don't want to miss a minute of this show."

"You can't do this!" Her voice was so shrill it would have hurt a dog's ears, her face red and contorted with rage. She turned and looked at the class, shrieking more obscenities. If looks could kill...

"I'll get whoever did this! You can't hold me—"

One of the cops disconnected her mic, cutting off the rest of her tirade. It squealed with feedback, as if it, too, was angry and offended.

The class was stunned silent as they dragged her off the stage.

The detective grabbed the mic. "Class dismissed."

The auditorium erupted in applause as Detective Wright followed the other two cops and Dr. Rogers out of the room through the instructor's entrance.

Dex grabbed his backpack. "And that's how you take down an evil professor." He was beaming. "Perfect timing."

You'd think with his face lit up like that he would have looked out of place. But everyone was jubilant and laughing, talking and speculating.

"Are you going to explain?" I slung my backpack over one shoulder.

"Not here. Let me buy you a cup of coffee."

I held my cup up. "You already have."

"Let me buy you a fresh one."

We filed out of the auditorium into the cold sunshine of a November morning. Frost covered the ground and our breath puffed around us.

"I thought you had class?" I said.

"Screw class. We need to talk."

He was so full of excitement and energy, I had to run to keep up with him.

He pointed at me. "Text Logan. He'll want to hear the news. From you especially."

I hesitated, confused, my heart pounding. "We're not talking. And I don't even know what's going on. How does this affect Logan?"

"Be the bigger person, Ellie. Put the bullshit behind you and reach out first. You'll be glad you did. Tell him Dr. Rogers has been arrested. He'll put two and two together. It affects him, trust me."

I pulled out my phone and texted Logan like Dex commanded. Sometimes it was easier not to fight Dex. Especially when he made a good point about being the bigger person. Maybe this would clarify where our weekend plans stood.

"I want you to meet my dad, too. He's eager to meet you."

I looked up from my phone. "Your dad's here already?"

Dex shrugged and grinned at me again. "Who do you think orchestrated this bust? I didn't have the resources to do it on my own."

"What did you tell him about me?"

"Only the good stuff."

"Like what?" I was really curious. I hadn't pictured Dex bringing me up to his dad ever.

"Like how you played lookout for us."

"You told him about the prank?" I couldn't keep the shock out of my voice.

"I had to." He led the way to the busy SUB cafeteria, which was already buzzing with the news. "Come on. Let's grab a table. Dad said he'd meet us here."

We found one in the corner in the middle of the buzz, but away from prying ears.

I set my coffee on the table and dumped my backpack in the empty chair next to me. "Okay, spill it before I die of curiosity. What's going on?"

He smiled. "You should have seen your face when the cops walked in—epic!"

"Shut up!" I leaned in and whispered to him. "I thought they were coming for us."

He laughed. "I know."

"Okay, what happened in chem? Why did the cops cuff Rogers?" Then I grinned. "That's fun to say."

"Oh, yeah." He nodded and leaned across the table. "You just saw Dr. Rogers being arrested on charges of manufacturing and selling illegal date-rape drugs."

I gasped. "Date-rape drugs? No way."

He nodded and whispered. "The night we went on our midnight excursion?"

"Yeah?"

"I went into her lab and office. I thought I'd just pull a last-minute prank. I had a few things in my backpack, some toilet paper and shit. That's when I found her equipment."

My eyes went wide as I realized why Dex had acted strange when he came out of the chem building that night.

My phone rang with the distinctive tone I'd set for Logan. I glanced at Dex and frowned. My hands shook as I picked the phone up. "A text from Logan."

Great news. With luck, you'll get an A now, haha. Hey, sorry about being an ass. You're right—I had no right to talk to you like that. You still owe me ;-) See you at seven? Can't wait for you to meet Dad.

"What does he say?"

"He thinks we're still on for the weekend." I couldn't keep the wonder out of my voice. I couldn't decide if Logan was being contrite, forgiving, or incredibly arrogant.

Dex grinned, looking smug. "Told you you'd be glad." He hesitated when he saw my expression. "You are going to do it?"

"I—"

"You *are* going to do it." His tone changed from question to command.

Finally, I nodded and texted Logan back. *Forgiven. See you at seven. Nervous about meeting your dad. You might have to hold my hand, haha.*

The phone buzzed right back. *Anytime.*

Dex watched me. "Let me see exactly what he said."

I flipped the phone around for Dex to read.

Dex's expression changed from smug to serious and sympathetic. "He's taking it well."

I frowned. "What aren't you telling me?"

"I found something else, Ellie." He took a deep breath. "There's really no way to say this. Dr. Rogers wasn't just making and selling GHB. She was using it on male students she thought were hot. I found pictures on her computer and in her desk. Of college guys. *Naked* college guys."

As the implication sank in, I felt lightheaded.

Dex took my hand again. "Hang in there. Take slow, even breaths."

I tried to focus on him.

"Along with the drug charges, she was arrested on over a dozen counts of drug-facilitated sexual assault."

Something about Dex's sympathetic tone and the way he was looking at me tipped me off.

The way Dr. Rogers ogled Logan when he came to fix the projector. His stiff manner. How he didn't look at her.

"Oh my God. Oh my God, Dex."

He squeezed my hand. "I know."

"Logan?" His name came out as almost just a breath. My eyes filled with tears. I felt guilty for pushing Logan. I wanted to hold him and tell him it was all right. I was overwhelmed with guilt for thinking he would ever willingly touch Dr. Rogers.

Dex nodded, confirming my fear. "I didn't see his picture. But given the evidence, I assume so." He squeezed my hand again. "The university IT department, including Logan and your boss Jason, has been helping with the investigation."

"Can guys..." I trailed off, unable to get the words out and trying not to picture it.

"Yes, Ellie. They can. Did you just collect the beer magnet and the condom and not pay attention during those stupid mandatory campus Sex, Booze, and Reality Checks? Sexual assault is any non-consensual sexual contact. Or any contact where drugs or alcohol impair judgment or consent."

"But the drugs don't..." I raised my eyebrows questioningly.

"Guys can still perform."

"I have to see him—"

Dex shook his head and kept his grip on my hand. "Give him time, Ellie. Being sexually assaulted isn't any easier for guys than girls. There's the sense of shame and guilt, the emasculation.

"He doesn't know you know. He doesn't even know what you originally suspected him of. Let him tell you when and if he's ready." Dex suddenly grinned and his tone became teasing. "Bet you're glad now you listened to me when I told you not to confront him."

Dex was such a back-patter and full of self-congratulations. It would have been annoying if he hadn't been absolutely right and such a good friend. He had warned me off from blowing things with Logan *permanently*.

"You're right. I absolutely do. Thank you."

For the first time ever, he almost looked embarrassed. "Let Logan tell you about it in his own time. *If* he ever wants to tell you. The cops seized Dr. Rogers' computers and drug paraphernalia. That bitch is going away for a long time."

Dex looked over my shoulder, recognized someone, smiled, and waved at a person behind me. "Dad! Over here."

I turned to look as Dex popped out of his seat. A wiry, middle-aged man with stylish glasses and a thin rim of graying hair approached, hugged Dex, and slapped him on the back. Like father like son, I thought. Dex was simply a younger version of his dad. Seeing them together was actually heartwarming and adorable.

Dex turned to me. "Dad, this is my best friend Ellie."

Best friend? Okay, those stupid tears threatened to come back.

"Ah, the partner in crime." His dad took my hand and shook it vigorously. "Dex has told me all about you and your *baking*." He winked conspiratorially. "Don't worry, Ellie. Our cooperation guarantees your immunity and anonymity. No repercussions. Ever. And sadly, no public glory." He laughed.

"Thank you for your part." I choked up.

He turned to Dex. "You sure know how to pick gorgeous study partners. I trained you well."

"*Dad.*"

Dex was actually blushing.

CHAPTER SEVENTEEN

I went back to my dorm room, stunned by the events of the day and jumpy because those damned paternity results could come back at any minute. At the same time, I wanted to run to Logan and just hold him in my arms, somehow communicate that I loved him no matter what before my mysterious past blew us apart.

At this point I didn't know whether I'd be more relieved if Jason was my father or not. If he wasn't, we could all go on as if nothing had happened and Logan would never have to know about this episode. But I'd be fatherless and sisterless again and clueless as to whom my real dad could possibly be. Maybe in the end that was less complicated.

Logan's aversion to Chem 202 made perfect sense now and so did his reasons for not talking or thinking about it. And why he thought that after the semester was over we might have a chance. Once I was out of the evil bitch's class, we could put it behind us.

I heard male dad-type voices in the hall outside my room. More and more dads were arriving every minute. Logan's dad would be here soon. As Logan's fake girl-friend, it was my job to impress him. Logan had said my natural self would be enough. I had my doubts.

I looked in the mirror and studied myself. The re-flection looking back at me was fresh-faced and natu-ral, but not stellar. Not a gorgeous, head-turning beauty like my mother. And then there was that nasty scar on my cheek. I tried to console myself—we're all scarred in some way. I would do what I always did—hide it.

I didn't know Logan's dad at all, and when I thought about him, I got angry at him for favoring Logan's brother Caleb the baseball star. But I was damn well going to impress him for Logan's sake. For all her hor-rendous faults, my mom knew how to charm men. She'd tried to teach me her tricks and I'd rebelled. That didn't mean I hadn't learned a few of them in spite of myself.

I glanced at the clock. I had nearly the full day to turn myself into something presentable. I went to my closet and looked past the rows of hoodies, jeans, and tennis shoes to my skirts and dresses. I found my brand new short black and white polka dot dress with the short flouncy skirt, spaghetti straps, and heart-shaped neckline that showed off my cleavage. Then I dug past my collection of tennis shoes for my heels and found the perfect pair of three-inch black heels with straps that tied up my legs. The combination of the dress and heels made my legs look long and sexy.

I looked at my ragged, unpolished nails. My toenails were in worse shape. I needed a mani and a pedi. And a trim. I hadn't had a haircut since before school started. I should have thought of all this earlier, but I'd been in the depths of depression, assuming the weekend was off. But now making a good first impression mattered. I grabbed my cell and started calling salons.

Six hours later, I studied myself in the mirror again. If there was one thing my mother taught me, it was that long hair turns men on. Most women get ready for a date by pinning it up. I listened to her advice and styled my hair in loose, flowing waves.

My nails were done and perfect. I was wearing my sexiest perfume and I'd applied my makeup using every technique I'd watched dear old mom use over the years. My scar was well concealed. I still wasn't a supermodel by any means, but at a quick glance I thought I could turn a head or two.

I waited nervously for Logan's text that they were on their way. He hadn't specified where we were going to dinner, except a casual mention that his dad had made reservations at his favorite restaurant, someplace expensive.

When my phone finally played Logan's ringtone, I jumped.

On our way.

I grabbed my cute black evening purse and my dressy black wool coat with the flared skirt and the tie around the waist. When Nic and Taylor saw it they were envious, calling it my Kate Middleton coat.

I waited for Logan and his dad in the lobby, heart racing and time going by at a crawl. Dad after dad and person after person came in before Logan finally appeared with the older man from the picture in his room with him. I had eyes only for Logan. I, the fake girlfriend, was throwing everything I had into this. I needed him to know I wasn't holding a grudge. I'd really forgiven him.

"Logan!" I ran to him, threw my arms around his neck, and kissed him passionately. Showily. Gave him a real movie kiss, the kind that makes the audience sigh, then smiled up at him and pushed a lock of hair away from his face.

"Wow, El, you look *gorgeous.*" With my lipstick on his lips and his hands on my waist possessively, he looked hot. And relieved. Happy.

I almost told him not to sound so surprised, but the way he said "gorgeous" thrilled me. With his hands on my waist and the way he was smiling at me, the world collapsed to just the two of us.

I wiped my lipstick off his lips gently with my fingertips. "Thanks." I grinned at him. "Pink's not your color."

"She certainly is exuberant."

Logan turned to his dad. "Dad, this is Ellie Martin, the girl I've been telling you about."

Even with the stress of introducing me to his dad, Logan seemed more relaxed than I'd seen him in months.

I smiled at his dad and extended my hand. "Nice to meet you, Mr. Walker. I've heard so much about you." Not much of it good, I could have added.

Rather than shaking, he took my hand and clasped it between his, looking me in the eye. "Please, call me Harlan." He had a commanding voice, a penetrating gaze, and a force of personality that might have been charisma if he chose to turn on the charm.

What he was looking for in me, fault? Did he think I was good enough for his son, or had he made a snap decision that his son had made another dumb mistake? Like choosing to trust a perverted cougar of a professor.

I made up my mind. I had nothing to lose by defending Logan and raising his estimation in his father's eyes. If that were even possible. I didn't care. At the first opportunity, I was giving it my best shot. This evening together was a fantasy that could all be blown apart at any minute. I was determined to throw my all at it. Make it another perfect memory to hold on to if I had to.

His father released my hand. I grabbed Logan's, threading my fingers through his and squeezing.

"We better get going," Harlan said. "We're parked in the loading zone."

I wanted to sit in the backseat and snuggle with Logan. Harlan insisted I sit in the front seat and make small talk with him. "Logan tells me you don't have a father."

That was direct. I glanced over my shoulder at Logan in the backseat for help. Mouthing "What have you told him?" He shrugged and grinned.

I turned around. "Yes, that's right. I was raised by a single mom."

"That's admirable. She must be a strong woman."

I was almost positive he was baiting me. I shrugged it off and went for broke. Logan had said not to hide who I was. "Not really. She had help from time to time. I've had three stepfathers." I laughed. What else could I do, really?

Harlan was looking at the road, maneuvering his way through throngs of dads and kids and traffic. I thought he set his jaw.

"Is that right? Must have been tough on you?"

"I wouldn't choose it for someone else, but you learn to live with what you're dealt. What else can you do?"

He glanced at me, looking baffled, like it wasn't the answer he'd expected. But I think I went up a notch in his estimation. "You've never met your dad?"

I bit my lip. This was exactly the question I had been afraid would come up. I was forced to either lie or hedge. Every lie I told felt like another wedge between Logan and me. I hedged. "Not to my knowledge." I laughed again.

"Not to your knowledge?" It was clear Harlan didn't intend to be distracted or let anything slip by.

I got the feeling he enjoyed having the upper hand in every situation. Putting people on the defensive was part of his strategy.

I smiled in the way my mom did when she was being charming and tried to imitate her tinkling laugh and her way of turning things back. "That's exactly right. Mom never told me who he is. I could have met him at any time and never known I was talking to my dad."

"Aren't you curious about him?"

"Curiosity wouldn't do me any good. Mom won't tell. But judging from Mom's taste in men, I have a pretty good idea of what he's like. And I'm not sure I want to meet him." I laughed like it was a joke and changed the subject. "How was your drive over the Cascades? They can be treacherous this time of year."

Harlan had chosen the best restaurant in town, which didn't mean it was five-star by Zagat standards, but it was the best the small town had to offer. The parking lot was busy. We had to cruise for a spot. Eventually Harlan found one on the street. Logan took my hand. We walked in the cold, our breath white and wispy against the clear night sky as we walked the half-block to Ricco's.

Although Ricco's was packed, we got right in and were seated at a prime table by a window. The lights were low. A candle flickered on the table next to a vase full of fresh fall flowers. I sat next to the window and Logan. Logan's dad sat across from us. He ordered a plate of appetizers for the table and a beer each for him and Logan. I ordered water.

"Cheap date." Harlan almost smiled at me.

I couldn't tell if he was insulting me or not.

"Ellie, has Logan told you about his younger brother Caleb? He plays baseball for the Chicago Cubs."

"Yes." I put my hand on Logan's arm and smiled at him. "Logan's really proud of him. He has Caleb's jersey framed and hanging in his room. Very impressive."

Harlan lit up. "Caleb had a hell of a season this year..."

He launched into a one-sided brag-fest about Caleb that lasted through appetizers, the salad course, and a second round of beers, interrupted only once when the waiter took our order.

I didn't know how Logan took it so patiently, nodding and smiling and making the appropriate murmurs of praise, agreement, and near idol worship for the great and mighty Caleb the fave. Harlan's enthusiasm, passion, and blatant preference for Caleb were so obvious I swore the waiter noticed it and shot Logan a sympathetic look.

Given the unfortunate accident that had taken Logan's dreams from him, Harlan's behavior seemed especially insensitive and boorish. With each new boast about Caleb, I felt Logan stiffen and a little bit of the life and fun of the evening leave him. Harlan seemed almost genetically incapable of asking about Logan's life. It was like Logan didn't even exist except to praise his brother.

By the time our entrées arrived, I'd had enough. I let the waiter grate a pile of cheese on my ravioli of autumn squash with balsamic vinegar and broke into the conversation, determined to take it over on my own terms. "Did Logan tell you he saved my life?"

"El—" Logan said, shaking his head subtly.

Harlan frowned. "You did?"

I smiled at Logan and gave his arm a squeeze. "He did. He's just being modest. He saved me from drowning at the cliffs."

Before Harlan could interrupt, I launched into the whole tale, making Logan the hero he was to me. Remembering brought tears to my eyes. The love I felt for him welled up.

"You went cliff diving again." Harlan's voice was hard. "I thought I made myself clear—cliff diving is too dangerous. Especially given your weak shoulder."

Logan stiffened.

A less angry me might have cowered and felt like I'd really stepped in it. But I had nothing to lose, really. I went ballistic. Without thinking, I pounded the table so hard the water glasses bounced and the ice in them tinkled, highlighting my point.

"Are you such an ass that you can't hear what I just said?"

Harlan's eye went wide. It was clear he wasn't used to being contradicted or called out. Or being called an ass.

"Saving my life is a *big* deal! Especially to me. And you just acted as if it doesn't matter at all that I'm alive and well. Because of *your* son.

"You should be bursting with pride. Saving a life is much more important than being able to catch a stupid baseball. But that's all you think about." I spat the words out with every venomous feeling I'd harbored toward Harlan. "It's time you grew up and got past living your own failed athletic aspirations through one son and realize you have two. Being proud of one doesn't mean you can't be proud of the other at the same time." I glared at him.

Next to me, Logan was silent. But his silence couldn't stop me.

"Keep this behavior up and you're going to lose the tenuous, totally not-so-great relationship you have with Logan now. Blatantly preferring one son to another is, like, one of the worst things a parent can do."

I pointed my finger at Harlan, letting all the frustrations of dealing with all of my bad stepdads roll out. "Want to know another great thing your son did?" I took a deep breath and went for broke. "He and Jason, our boss, just helped the police crack the case against my perverted, nasty chemistry professor, Dr. Rhonda Rogers.

"She was making and selling date-rape drugs. Making, selling, and *using* them on male students she had a thing for. Luring them to her place, drugging and photographing them.

"She's sick and awful. And without Logan's help and bravery she'd still be selling drugs, still assaulting students and making it possible for others to, too." My voice broke with emotion. I couldn't look at Logan for fear I'd give away what I knew about him. Instead I stared at Harlan, daring him to come back at me and defend his position.

"Is that true, Logan?" Harlan's voice was soft and stunned. Suddenly I didn't exist.

Logan looked at his dad and nodded.

"All of it?"

Logan nodded again. "Yeah, Dad."

Harlan scooted his chair back so quickly it startled me and made the candle on the table flicker. He came around to Logan's chair, pulled Logan to his feet and into a fierce hug, holding him like a dad does when protecting a small boy. The tears in his eyes were evident even in the dim light.

"I'm sorry, son. I'm sorry I didn't believe in you." His voice was choked up as he kept repeating it. "It's okay now. It's going to be all right." He pulled back and slapped Logan on the shoulders. "You okay?"

Logan nodded.

"I don't say it enough, but I love you, kid." His smile was wobbly.

"Love you too, Dad."

"Your mom will be relieved." He paused. "I can tell her? Or do you want to?"

"Go ahead," Logan said.

Both men nodded and smiled at each other, slapped each other on the back, hugged each other quickly, and returned to their seats.

I was so stunned I couldn't speak. I'd never seen anything like it. I looked from one to the other as they each picked up their forks and resumed their dinner like nothing had happened.

Logan's dad looked at me with new admiration, and a little bit of sheepishness, like possibly he'd let some cat out of the bag that he shouldn't have.

"Thank you, Ellie. It takes a confident woman to do what you did and put me in my place." He smiled at his son again. "You picked a good one this time."

CHAPTER EIGHTEEN

Harlan drove us to Logan's apartment after dinner. He parked and walked us up.

Logan let us in. "Take your coat, Dad?"

Harlan shook his head. "Sorry. Can't stay. Got to get back to the hotel. Work to do." Harlan laughed. "Global business stops for no one and nothing, not even Dad's Weekend. I'll leave you two kids alone. I'm sure you're tired of hanging with your old man by now anyway."

He slapped Logan on the back and gave me a quick, one-armed hug. "Good to meet you, Ellie. Looking forward to seeing you at the tailgate party and game tomorrow. We have damn good seats."

Harlan squeezed Logan's shoulder once more. "'Night." And then he left.

As Logan closed the door behind him, my phone buzzed. My heart pounded as I pulled it out of my purse, shielding it so Logan couldn't see the screen. A text from Jason. I read it, expecting either the best or the worst, and not really knowing what would be best. *The results should be in anytime now. Are you as nervous as I am?*

More, ha ha, I texted back. False alarm. I let out a deep breath.

"El? Who was that? What's up? Hope you're not planning to dash out of here, too?" There was a hint of tease and promise in his voice and an underlying pleading for me not to go.

"What?" I slid the phone back into my purse, trying not to look guilty and wishing my heart would stop racing. "That was nothing. Leave? Not a chance." I unbuttoned my coat and let him help me out of it, watching as he hung it in the closet along with his, liking the sight of our coats hanging side by side. I set my purse on the console table next to Spartacus, who floated in his fishbowl, ignoring us. Logan came to me, pulling me close against his chest, wrapping his arms around me, and leaning his chin on my head. "Thanks for tonight, El."

I wasn't sure what he was saying, or how far the thanks extended, only that it sounded heartfelt. "I'm sorry." I pressed my head against his chest, listening to the strong, steady beat of his heart and wishing it really belonged to me. "I shouldn't have called your dad an ass."

His chest shook with laughter. "Yeah, you're right. 'Ass' was lame. You should have called him something stronger. I wish I'd had the courage to tell him off myself. Shit, El, you saved me."

Praise usually made me uncomfortable. I never knew how to respond to it. Except with Logan. His praise made me glow. I felt that fierce protectiveness toward him that made me unafraid to take any risk to defend him. "Anytime. Besides, I owed you."

He stroked my hair. "You're not getting off that easy. I get to call in the debts. You still owe me one."

I smiled into his shirt and pulled away just enough to look Logan in the eye. "What *happened* at dinner? Are you two good now?" I had my doubts. Life was rarely that simple.

He gave me a lovable half-grin, the one that always melted my heart. "Hardly. That was the understated Walker way of saying we're sorry, bygones, and all that shit.

"We're better. We're good. For now. Be warned— he'll be back on his Caleb kick at the game tomorrow. But he's forgiven me and reminded me I may only be his second favorite son out of two, but he loves me. If the Caleb-fest gets out of hand tomorrow, feel free to slap him down again."

"No way. Not until you teach me some stronger language. I'm not going in armed only with lame insults again."

"I like your language the way it is." He paused and leaned his forehead against mine.

"Yes?"

"How did you know about our investigation?" He paused again like he was collecting his thoughts. "Did Jason tell you?" His brow furrowed and puzzlement and concern sounded in his voice, like he thought Jason had betrayed him.

I rushed to set him straight and clear Jason. "*No.* I heard it...someplace else." I realized too late I'd acted on impulse and not thought things through properly before acting. Of course he would blame Jason.

"Where?" The crease in Logan's forehead deepened. "*No one* else knows, El." He was silent. "Except..."

I didn't waver under his intense stare.

"You weren't involved in sabotaging her projector?"

My heart hammered. I hated lying to him, but I'd promised Dex and the guys. We'd sworn an oath never to squeal on each other. *Ever.*

"Me?" I frowned like I was confused, too, and made a sweet, sexy pout, like how could he accuse me of such a thing?

He looked confused, but backed off and took a deep breath. "Thanks for defending me to my dad." He paused again. "And setting him straight about Dr. Rogers. He believed—"

I gently laid two fingers against his lips, cutting him off. "We swore never to talk about chem. I'm standing by that. You don't have to say *anything*. Ever. I understand."

He kissed my fingers and pulled my hand away from his lips, holding it firmly in his. "But somehow you knew?" His voice was soft.

"I pieced it together."

He dropped my hand and pulled me into him again, pressing me against his chest with his hand cupping my head like he would never let me go, like he was holding me safe against his heart. "You believed in me." His voice broke with emotion. "God, I love you, El."

My heart literally skipped a beat. I was overwhelmed with an emotion so complex it was hard to explain— love, joy, guilt. How could I tell him *Dex* was the one who had believed in him and had stopped me from making a horrible mistake? I couldn't, and maybe it didn't matter. I believed in him now with my whole heart. I loved him. He cut me off before I could tell him.

"She lured me to her house with the excuse she was having trouble with her modem and internet connections. She knew I worked for Jason in the IT department because I'd worked on the equipment in her classroom. Sometimes I had the feeling she had a thing for me and made up reasons to call me to her classroom or lab to fix things. She liked to hang around while I worked and watch. She flirted. I wasn't turned on, but it seemed harmless. I didn't shut her down because I wanted to stay on her good side. Later, I felt guilty about that. Like I'd led her on.

"She hinted that if I helped her out she'd go easy on me on the next exam, maybe even give me bonus points at the end of the semester to raise my grade. Give me the benefit of the higher grade if I was on the edge.

"Like everyone else, I was barely hanging on in her class. Studying my ass off and getting D's. My dad was breathing down my neck, on my case about my grades slipping, my drinking and partying. I was on heavy-duty prescription narcotic painkillers. Coping with my injury and the end of my baseball career by drowning my sorrows and partying until I forgot who I was. Dad was afraid I was going to do something stupid—like overdose or take a lethal combination.

"In retrospect, he was right to be worried. But his fear and concern for me manifested as disapproval and anger. I was on his shit list. So I figured, what could it hurt to play up to Dr. Rogers? Play the game, right? The politics? It's what Dad does in business all the time.

"So what if I fixed her equipment and she looked kindly on me? It was just one of those scratching each other's backs things Dad is always bragging about." His voice was distant and faraway, almost like he was in a trance.

I would have stopped him, but it was clear he needed to talk. He trusted me to listen and I wouldn't violate that.

"When I got to her home, she opened two bottles of beer with her back to me, turned around, and handed me one. She started talking and openly flirting with me.

"She was more obvious than before, ogling me like I was man candy, standing too close to me, finding excuses to touch my shoulder and back. The way she was acting made me uncomfortable, but I thought 'no problem.' I could handle it. She was probably just lonely. She showed me to her home office and pointed me to the modem.

"'Well? Can you fix it? Or is it hopeless?' She laughed and put her hand on my shoulder, leaning in close behind me and pressing against me so her breasts brushed against my back as she whispered in my ear.

"As I tried to sidestep away from her, I started feeling strange. Thickheaded and fuzzy. I turned around so I was facing her.

"'I don't feel well,' I told her. 'I have to go.'

"All I wanted at that moment was to get the fuck out of there. She put her hand on my chest and squeezed my nipple through my shirt. She had an excited look in her eyes. 'I like you, Logan. Don't you like me?' She grabbed my head and kissed me."

He shuddered, like the memory was revolting. I held him tight.

"I don't remember anything after that until I woke up in my own bed the next morning with a pounding headache that made me nauseous. I was hung over. But on just a few sips of beer?

"I felt an overwhelming sense of dread and revulsion. Violation. Images, just snatches, like scenes from a nightmare. The kind where I'm making love with a girl I'm hot for and she suddenly morphs into someone repulsive popped up out of nowhere and made me break into a cold sweat. Dr. Rogers naked. On top of me." He shuddered again and held me ferociously. "I was hoping it was all just a bad dream. While I was on the pain meds I got a lot of them."

He took a minute to compose himself. "I vaguely remember Collin driving me home in my car, but my thoughts were jumbled. Later I learned Zave had dropped him off. Dr. Rogers told them I'd had a bad reaction from mixing beer with painkillers. Shit! I'd only had a few sips. She made it sound like I was out of control again." He took a deep breath. "I threw away the rest of my bottle of painkillers. Went off them cold turkey.

"The next day in chem, a wave of panic washed over me when Dr. Rogers took the podium. I couldn't breathe. My palms sweated. My heart raced so fast I thought I was going to have a heart attack or some shit.

"She stared right at me, smiling, her eyes filled with lust. I grabbed my backpack and crap and stood to leave. She called me out.

"'Mr. Walker, sit down. If you leave my class, I'll fail you. See me in my office after class.'" His heart was racing again.

"Logan, you don't have to—"

"It's all right. It feels good to tell you." He stroked my hair. "When I went to her office, Dr. Rogers came on to me, telling me how good I was in bed and how hot she was for me. I was disgusted. She was revolting. I told her I'd never touched her and hell would freeze over before I ever would.

"With a triumphant look, she dragged me to her desk and showed me her computer with her private picture of me naked in her bed.

"'See,' she said. 'You're hot for me.'" His voice quaked with rage. "I wanted to grab that damn thing and throw it out the window along with her.

"She must have seen how I felt, but she ignored it. She touched my arm and said we could have more good times together. The more I did for her, the more she would do for me. She could get me drugs that would take away my pain. Give me an A in her class. Write me letters of recommendation for internships. Whatever I wanted.

"I told her she was talking shit and that I'd never touch her again. Wouldn't have in the first place if she hadn't drugged me.

"Her face went red and mottled with rage. She hissed at me, saying I'd regret spurning her and if I ever talked, she'd claim *I* had raped *her*. And she had proof."

I gasped.

He kissed the top of my head like I was the one who needed comforting. "I went to my dad. He accused me of being a dumbass for going over there in the first place, for getting drunk and sleeping with a prof. For being stupid enough to drink while I was taking narcotic painkillers. He made me talk to our family lawyer to see what we had to do to cover our asses.

"Our lawyer was sympathetic, but basically said I was screwed. So I kept my mouth shut." He exhaled loudly. "I had no idea about the other shit—that she was making date-rape drugs and had done this to other guys. I thought it was just me. I was embarrassed. If I'd known..." He took another deep breath.

I stroked his back. "It's all right. I *know* you would have." I hesitated. "The way she looked at you when you came to fix her projector after that prank..." I shuddered. "Did she ever come on to you again?"

He nodded. "A couple of times. She begged me to come over. Tried to lure me to her office. Caught me alone once in the lab when I was there working on some equipment. She said she couldn't stop thinking about me. Was obsessed with me. That we were so good together.

"I told her to go to hell and threatened to have our lawyer issue a restraining order if she didn't leave me alone. She backed off after that.

"I went to Jason and told him the story. He made sure I was never assigned any jobs for her. Until that last one, the prank. But I said that was okay. I could handle it. What could she do in front of hundreds of students?

"We've been working to catch her ever since the night I went to her house, unsuccessfully. Until the cops came to us with their suspicions."

He paused and sighed. "I still can't decide if she gave me that damn A to spite me and remind me of her, or to bribe me back, or pay me off." He shook his head. "Kels was the only one who understood. She was a victim of drug-assisted sexual assault, too. Her freshman year. That's why we're close. We understand each other."

He tipped my chin up. "But there's nothing between us now other than friendship. I've never felt anything for her like I feel for you."

I didn't like the way he said "now," as if there had been something more once. And I thought he was wrong about Kelsie—she still felt something for him, even if he didn't reciprocate. "I love you, Logan."

His eyes lit up. As he angled his mouth toward mine, the front door flew open and Collin stumbled in.

"Oops!" Collin laughed. "Looks like I'm interrupting something."

Logan rolled his eyes. "What are you doing back so early? Where's your dad?"

"At his hotel. Work to do."

"Sounds familiar." Logan grinned at me, shrugging off the bad memories and putting on his easygoing persona for Collin. "He and my dad probably have a poker game going." Logan took my hand and pulled me toward his bedroom. I grabbed my purse on the way.

"Where are you two going? Aren't you going to keep me company?"

"Good night, Collin." Logan closed the door after him and pulled me down onto his bed next to him.

I leaned over, set my purse on the nightstand beside the bed, and pulled him on top of me between my knees as the skirt of my dress rode up, exposing my black lace panties. I wanted to feel his desire and hardness against me. I wanted him to know I loved him and understood. As he perched over me, I wrapped my arms around his neck and smiled at him. "I'm glad you told me."

"Yeah?"

"Yeah." I had to reassure him that he didn't look weak or guilty or naïve to me. That I wasn't judging him. I understood being a victim.

"You're beautiful, El, all the time." His voice was low and sweet with emotion. "But tonight, you're stunning."

"It's the makeup." I touched my cheek, conscious of my scar.

He kissed it with a brush of his lips so soft and tender it brought tears to my eyes. "I never notice the scar, El. To me, it's a beauty mark, a part of you." He brushed the hair away from my face and neck and whispered in my ear. "I like the way you look when you're fierce and worked up and defending me. You're like a she-devil. It's sexy."

As he kissed my neck, my entire body tingled with pleasure, radiating out from the warmth of his mouth on my skin to the tips of my fingers and my toes, lingering between my legs. I wanted him with an ache that was simply gorgeous and an intensity I'd never thought possible. I moved his hand to my breast and sighed as he gently cupped it.

Letting Logan close to me, letting him touch me, frightened me as much as it excited me, but I was powerless to stop the longing for him. I was losing my heart to him so deeply and completely, he had the power to crush me. I'd sworn never to give anyone the strength to do that again, but somehow Logan had penetrated my defenses. It was reckless, a simply reckless longing.

His lips traveled down the side of my neck and over my shoulders to the hollow of my neck. I circled my arms around him, running my hands over the taut muscles of his back, memorizing the feel of him, clutching handfuls of his shirt, wishing I could hold him forever. He licked, making slow, lazy circles with his tongue in the hollow of my throat.

"Your pulse is racing," he whispered.

I wrapped my legs around him, pulling him so tightly against me we were almost one. I pressed my hand to his heart. "So is yours." I curved my neck to meet his lips and pulled his shirt loose from his jeans.

As I ran my hands up his back, skimming my fingers lightly over his skin, he shivered beneath my touch. But nothing distracted him as he trailed hot, beautiful kisses up my throat, licking while I trembled with pleasure until he found my mouth.

I opened it to him, wanting the heat of his lips on mine, relishing the intimacy. He wouldn't be rushed, gently sucking my lower lip, tracing the outline of my mouth with his tongue until I shivered and almost begged for more.

I ran my hands through his hair, knowing I was running down a path that could lead to heartache. And not caring. He covered my mouth with his, kissing me urgently, passionately, perfectly. His tongue danced with mine and I was his, wrapped up in him, caught up in him. Nothing else existed except for him and the tight, building ache for him.

I sighed, wanting more. Then he broke away, trailing kisses down my body until he slid the spaghetti straps off my shoulders and kissed the tops of my gently heaving breasts.

I unbuttoned the buttons of his shirt until it fell open around me and ran my hands along the hard planes of his chest until his nipples budded. I squeezed them while his hand slipped beneath my dress and pushup bra.

I felt his hard-on through his jeans and reached for his fly while my heart pounded and I wondered what I was doing. I wanted him, but I was afraid of the risk of making love. Afraid of making a mistake like me.

He stared at me with heart-wrenching honesty and love in his eyes. "Just touching this time, El. No pressure." He pulled me into a sitting position and reached for the back zipper of my dress and unzipped it.

I held my arms up as he pulled it off over my head, dropped it over the edge of the bed, and unfastened the back hook of my bra. I clutched my bra to me. "Take off your shirt."

"Shy?"

"Fair's fair."

He grinned and shrugged his shirt off, letting it fall over the side of the bed.

I dropped my hands from where they cupped my bra against my breasts and let him pull the bra away. His eyes went wide when he saw my budded breasts, excited because of him. "You're so beautiful."

I arched back so they pointed directly at him. As he leaned forward to suck them I pointed at his pants. "Take them off."

"Bossy."

"I want to feel you, too."

He slid his jeans off and tossed them over the edge with the rest of our clothes. We stared at each other. And then he leaned over and sucked my breasts, easing me back on the bed. The tightness between my legs built until I thought I couldn't stand it.

Finally, he slid one hand beneath the lace of my thong panties and slowly began stroking and probing me. He worked magic with his fingers, the same way he did with my heart. I blossomed for him.

I pulled his hard-on out of his briefs, turned on by the long, pulsing firmness of it, and began stroking him, too. As waves of pleasure built, I gasped. The sense of oneness with him grew until I was almost overcome with the power of it.

"Logan." I whispered his name and stroked him harder.

And then, just when I felt like I couldn't stand the aching need, wave after wave of pleasure crashed over me. I lost my grip on Logan, caught up in my own passion.

Just as I was about to apologize for being an insensitive, selfish lover, he stiffened and his warm spray covered my abdomen.

"I'm sorry, El. I'll get a towel."

I smiled at him and held onto him. "You have absolutely nothing to be sorry about. This is beautiful." I was still breathless as I leaned back against the pillows that smelled like him and sighed with happiness. I cuddled into him. We lay there, wrapped in each other's arms. I thought this was perfection, that nothing could be better.

He wiped my stomach with the edge of the sheet and kissed my bellybutton. "This is beautiful, too. If you hadn't gotten it, we never would have met. Have I ever told you that girls with bellybutton rings are hot?"

"Once or twice." I smiled at him.

We lay sleepily intertwined for a long, peaceful time. Finally, Logan slid out to use the bathroom. "Be right back."

I missed his warmth the minute he left the bed and cuddled into the hollow his body had made on the mattress, soaking up the scent of him. As he disappeared into the bathroom, my phone buzzed in my purse on the nightstand. I literally jumped. My heart stood still. I stared at my purse, completely frozen for a second before frantically reaching for it. My hands shook as I pulled the phone out.

A text from Jason. *I got the results. Looks like I'm the one. Don't share this with anyone. We need to talk.*

I have a dad. It was wondrous. Terrifying. And totally complicated everything. For both of us. I blinked back tears. Hands shaking so badly I could barely type, I started to reply and stopped myself short. I took a deep breath. I needed time to process.

I'd waited nineteen years to find my father and my true love. Now I had both, at least for tonight. I wanted to hold on to the beauty of that for as long as I could. I turned the phone off and slid it back into my purse. *This night belongs to Logan.*

Logan came out of the bathroom. "Miss me?" His tone was playful and flirty.

Silhouetted by the bathroom light, he looked like every dream of Prince Charming I'd ever had—tall and sexy, perfectly sculpted. The thought of ever losing him broke my heart.

I swallowed the lump in my throat. "Terribly. Almost tragically." I patted the bed next to me and held my arms out for him, needing him to hold me. "Come keep me company. Hold me."

He slid into bed beside me and pulled me close, wrapping me in his arms, cradling my head against his chest like he was protecting me from the world. If only he really could. I wanted to tell him to hang on to this minute. That no matter what I'd done or how things seemed, or how many secrets I'd kept from him, I loved him. And that was all that mattered, none of the rest of it. If our love was true, we could work things out.

"You're shaking," he said. "Is everything okay?"

"It's perfect. Everything's perfect."

"Good." He didn't sound convinced. He stroked my hair and kissed the top of my head. "El, I *really* do love you."

I lifted my head and looked into his eyes. I wanted him to see the truth shining in mine. "I love you, too." I paused, searching for the right words. "Promise me, no matter what happens, you'll never forget that."

"What could happen, El?" He grinned at me like he was trying to reassure me. "Nothing could ever change the way I feel about you. *Nothing.*"

He sounded so confident I almost believed him. *Almost.*

"Just promise me, okay?" I couldn't keep the urgency out of my voice as I rested my head on his chest again and listened to the reassuring beat of his heart.

He held me tighter. "Don't be insecure. How could I ever forget? And why would I want to?"

He was right. He *had* to be. Our love could overcome any obstacle. And if not, I would always have this night,

this perfect night when I had Logan's love and the father I'd been looking for. I would deal with the rest of
it tomorrow.

Author's Note

When I was in college, my roommate and I really did use baked goods as bribes, mostly chocolate chip cookies and the occasional snacking cake. One time my roommate ran out of chocolate chips and substituted raisin bran. Yeah, not really the best. But the guy she gave them to wolfed them down. Go figure.

In case you ever need to bake a bribe, I've included the recipe for Ellie's Top-Secret Cobblestone Bars. This recipe really is adapted from an industrial-sized recipe from a major Pac-12 university dining hall. And they are yummy and decadent!

Happy baking!

Gina

Ellie's Top-Secret Cobblestone Bars

Crust

1 stick (1/2 cup)	butter, softened
1 cup	sugar
4 Tbsp.	Dutch baking cocoa
1 tsp.	vanilla extract
heaping 1/4 tsp.	baking powder
3/4 cup + 1 Tbsp.	all-purpose flour
1 extra large	egg

Cream butter and sugar. Add eggs and vanilla. Mix well. Add all dry ingredients and mix well. Spread into 13x9 pan.

Filling

1/2 stick	butter, softened
6 oz	cream cheese
1/2 cup	sugar
1/2 tsp	vanilla extract
1 small	egg
2 Tbsp.	all-purpose flour

Cream butter, cream cheese and sugar. Add eggs and vanilla. Mix well. Add flour and mix until smooth. Spread over the crust evenly.

1 cup	semi-sweet chocolate chips

Sprinkle evenly over the filling. Bake at 350 degrees for 30 minutes.

| 2 1/2 cups | mini-marshmallows |

Sprinkle on the baked crust/filling and bake an additional 2 minutes.

Frosting

4 Tbsp.	butter
2 oz.	cream cheese
2-1/2 cups	powdered sugar
1 tsp.	vanilla extract
1/3 cup	2% milk
2-1/2 Tbsp.	Dutch baking cocoa

Cream butter. Add cream cheese. Add half the powdered sugar. Add the milk and vanilla. Mix until smooth. Mix cocoa and remaining powdered sugar together. Add to the milk mixture. Mix until smooth. Pour over the melted marshmallows and swirl together. Cool. Cut into bars.

Servings: About 18 bars.

ABOUT THE AUTHOR

Gina Robinson lives in the Pacific Northwest with her husband and children. She was not a prankster in college, although she knows a good many people who were. They will remain nameless to protect the guilty.

She married her college sweetheart and has never forgotten that wonderful feeling of falling in love.

Most days she writes while wearing slippers, flip-flops, or tennis shoes, depending on the season. But she loves a great, sexy heel and has a closet full for special occasions.

Connect with Gina online at www.ginarobinson.com